The Clockwork Testament or: Enderby's End

Manchester University Press

The Irwell Edition of the Works of Anthony Burgess

Series editors: Andrew Biswell and Paul Wake

Anthony Burgess (1917–1993) was one of the most prominent novelists and critics of the twentieth century. He wrote thirty-three novels, twenty-five works of non-fiction and two volumes of autobiography. Pursuing a parallel career as a classical composer, he wrote a symphony, a piano concerto, a violin concerto for Yehudi Menuhin and more than 250 other musical works.

The Irwell Edition takes its title from a collected edition outlined by Anthony Burgess himself in the 1980s but never achieved in his lifetime. Each volume in the series presents an authoritative annotated text alongside an introduction detailing the genesis and composition of the work, and the history of its reception.

Titles previously published in this series:

The Irwell Edition of the Works of Anthony Burgess

The Clockwork Testament or: Enderby's End

Edited with an introduction and
notes by Ákos Farkas

Manchester University Press

Published by Manchester University Press
Oxford Road, Manchester M13 9PL

www.manchesteruniversitypress.co.uk

British Library Cataloguing-in-Publication Data
A catalogue record for this book is available from the British Library

ISBN 978 1 5261 6348 6 hardback

First published 2023

The publisher has no responsibility for the persistence or accuracy of
URLs for any external or third-party internet websites referred to in this
book, and does not guarantee that any content on such websites is, or will
remain, accurate or appropriate.

Typeset
by Cheshire Typesetting Ltd, Cuddington, Cheshire
Printed in Great Britain
by TJ Books Limited, Padstow, Cornwall

Contents

General Editors' foreword

John Anthony Burgess Wilson (1917–1993) was one of the most prominent novelists and critics of the twentieth century, but in the years since his death most of his work has been unavailable. A polyglot and polymath, Burgess wrote thirty-three novels, twenty-five works of non-fiction, and two volumes of autobiography. Pursuing a parallel career as a classical composer, he wrote a symphony, a piano concerto, a violin concerto for Yehudi Menuhin, and more than 250 other musical works. He translated novels, stage plays and poems into English from French, Italian, Russian and Ancient Greek. As a journalist and cultural critic, he was a regular contributor to the *Observer, Times Literary Supplement, New York Times, Corriere della Sera* and the *Yorkshire Post*.

The Irwell Edition of the Works of Anthony Burgess is the first scholarly edition of Burgess's novels and non-fiction. By restoring 'lost' works to the available canon, it aims to encourage a new climate of reception, enabling readers to reconsider Burgess's literary career as a whole. The edition will include work in a variety of genres, such as stage plays, musical libretti, short stories and essays.

The Irwell Edition takes its title from a collected edition outlined by Anthony Burgess himself in the 1980s but never achieved during his lifetime. The River Irwell runs between Salford and Manchester, where Burgess spent his boyhood. Each volume is edited by an expert scholar, presenting an authoritative annotated text alongside an introduction detailing the composition of the work and the history of its reception. Commentaries on the genesis of each book draw on editorial correspondence, along with manuscripts, the author's notebooks and other working notes. Particular attention is paid to critical reviews published in the United Kingdom and the United States during Burgess's lifetime. The appendices make available previously unpublished documents from the Anthony Burgess archives held at institutional libraries in Europe and North America, in addition to rare and out-of-print materials relating to the thematic concerns of each volume. The endnotes translate words and phrases in foreign languages, explain obscurities and establish new connections with the wider body of Burgess's fiction, autobiographical writing and literary criticism.

The Irwell Edition is designed for students, teachers, scholars and general readers who are seeking accessible but rigorous critical editions of each book. The series as a whole will contribute to the ongoing task of encouraging renewed interest in all aspects of Anthony Burgess's creative work.

Andrew Biswell
Paul Wake
Manchester Metropolitan University

Acknowledgements

I received invaluable help from the staff and management of the International Anthony Burgess Foundation (IABF) in my efforts to reconstruct, by collating the first editions and the original typescripts, what is meant to be a definitive version of the third Enderby novel. In particular, I wish to express my sincere gratitude to the Foundation's director, Professor Andrew Biswell, whose generosity with his time and resources spared me the embarrassment of saying either too much or too little in the introductory passages and the endnotes. I also wish to thank senior archivist and fellow-Burgessian Anna Edwards at the IABF for unearthing for me every last bit of written or recorded document potentially relevant to my work. Matthew Frost of Manchester University Press also deserves very special mention here for his needful editorial advice at the beginning of my undertaking. I also had the support of my colleagues and graduate students at the Department of English Studies at my university where I was often relieved of my routine educational and administrative duties. Here I was also provided with unlimited access to the impressive knowledge of Professor Ferenc Takács and Dr Zsolt Czigányik concerning Burgess's international significance and to fresh information on the generic peculiarities of the campus novel coming from my doctoral student Yuliia Terentieva. On a more personal note, I owe a massive debt of gratitude to my wife Dr Mária Palla for her inexhaustible reserves of patience, affection and professional advice.

Finally, I would like this edition to stand as a tribute to the memory of Burgess's late widow Mrs Burgess née Liana Macellari and the also sadly departed Professor Alan Roughly and Dougie Milton of the Foundation and *The End of the World Newsletter*, whose early encouragement had a lasting effect on my Burgess-related work.

Ákos Farkas
Eötvös Loránd University, Budapest

Introduction

Genesis and composition

The prehistory of *The Clockwork Testament* begins in late January 1972, in a New York hotel named after the indigenous Americans whose mythology Anthony Burgess had borrowed for his 'structuralist' novel about incest, published the previous year under the title *MF*. It was here, at the Algonquin Hotel, that agents of Warner Brothers promoting Stanley Kubrick's film adaptation *A Clockwork Orange* had booked a room for Burgess, flown in from Minneapolis, where he was engaged in the staging of his translation of Edmond Rostand's play *Cyrano de Bergerac* (1897), including entr'acte music composed by himself in 1971 and 1972. The invitation extended to the writer by the film people served the express purpose of having him accept two prestigious prizes won by the *Clockwork* movie to be awarded on 23 January at Sardi's, a fashionable Manhattan restaurant. Thanking the New York Circle of Critics' awards for best film and best directing, on behalf of the American Kubrick busy 'paring his nails' back in England,[1] Burgess delighted his audience with a witty oration animated by the brio of its delivery.[2] The acceptance speech followed by the razzmatazz involving the consumption of

---

1 Anthony Burgess, *You've Had Your Time* (London: Heinemann, 1990), p. 253.
2 See 'Anthony Burgess Acceptance Speech at Sardi's, 1970s', www.anthonyburgess.org/tape/anthony-burgess-on-a-clockwork-orange/ (accessed 31 March 2021).

sophisticated beverages served at Sardi's made Burgess lower his defences. Retiring to his room in the Algonquin brought little relief to the writer beleaguered by unwelcome personal visits and telephone calls coming from variously enthusiastic or outraged viewers of the hotly contested film based on his novel.[3]

Burgess's unexpected callers at the Algonquin included one Thomas P. Collins, 'a former Jesuit priest' turned book promoter,[4] or 'shadowy packager' as the man was described by Robert Gottlieb, editor-in-chief of Alfred A. Knopf, one of the American publishers later contacted by Collins about his Burgess scheme.[5] Apparently, the 'president' of the obscure, now defunct company Collins Associates managed to exploit the chronically overworked and underpaid writer's momentary lack of caution. That was how this unbidden guest managed to persuade Burgess to consider a book project that he should have regarded as a wild goose chase at best and a self-serving scam at worst. The project, suggested by Collins with the ostensible intention of earning Burgess the fortune befitting his newly acquired celebrity status, would have involved the writing of a sequence of great men's lives, the major connecting link between successive parts of the proposed trilogy being the shared first name of the protagonists: King George III, General George S. Patton and the composer George Gershwin. Another, less fortuitous, thematic feature shared by these bio-fictions would have been the significant part played by each of the three Georges in the unfolding history of America, a quality to be a major selling point in the United States. However, a fully awake and mostly sober Burgess kept dragging his feet – his answers to Collins's urgent letters Burgess sent back to New York from Italy with considerable delay offered all sorts of excuses, such as his having no access to his library left in his now occupied former home in

---

3 Burgess, *You've Had Your Time*, p. 255.
4 *Ibid.*
5 Robert McCrum, 'The "Lost" Novels that Anthony Burgess Hoped Would Make Him Rich', *Observer*, 19 March 2017. The Collins letters are in the archive of the International Anthony Burgess Foundation (IABF), Manchester.

Malta, his other pressing obligations and the lack of clear financial arrangements.[6]

His growing reluctance notwithstanding, Burgess did not back out of the deal at first. Although he discarded Collins's idea of building a fictional narrative around the life and times of George III to be called 'The Man Who Lost America', he went on to produce outlines for the rest of the 'George trilogy' – 'The True Patton Papers' and 'The Rhapsody Man', about the soldier and the musician respectively.[7] In a synopsis of these novels, he promised to eschew the 'tortuous syntax' and 'wanton wordplay' attributable to some of his earlier work. Yet another ploy to corner the United States market was to turn the 'rich though brief' Gershwin book into 'a muted celebration of American achievement', making the story 'highly entertaining as well as thoughtful and moving'.[8] Adding a third title to replace the historical novel on America becoming independent, Burgess proposed a Biblical story titled 'The Fifth Gospel' meant to provide a boy's-eye-view of the Gospel narrative told in an idiom reflecting the age and times of the narrator – a ruse familiar from *A Clockwork Orange*.

Despite Burgess's initial willingness to comply, testified by the outlines of these imaginary novels he sent to Collins, and the book packager's eagerness, demonstrated by his busy correspondence with such high-profile representatives of the publishing industry as Robert Gottlieb in New York and Tom Maschler of Jonathan Cape in London, the trilogy intended to make Burgess and Collins rich failed to materialise. Collins's summary of these outlines is reprinted as Appendix 3. What has been left of them is just as valuable as, if not more valuable in fact than, the two-Georges-plus-one conception could have become. The European battlefields in what never became 'The True Patton Papers' are surveyed, in vivid detail, in Burgess's *Napoleon Symphony*, Gershwin's place as a musician is taken by he even more solidly canonised composers Mozart and Beethoven in

6 Anthony Burgess, letter to Thomas P. Collins, 13 March 1972 (IABF).
7 Book proposals attached to Collins's letter to Robert Gottlieb, 18 September 1972 (IABF).
8 *Ibid.*

Mozart and the Wolf Gang and, again, *Napoleon Symphony*, while
the New Testament story first conceived for the unwritten 'Fifth
Gospel' is recounted in Burgess's film narrative *Man of Nazareth*
and, reworked from an outsider's perspective, in the novel *The
Kingdom of the Wicked*.

More importantly than any thematic or compositional ideas recy-
cled by Burgess in his later work, the Collins interlude led to the
writing of the third volume of the Enderby series, *The Clockwork
Testament*. The proposed million-dollar trilogy about the great but
unrelated Georges was, right at the outset, meant to be preceded by
the warm-up exercise of a single, photographically illustrated volume,
filled with pertinent maxims selected and explained by Burgess. The
emerging combination of quotation, picture and comment was supposed to encapsulate the writer's comprehensive view of 'the human
condition' – deformed into a mechanised, 'clockwork', shape. The
miscellany of quotations to be selected and interpreted by Burgess
would have been something like Aldous Huxley's compilation of
metaphysical speculations cited from others and conclusions drawn
by himself in *The Perennial Philosophy*, or Cyril Connolly's similar
collection of quotations fitting the melancholy mood of the writer's
recollections and reflections in *The Unquiet Grave*. Lacking the the-
oretically trained mind of Huxley, who Burgess believed helped 'to
equip the contemporary novel with a brain',[9] or the egotistic intellec-
tualism of Connolly, who subtitled his anthology a 'A World Cycle',
Burgess accepted Collins's suggestion to produce something entirely
his own, based on his lived personal experience – his travels with
his wife under the 'Orange Cloud'.[10] The volume thus reconceived
would have contained nothing but Burgess's writing, now extended
to three or four times the originally proposed length of fifteen thousand words, and aiming 'strongly to speak to the wide audience
prepared' by Kubrick's film for its governing theme identified in the
resonant title 'The Clockwork Condition'.[11]

9 Anthony Burgess, *Ninety-Nine Novels: The Best in English Since 1939*
(London: Allison & Busby, 1984), p. 85.
10 Thomas P. Collins, letter to Burgess, 3 November 1972. (IABF).
11 Thomas P. Collins, letter to Tom Maschler, 7 June 1972 (IABF).

Whether because of Burgess's diminishing self-confidence, eroded by Collins's dismissal of the first batch of twelve type-written pages, or on account of direct rejection by one or another potential publisher, the 192-page typescript of the unfinished 'Clockwork Condition' never saw print. The manuscript, together with notes, outlines and fragments, lay forgotten in the Burgesses' house in Bracciano, Italy, until it was transferred to the archive of the Manchester-based International Anthony Burgess Foundation (IABF), where it awaits publication. The short extract made available on the internet by Andrew Biswell, director of the Foundation,[12] reveals Burgess's long-term preoccupations related, in one way or another, to some major unresolved issues of faith, ethics, aesthetics and the effects of technological modernity appearing in *A Clockwork Orange* and haunting Burgess long after the release of the film adaptation. This extract offers valuable insight into the literary and philosophical inspirations derived from the quotations of the abandoned anthology.[13] Burgess's discussion here of the relative importance for the human condition of the four scholastic 'transcendentals' – truth, beauty, goodness and oneness – brings to mind at least two of his major precursors: the already mentioned Aldous Huxley, and the writer to whom Burgess had devoted two full monographs, James Joyce. Burgess's observation in 'The Clockwork Condition' that 'through the pursuit of beauty, [one] may gain ... an indirect experience of the quiddity or whatness of God' can be seen as a fair summary of Stephen Dedalus's exposition of the true artist's calling in *A Portrait of the Artist as a Young Man*.[14] This involves the task and the ability to apprehend the radiance, or whatness, of the thing represented, a 'supreme quality' termed *quidditas* in Church Latin.[15]

12 Andrew Biswell, 'MetCast Episode 8: Anthony Burgess and The Clockwork Condition', 18 February 2019. www.mmu.ac.uk/news-and-events/news/story/9535/ (accessed 31 March 2021).

13 *Ibid.*

14 Andrew Biswell, 'The Clockwork Condition: Lost Sequel to *A Clockwork Orange* Discovered in Anthony Burgess archive', 25 April 2019. www.mmu.ac.uk/news-and-events/news/story/10185/ (accessed 31 March 2021).

15 James Joyce, *A Portrait of the Artist as a Young Man* (New York: Penguin, 1976), p. 213.

The pursuit, commended by Burgess as the highest human aspiration, of the ultimate reality, 'the final monad', residing in the aesthetically communicable quiddity of things is also analogous to what Huxley called 'man's final end ... the unitive knowledge of the Godhead'.[16] What we witness here, once again, is an important manifestation of Burgess's indebtedness to his various modernist precursors behind the strong thematisation in *The Clockwork Testament* of the poet's duty to serve his art and nothing but.

A further connection between Huxley and Burgess related to the genesis of *The Clockwork Testament* is the onscreen representation, provocative at the time, of full-frontal nudity and shockingly naturalistic shots of brutal violence. The film titled *The Devils*, Ken Russell's 1971 adaptation of *The Devils of Loudun*, Huxley's non-fiction treatment of a seventeenth-century case of 'demonic possession', and then Kubrick's *A Clockwork Orange*, based on the American edition of Burgess's novella of the same title, shared the quality of 'highly coloured aggression', as Burgess saw it.[17] The difference, for Burgess, was that of artistic quality. While he admired Kubrick's 'brilliance of [visually] responding to the wordplay' in the source text, Burgess despised Russell's exploitation of his audience's basest urges or producing nothing but meaningless noise.[18] In an April 1972 instalment of the American talk-show *Sound on Film*, discussing the controversial reception of Kubrick's film, Burgess said he was glad that his book had not fallen into the hands of Russell who, as he put it, 'would have gone to town on the pornographic possibilities of the film'.[19] The graphic representation of brutal violence and base pornography in the fictional film adaptation, based on Enderby's 'idea' in *The Clockwork Testament*, of Gerard Manley Hopkins's long poem 'The Wreck of the Deutschland', is a transition

16 Aldous Huxley, *Perennial Philosophy* (London: Chatto & Windus, 1947), p. 1.
17 Burgess, *You've Had Your Time*, p. 245.
18 *Ibid.*, p. 317.
19 *Sound on Film: What's it going to be then, eh? A look at Stanley Kubrick's A Clockwork Orange*, transcript (New York: Ervin Frankel Productions, 1972), p. 3.

between what Burgess attributed to Ken Russell's and Kubrick's work – cheap visual sensationalism here, aesthetically valuable, if theologically questionable, cinematic art there.

As Burgess's favourable initial impressions of Kubrick's achievement faded, he felt more and more dubious about the cult status of the film and indeed the value of his own work adapted for the screen by the American director. Rightly or wrongly, Burgess believed the novel to be marred by the inadmissible didacticism in its sermonising treatment of *liberum arbitrium* or free will.[20] This, however, did not prevent him from rewriting *A Clockwork Orange* for the stage in 1987 and returning to it in learned essay after new introduction after broadcast interview in the years to come. As Biswell sums it up in the podcast interview cited above, whether he liked his own or Kubrick's work or not, Burgess could simply not leave *A Clockwork Orange* alone.[21]

The Clockwork Testament growing out of 'The Clockwork Condition' and Burgess's first-hand experience of American academia and showbiz is, among other things, a major document of its writer's obsession with the creation, editing, filming and, most important of all, the reception of his best-known novel. Also, the fourth Enderby book fulfilled, although in a radically altered form, Burgess's contractual obligation to produce a book, any book, for that literary go-between first met in the Algonquin, Thomas P. Collins. When both the George trilogy and 'The Clockwork Condition' were finally laid to rest, *The Clockwork Testament* was written, at a pace super-fast even by the standards of Burgess's amazingly rapid rate of composition: in two weeks in Bracciano, Italy, some time in the summer of 1973, as testified by Burgess in his interview with George Armstrong shortly after he had completed the novel.[22] 'Anthony Burgess said today that he has prepared an answer to magistrates in Britain and in Australia who are denouncing

20 These are Burgess's own words: 'I admire it [*A Clockwork Orange*] least of all my books. That is because *it is* too didactic' (*ibid.*, p. 13).
21 Biswell, 'The Clockwork Condition'.
22 George Armstrong, 'Pith of the Orange', *Guardian*, 30 July 1973, p. 1; In another interview Burgess spoke of three weeks, which included one week for

the Kubrick film for having inspired gang assaults', according to Armstrong.[23] Burgess added that the plot of the fifty-thousand-word novel revolved around copy-cat crimes inspired by a seemingly religious but in fact very violent and blasphemously pornographic film based on Hopkins's 'The Wreck of the Deutschland'. The published novel is shorter, but in its story more complex, than what is suggested by Armstrong's outline cited here.

The speed at which the typescript of the novel was created is all the more amazing as a number of false starts must have impeded its composition. Two such fragments are held in the Burgess Foundation's archive – one just a shortish paragraph, the other running to five densely typed pages. Of these, the brevity of the first and the position of the eight lines at the top of an A4 sheet suggest that the fragment starting with the words 'Temporary Professor Enderby' was probably meant to serve as the opening of the novel's body text but was then left unfinished and discarded.[24] Rightly deemed less than satisfactory, this fragment was replaced with what is a more eye-catching and less tortuously witty opening in the novel's English-language editions. On the other hand, the Roman numbers at the bottom of the five typewritten pages filled with what is referred to as the 'French Overture' indicate that this five-page text is likely to have been intended to appear *before* the first chapter as a thematic preview of sorts.[25] As a musical overture does, the episode involving the poet Enderby giving a lecture, delivered in hesitant and at points hilariously garbled French, to the patrons of a provincial literary salon run by former French colonials in Casablanca, offers a compact exposition of the major themes to be developed in the novel. Presented here is the figure of the intransigent-aesthete-cum-frustrated-lecturer, in the person of Enderby, the émigré poet comically alienated from his baffled and bored audience. Also introduced in the 'French Overture' is a caricature of xenophobia, here in the shape of anachronistic

revision, See James B. Hemesath, 'Anthony Burgess Interviewed by James B. Hemesath', *Transatlantic Review*, May 1976, pp. 96–102, p. 101.

23 Armstrong, 'Pith of the Orange', p. 1.

24 Anthony Burgess, 'Temporary Professor Enderby' typescript, IABF.

25 Anthony Burgess, 'French Overture' typescript, IABF. See Appendix 1.

Francophobia, together with suggestions of how Enderby has found himself at the way-station of Casablanca between his inherited seaside bar La Belle Mer (or *Belle Mère*, meaning mother-in-law, as he jokes awkwardly) in Tangier and his destination in New York. All this is given the virtuoso treatment of multilingual puns and deliberate misconstruals, which readers of the first two Enderby novels have come to expect. This critical edition provides, in an appendix, the 'French Overture' missing from all previous English-language editions of *The Clockwork Testament*.

Publication history

The typescript of *The Clockwork Testament* was forwarded by Thomas P. Collins to publishers in London, New York, Paris and, possibly, Munich. Either Collins deliberately avoided the publishers of Burgess's previous books, or his approaches were rejected by them. What makes the first assumption more likely is that, following advice from his London agent Deborah Rogers, Burgess had dropped Heinemann in 1968, while it could have led to some unpleasantness if his New York agent Robert Lantz had learnt, from W.W. Norton, of his being sidestepped.[26] Another reason why Norton was not considered could have been the fact that Burgess bore a grudge against the company's vice president Eric P. Swenson as the man making him accede to the 'lopping' of the last chapter of *A Clockwork Orange*.[27] As for Burgess's other London publisher, there is no evidence that Jonathan Cape's managing director Tom Maschler, who had been approached by Collins with the subsequently discarded idea of 'The Clockwork Condition', had any great confidence in Collins and Burgess delivering a similarly titled book in the shape of *The Clockwork Testament*.

---

26 This is in spite of the fact that Burgess had little reason to feel bound to Lantz and the house the latter represented, as the two of them had first met just a few minutes before Burgess bumping into Collins after his acceptance speech at Sardi's. In short, these two book-people had just about equal claims – if indeed any – on Burgess's loyalty.

27 Burgess, *You've Had Your Time*, p. 60.

Whoever were or were not contacted about the new project, the first edition of *The Clockwork Testament or: Enderby's End* was published in June 1974, by Hart-Davis, McGibbon, a British firm of relatively recent establishment at the time. Collins apparently managed to win over for the cause Robert Gottlieb of Alfred A. Knopf in New York, too. Consequently, the first American edition of *The Clockwork Testament*, issued in 1975, bore the imprint of a truly major publishing house. In addition, this edition was illustrated by the Brothers Quay, identified as The Quays in the imprint, exceptionally talented twins whose work as animators was to earn them international recognition.

Set side by side, the first two editions of *The Clockwork Testament* reveal much about the publishing philosophies of the companies involved. The cover design of the first UK version was obviously meant to catch the prospective buyer's eye with a rather garish set of oversize block capitals printed in pop-art colours and shapes – ironically, a style exposed to derision in the novel itself. In stark contrast with the emphatic trendiness of the Hart-Davis, McGibbon edition are the restrained colour scheme and blurry figural illustration on the cover of the earliest American version. The hardback binding, together with the high-quality bond paper and carefully selected typeface used for both editions are of the same standard. However, the inclusion of topic-adjusted illustrations – such as a small clock-face superimposed on a miniature portrait of the protagonist heading each chapter to indicate the appropriate time of day – together with the feathered, slightly uneven, fore edge of the book lends a touch of old-world elegance to the first American edition of *The Clockwork Testament*.

The differences between the impressions created by the two editions' external appearance are reinforced by the effect of the divergent editorial practices followed by the two publishers. Whereas the editors at Hart-Davis, McGibbon felt free to make 'corrections' whenever their language instinct prompted them to intervene, their colleagues at Alfred A. Knopf adopted a more conservative approach, being chary of altering even the most idiosyncratic locution in the typescript. As an example, the unfamiliar, possibly non-existent, past tense verb *hizzed* in the typescript is 'corrected' to *hissed* in the British version but left unchanged in the Knopf edition.[28] What was overlooked by the British but apparently acknowledged by the American editor is the onomatopoeic function of the 'mistaken' form, and the awkwardness, or even absurdity, attributed to the speaker's feminist outburst by her interlocutor. Enderby's unbidden guest takes her professor and interviewee to task over referring to God as a masculine entity like this: "'Why do you say *his*?" she hizzed' as the typescript and the American edition have it.[29] In the British edition, the verb in the clause quoting the young woman's question is *hissed*, a grammatically correct but less expressive or phonetically appropriate form.

In another example, it is not a *hapax legomenon* but an apparent error of style that spurred Hart-Davis, McGibbon's editors to act. To end one paragraph and then begin the next with the exact same words must have struck the editors at the London publisher as redundant. The author, as it must have been assumed, had forgotten having concluded his previous paragraph with the phrase 'at this point', otherwise he would not have started the next one with the same adverbial. The second instance of 'at this point' was thus deleted. The editors in New York seem to have been more attentive readers here than to assume inattentiveness rather than authorial intention. Whatever the editorial motivation may have been, the immediate context makes it clear that the repetition must be functional: Enderby 'walked down chill blowing Broadway as far as 91st Street, then crossed towards Columbus Avenue. *At this point. / At this point* it happened again' (slash and emphasis added).[30]

What happens to Enderby 'at this point' is an episode of cardiac arrhythmia involving an extrasystole, namely, the normal contraction of the heart followed by yet another, premature, systole,

---

28 Anthony Burgess, *The Clockwork Testament* (London: Hart-Davis, McGibbon, 1974), p. 31.
29 Anthony Burgess, IABF typescript of *The Clockwork Testament*, July 1973, p. 21; Burgess, *The Clockwork Testament* (New York: Alfred A. Knopf, 1975), p. 37.
30 Burgess, IABF typescript of *The Clockwork Testament*, p. 76.

or contraction, rather than a diastole, or the relaxation of the heart muscle, which would have its turn in the normal sequence of healthy heartbeats. After this comes a prolonged pause, and then an abnormally intense contraction. And indeed, 'pain was pumped rapidly into his chest and he stopped breathing' as Enderby experienced the event.[31] This is a textbook case of the cardiovascular episode: palpitations attendant on the ischaemia of the heart tissue. In short, the stylistically irregular repetition of the phrase 'at this point' verbally replicates the also irregular repetition of the same muscular action in the heart. Burgess provides the appreciative reader with a prime example of what can be termed, in the style of classic 'New Criticism', expressive or imitative form. The Irwell Edition of the Works of Anthony Burgess aims to restore the texts of Burgess's books to the state of the first published UK editions – with a minimum of interventions. The arguments set forth here legitimise the minimal intervention, resorted to on very rare occasions, of prioritising Burgess's choices over those made by the editor of the first print version of *The Clockwork Testament*.

Of the first batch of editions, the German translation stands out as a remarkable curiosity. Issued by the Munich-based company Wilhelm Heyne Verlag, the paperback entitled *Das Uhrwerk-Testament* is unique among the many translations of Burgess's novels on account of its being brought out simultaneously with the first English-language original in 1974. Another notable feature of Walter Brumm's German rendering of *The Clockwork Testament* is that it is not based on any existing English-language edition. This could not have been otherwise, given the very close proximity of the German-language novel's publication date to that of the first British edition. Instead of following the latter, Heyne Verlag's German text appears to be based on the typescript, even at points where the British edition departs from it. Examples include the ones cited above as well as the locus where the unknown British editor corrected Burgess's *ice* to *nice*, assuming that the brackish liquid in Enderby's 'ALABAMA'

---

31 *Ibid.* (I thank Balázs P. Farkas MD for the medical information underlying my argument here.)

mug used to be tea, which, when freshly brewed must be *nice*, rather than what the slop in fact is – dirty, melted *ice*. Believing their eyes rather than their language instinct, the German editors – and, incidentally, their American colleagues – here understood Burgess's intentions better than their British colleagues.[32]

Another, even more striking, feature setting *Das Uhrwerk-Testament* apart not only from the Hart-Davis, McGibbon version but from all known English editions is that it contains a '*Französiche Ouvertüre*', the German translation of the prefatory episode discarded by the author or his Anglo-American editors. It is quite conceivable that the latter wished to spare the sensibilities of the novel's French readers, whose fictional compatriots are rather viciously satirised here. Such tact was apparently not part of Wilhelm Heyne Verlag's editorial policies. What they had to offer instead was a painstakingly precise German rendering of Enderby's broken French oration in the footnotes, where every last multilingual pun receives its verbatim translation. As neither the self-contained typescript nor any of the English-language editions includes the 'French Overture', the prefatory chapter is given in Appendix 1 here as a curiosity rather than an integral part of *The Clockwork Testament* as a coherent work of literary art.

Subsequent editions, including single-volume paperbacks of *The Clockwork Testament* and bulky anthologies containing the first three or all four Enderby volumes, vary in external appearance and editorial practices. It would require a study of its own to explore how the cover design changed from figural caricature to abstract pattern and, more importantly, why one edition followed Hart-Davis, McGibbon's interventionist method while another preferred to leave things as found in the typescript or the Knopf version. *The Complete Enderby*, the full Enderby quartet respectively published by Penguin Classics in 1995 and by Caroll and Graff in 1998 contains *The Clockwork Testament* in two noticeably different versions.

32 Anthony Burgess, *Das Uhrwerk Testament* (München: Wilhelm Heyne Verlag, 1974), p. 78. See also Burgess, *The Clockwork Testament* (Hart-Davis, McGibbon), p. 67; Burgess, typescript of *The Clockwork Testament*, p. 50; and Burgess, *The Clockwork Testament* (Knopf), p. 84.

Where the latter is identical in almost all its examined particulars with the first US edition, the former stays closer to the first British edition, from which it departs on occasion in favour of the type-script. This new edition, while respecting the first British edition, explains the rationale of its few departures from the Hart-Davis, McGibbon text in the annotations.

Background and contexts

On a late August day of 1972, Burgess boarded, with his small family of wife Liana and son Andrea, the ocean liner *Raffaello*, heading from Naples to New York. Here he was to occupy the post of Distinguished Professor at the City College, New York in upper Manhattan, where he would teach undergraduate courses in creative writing and literary history in both semesters of the academic year 1972–73. Far from looking forward to being lionised in the New World as the international celebrity he was on the way to becoming, Burgess complained, in one of the short autobiographical notes he regularly contributed to the *Times Literary Supplement*, of being dragged about the world by 'the need to earn money'.[33] This, how-ever, was nothing to be ashamed of: Burgess recognised, in himself as well as others, 'the healthy urge to make pots of money', the chief attraction of the Big Apple for successive waves of immigrants coming to the metropolis to which he later devoted an illustrated guidebook titled *New York*.[34]

Respectable as he believed the wish to secure for his loved ones the standard of living he thought their due, Burgess was not happy about the state of affairs in which 'the rewards of authorship … reside not in published work but on the margins', as he put it in another *TLS* article, published on 13 October 1972.[35] The margins of publishing meant, for Burgess as for many of his predecessors and contemporaries from Aldous Huxley to Harold Pinter or Joseph

33 Anthony Burgess, 'Viewpoint', *Times Literary Supplement*, 13 October 1972, p. 1224.
34 Anthony Burgess, *New York* (Amsterdam: Time-Life, 1976), p. 81.
35 Burgess, 'Viewpoint', p. 1224.

Heller, Burgess's colleague at CCNY, a visiting professorship or working in the entertainment industry – in Burgess's words: 'academic or showbiz'.[36] He claimed to have been the first to have known, simultaneously, 'two aspects of New York life from the inside – academia and the musical theatre'.[37] And yet, he felt increasingly restless under the dual pressures of his academic and theatrical responsibilities. Teaching Joyce, Shakespeare and the rudiments of literary composition to students he saw as ill-educated and uninterested, while churning out ever newer versions of his lyrics for the musical *Cyrano*, left him with little time or energy to work on what he would most have wanted to work on. This was supposed to be *Napoleon Symphony*, a daringly innovative, dauntingly difficult, but equally rewarding novel, just started in the summer of 1972.

The situation was exacerbated by the fallout of the controversial reception of the *Clockwork Orange* film. Burgess's personal involvement in the aftermath started soon after the film's release in early 1972. The promotional tour he was sent on with Malcolm McDowell, the actor who had played the part of Alex in Kubrick's movie, took Burgess to a number of television and radio studios. Attending the Cannes festival in April to publicise Kubrick's work, shown *hors de concours* as a non-competing entry, and enjoying the table talk of people like Groucho Marx was walking on the bright side.[38] The other, darker, aspect of the 'Clockwork affair' involved having to defend the film and his own work from their detractors. Before the Cannes detour, Burgess stopped off in London, having, as he puts it in his autobiography, 'to appear on a BBC radio programme to defend Stanley Kubrick's art and the apparent depravity of a book that few had read' – meaning *A Clockwork Orange*.[39] The stopover likely took him to the 'Paris Studio' in Lower Regent Street where

---

36 *Ibid.*

37 Burgess, *New York*, p. 117. Biswell describes this as 'a typically Burgessian fusion of "high" and "low" culture' in *The Real Life of Anthony Burgess* (London: Picador, 2005), p. 348.

38 For Burgess's account of the experience see *You've Had Your Time*, pp. 262–3.

39 Burgess, *You've Had Your Time*, p. 256.

BBC talk shows hosted by Jimmy Savile,[40] a disc-jockey noted, as Burgess put it, for 'his love of the young', were recorded before an invited audience.[41] The discussion programme, by all probability a spring instalment of Savile's *Speakeasy* series, ended with the seemingly unbiased anchor asking an ex-convict in the audience to explain whether 'his reading [had] influenced his criminal behaviour'.[42] The man's unequivocal 'yes' ended the programme, abruptly depriving Burgess of the chance to respond in defence of everyone's God-given liberty to choose the course of action, good *or* evil, to follow and the accountability attendant on such freedom.

It was in the same programme that, according to Burgess's recollections, 'a member of the audience cited the Poughkeepsie, New York, rape of a nun', supposedly incited by the perpetrators having seen Kubrick's film.[43] The location of the incident is commemorated in *The Clockwork Testament* where a deranged but attractive woman invades Enderby's Manhattan apartment in order to avenge her fixation on the man's poetry. The attacker turned – ultimately satisfied – victim absconded from her home in Poughkeepsie, New York, the scene of the real-life crime brought up in the Savile show. The target of another copycat crime, allegedly provoked by the Kubrick movie and given wide circulation in the British press, was a young woman raped 'by a gang of youths who sang "Singin' in the Rain" … just as Alex and the droogs did in the film' – this also found its way into *The Clockwork Testament*. In an earlier episode a journalist, hailing from England like Enderby, phones the poet to corner him with the news that a 'nunslaughter' was perpetrated by a gang of hooligans claiming to have been inspired by a violence- and pornography-filled film based on Enderby's 'idea' of Hopkins's 'The Wreck of the Deutschland'. The scene of the fictional incident is Burgess's native county of Lancashire.

40 'Genome Beta – Radio Times 1923–2009' https://genome.ch.bbc.co.uk/schedules/radio1/england/1972–03–12 (accessed 31 March 2021).
41 Burgess, *You've Had Your Time*, p. 256.
42 *Ibid.*, p. 257.
43 *Ibid.*, pp. 256–7.

In spite of the occasional references to the old country in it, *The Clockwork Testament* is an 'American' novel or, rather, a novel addressing Burgess's engagement with the American experience. America is, of course, too big to be summed up in a single book, which is why Burgess limited his focus to one particular city in itself large and multifaceted enough to stand for the rest of the continent-wide country – New York. That is one aspect in which *The Clockwork Testament* differs from other, earlier novels, about the (mis)adventures of the hapless – but snobbishly superior or even bigoted – European in America, whether the setting is a media-magnate's sprawling California estate in Aldous Huxley's *After Many a Summer*, a provincial university in Vladimir Nabokov's *Pale Fire* and in Kingsley Amis's *One Fat Englishman*, or a Mid-Western theatre as in Burgess's own *Enderby's Dark Lady*, the latter bringing Enderby back from the dead 'to placate kind readers of *The Clockwork Testament* ... who objected to' his 'casually killing' his hero.[44]

An important difference setting it apart from other novels of the 'Englishman-in-America' scenario is that *The Clockwork Testament* is not merely of its own place but very much of its own time, too. The novel is not only a commentary on Burgess's exposure to the now unreservedly celebratory, now violently adverse, reception of the *Clockwork Orange* film thinly disguised in the novel as *The Wreck of the Deutschland*. It is also a semi-autobiographical review of living in an apartment sublet to a visiting professor by a colleague on research leave (the real-life model here is the poet and educator Adrienne Rich) located in a fortress-like but cockroach-infested tenement building in Upper Manhattan, just south of Harlem.[45] More importantly, the novel offers a series of aesthetically rendered philosophical reflections on the surface texture and the deeper structures of 'the human condition' as seen and felt in a specific place at a particular time. Both the context of its writing and the setting of its plot

---

44 Anthony Burgess, *Enderby's Dark Lady* (London: Hutchinson, 1984), p. 5.
45 Burgess, *You've Had Your Time*, p. 269. The location of the apartment is referred to as Riverside Drive, Manhattan, in Burgess's autobiography but the address appearing on a letter from Thomas P. Collins is 670 West End Avenue New York, New York 10025 (IABF).

are largely determined for *The Clockwork Testament* by a specific decade. This is the 1970s, a period famously characterised by the ascendance of the counterculture mostly in response to the Vietnam War providing the public background to Enderby's private lecture given to a student visitor on the differences between right and wrong as opposed to good and evil.[46] Memories of the Mỹ Lai massacre perpetrated by a bunch of renegade American soldiers in Vietnam were still fresh in the minds of Burgess and his readers.[47]

Another, related, aspect of the turbulent times visiting professor Enderby is caught up in is the controversial democratisation of higher education in America, involving widespread experimentation with open admission policies, and the questioning of 'the Western Canon' – issues addressed by Burgess in open letter after public speech after published interview as well as the novel itself. Also highlighted in *The Clockwork Testament* and in Burgess's non-fiction are the perceived excesses of the women's liberation movement. Added to all this was the apparently unresolvable ethnic conflicts whose severity in New York was as disconcerting for Burgess as for his self-parodic avatar Enderby, both coming from the Old World as yet unused to the searing heat of emotions surrounding the issue in America. But then the USA, that trend-setter of the Rest of the West, and New York City, itself a synecdoche of America as Burgess saw it, portended the future of humanity at large. The schoolteacher guiding her time-travelling pupils visiting the America of Enderby's present from the distant future has every reason to point out New York to her charges as a universal representative of '*la condition humaine*'.

Critical reception

While stopping at the University of Iowa on a lecture tour in October 1975, Burgess gave an interview to *Transatlantic Review*. Responding to the student reporter's question about the critical

46 The 'heavy presence' of Greene in this respect is pointed out, among others, by Stinson. See Stinson on Hopkins (2000), p. 19.
47 For more detail see Burgess, *You've Had Your Time*, p. 271.

reception of *The Clockwork Testament*, published the previous year in America, he had this to say: 'The novel went down well in both England and the United States. ... The critics said it was honest, sound, human, humane, and all that.'[48] Such is not quite the impression one is left with after sampling a representative collection of reviews published in the major papers, magazines and journals of the period. This is not to say, however, that Burgess himself got it all wrong; neither did scholarly critic John J. Stinson have it right when concluding, in 1981, that Burgess's last four or five novels, with *The Clockwork Testament* among them, had 'met with either contempt or patronage'.[49] The evidence of more than twenty high-profile reviews suggests that the truth lies somewhere between the extremes of the writer's unreservedly optimistic and his scholarly commentator's starkly pessimistic summary of how *The Clockwork Testament* had been treated by its reviewers.

The contemporary press coverage did include a number of enthusiastic, even celebratory, appraisals. Some of the 'rave reviews' came from Burgess's naive-sounding admirers, such as the correspondent of the *Baltimore Sun* who, referring to Burgess as 'the greatest living English novelist', expressed her impatience to see 'another monolithic novel' to be produced by her hero, gladly settling for the brevity of *The Clockwork Testament* 'for the nonce'.[50] Praise of a more nuanced kind was not missing from the early reviews either. Auberon Waugh, while deeming the implied commentary on Kubrick's film adaptation of *A Clockwork Orange* in the new novel less than wholly fair, described the 'burlesque on Hollywood treatment of a work of art' as 'unrivalled'.[51] There is nothing unexpected about Waugh, son of the man who wrote *The Loved One* ridiculing America's philistinism, to have loved 'every word of the novel', which he took to be

48 Hemesath, 'Anthony Burgess Interviewed', p. 99.
49 John J. Stinson, 'Better to Be Hot Or Cold: "1985" and the Dynamic of the Manichaean Duoverse', *Modern Fiction Studies*, 27:3 (1981), pp. 505–16 (p. 505).
50 Cecile Sullivan, 'Ugly, Hair, Fat – Ah, Yes, He Always Was', *Baltimore Sun*, 23 February 1975 (IABF reviews file).
51 Auberon Waugh, 'Good? Evil? OK – Let's Film It', *Evening Standard*, [no date] (IABF reviews file).

a satire of the 'filthy, unspeakable world' Enderby sees all about him in New York.[52] Another review more guardedly sympathetic but at least as insightful as Waugh's appeared in *The Times* on 6 June 1974 over the name of Antonia S. Byatt. The fellow-novelist discussed, with the erudition of a true scholar, the system of mythic archetypes behind the female figures and the aesthetic as well as ethical implications of the Enderby trilogy. According to a note sent to Burgess,[53] and the testimony of the biography written about her fellow-juror on the Booker Prize committee Elizabeth Jane Howard,[54] Byatt affirmed that *The Clockwork Testament* should have received the prize awarded to the best British, Irish or Commonwealth novel of the year. No wonder that Byatt in *The Times* had every praise for the various *tours de force* in the latest Enderby sequel. These included an 'excruciating illiterate transcript' of a television show 'full of double entendres', as well as the rendering of visiting professor 'Enderby's encounters with the Creative Writing of his students'.[55]

The review suggestively titled 'Exile's Return', published by William Pritchard in the *Listener*, the BBC's now defunct weekly,[56] represents a middle-of-the road position befitting the balanced approach to be expected of a public-service medium. The review provides a transition between the overwhelmingly favourable and the predominantly adverse criticism accorded to *The Clockwork Testament*. While describing the 'chunks of poetry-in-progress' given by Burgess to Enderby as less than engaging, and detecting 'an air of contrivance' about the novel as a whole, Pritchard finds 'moments of high entertainment' infused with considerable 'stylistic

---

52 *Ibid.*
53 IABF.
54 This is what Byatt told Howard's biographer: Elizabeth 'dismissed my own favourite – Anthony Burgess – because "he gets drunk and falls down stairs".' For more detail see Artemis Cooper, *Elizabeth Jane Howard: A Dangerous Innocence* (London: John Murray, 2016) p. 230.
55 A. S. Byatt, 'All Life Is One', *The Times*, 6 June 1974, p. 8.
56 Pritchard was the author of one of the earliest critical essays on Burgess's novels, published in the *Massachusetts Review* in 1966. He also arranged Burgess's first US lecture tour in the same year.

energies'.[57] This inclines the reviewer to forgive Enderby and, possibly his creator, his 'self-pity and misanthropically slobbish grunts toward life'.[58] It is its profusion of verbally dazzling comedy that even the novel's less than sympathetic critics considered as something of a saving grace: it is not only Byatt who finds *The Clockwork Testament* 'ferociously funny'. Jonathan Raban, reviewing the novel for *Encounter*, notes the writer's purported 'savage, anti-American illiberalism', but is willing to overlook such negative sentiments in light of such 'marvellously funny' parts as the transcription of Enderby's appearance on a recorded but shelved TV talk-show.[59] Stinson, who has few nice things to say about this particular novel of Burgess's, concedes that it is 'genuinely funny'.[60] While the 'Sperr Lansing Show' is undoubtedly a critics' favourite, absent-minded Enderby's exercise in creative literary history, his controversial Creative Writing class and even the Rabelaisian descriptions of his digestive malfunctions also receive a number of votes as the novel's funniest episodes.

Although 'funny' is the operative word in most cases, not everyone was amused. Philip Toynbee, another famous father's son, was among the first to denounce Burgess and his newest novel in a June issue of the *Observer* in 1974. The left-leaning writer-publicist did not mince his words, calling *The Clockwork Testament* the worst that 'Mr Burgess has ever done', concluding that 'raw hatred is a rotten motive-power both in life and letters'.[61] Equating the teller with the tale, overlooking the differences setting flesh-and-blood writer apart from implied author and both from character is a recurring feature even of some scholarly assessments of *The Clockwork Testament*. In vain did Burgess point out, in the Iowa interview and elsewhere, how such character traits of Enderby as his narrow and

57 William Pritchard, 'Exile's Return', *Listener*, 13 June 1974, pp. 776–77.
58 *Ibid.*
59 Jonathan Raban, 'What Shall We Do about Anthony Burgess?', *Encounter*, November 1974, p. 83.
60 John J. Stinson, *Anthony Burgess Revisited* (Boston, MA: Twayne, 1991), p. 97.
61 Philip Toynbee, 'Kicking the Bucket', *Observer*, 2 June 1974, p. 33.

intense misogyny – meaning the morbid fear and hatred of women, rather than just arguing against the ideology of radical feminism – or his sloppily inept culinary habits were clearly distinct from his, Burgess's, admiration for womankind and his well-known proficiency in fine cooking, as noted by Martin Amis and others.[62]

Whatever Burgess or his character-witnesses had to say, most critics of *The Clockwork Testament* would certainly have answered the Iowa interviewer's question whether Enderby was 'pretty much' the novelist himself with a definite yes.[63] True, contemporary reviewers did not have the benefit of Burgess's fellow writer-in-residence at CCNY Joseph Heller's testimony of his former colleague's 'inner generosity' rendering him incapable of 'looking down on people' as the writer of *Catch-22* said in an interview published by Andrew Biswell in his major Burgess biography.[64] Such lack of relevant information, together with the exigencies of a journalist reviewer's trade, might explain the hasty attribution of Enderby's 'scorn and dislike' to his 'creator' by the anonymous reviewer of the *Times Literary Supplement*.

Similarly, the condemnation by the critic of the *New Statesman* of Enderby-Burgess having supposedly 'been translated from his easy-going bigotries of his native turf to [the] tense, angry city' of New York is likely attributable to the politics of the magazine where Peter Prince's review appeared.[65] Equally understandable is the animus felt by Greg Lawless, reviewer of the campus daily *Harvard Crimson*, for the novel's protagonist, and behind him for the author, supposedly loathing his 'students for their eating habits and for their

---

62 'My first thought when I wake up every morning is – My God. The kitchen! My wife, you see, doesn't go in for that kind of thing', said Burgess to Martin Amis in 1980. Quoted in Martin Amis, *Visiting Mrs Nabokov* (London: Jonathan Cape, 1993), p. 244.

63 Hemesath, 'Anthony Burgess Interviewed', p. 99.

64 Biswell, *The Real Life of Anthony Burgess*, pp. 348–50.

65 Peter Prince, 'Intramural', *New Statesman*, 21 June 1974, p. 894. Attributing too much importance to the ideological bias of either the author of the article or the medium where his piece appeared requires some caution, as the literary editor of the *New Statesman*, who assigned the book to Peter Prince, was Martin Amis, and he can hardly be easily accused of leftist radicalism.

anti-intellectualism' and even hating 'his brightest student because he knows too much'.[66] The student-reviewer ignores both Burgess's repeated public expressions of his care for his 'dear students' and the novel's subtle representation of how Enderby's initial annoyance modulates into the grudging recognition of the student-character – the 'Kickapoo knowall' – as a fellow-writer in the making.[67] Such critical oversights can be explained if one takes into consideration the obligatory loyalties of an undergraduate paper's contributor. It is harder to understand how such a knowledgeable monographer of Burgess's as John J. Stinson could have overlooked the accumulating external and obvious internal evidence of Burgess's lack of sympathy for Enderby's undeniable misogyny, elitism and xenophobia. Not only did Stinson approvingly quote, in *Anthony Burgess Revisited* (1991), Prince's harsh words about the representation of Enderby's bigotries,[68] but he went on to reiterate, nine years later, the trite critical misconception that at certain points in *The Clockwork Testament* 'Burgess and his character Enderby are indistinguishable'.[69]

Despite all the ill-advised or ill-disposed misinterpretations in the critical reception of *The Clockwork Testament*, the early reviews surveyed for this introduction are not without some sound critical observations. Even such less than friendly assessments as those made by Lawless or Stinson contain bits of valuable insight concerning the novel's formal properties. Although he finds the prose 'lofty and burdensome' at points and dismisses the talk-show transcript as implausible, the Harvard reviewer is alert to what he calls 'traceries of stream of consciousness'.[70] Together with the Eliotian parallels also noted in his review, such alertness to a novel's allusiveness bespeaks an education incomparably more effective than whatever Enderby's students had access to before making use of the open admission

66 Greg Lawless, 'A Clockwork Lemon', *Harvard Crimson*, 13 February 1975, www.thecrimson.com/article/1975/2/13/a-clockwork-lemon-pbabntho ny-burgess-would/ (accessed 31 March 2021).
67 Burgess, 'A Letter', *New York Times*, 19 November 1972, section SM, p. 20.
68 Stinson, *Anthony Burgess Revisited*, p. 97.
69 John J. Stinson, 'The Gratitude for Influence: Hopkins in the Work of Anthony Burgess', *The Hopkins Quarterly*, 7:1–2 (2000), pp. 18–43, p. 30.
70 Lawless, 'A Clockwork Lemon'.

policy employed by 'the University of Manhattan' and its real-life model CCNY. Indeed, the erudite remarks made by this critic have more in common with such learned discussions of the novel's amazingly complex intertextuality as those found in academic exegeses produced by the calibre of Geoffrey Aggeler or Samuel Coale than with the impressionistic evaluations characterising some of the book reviews produced at the time. Noteworthy in this connection are the novel's strategically important borrowings from and references to the works of Rabelais and Cervantes, Milton and Blake, Hopkins and Joyce, or Dostoevsky and B.F. Skinner, whose names most frequently crop up in the scholarly evaluations made in Burgess's lifetime of *The Clockwork Testament*. Among these must be counted Stinson's altogether unfavourable assessment, which nevertheless takes stock of the novel's aesthetic merits, too. These include, beyond Burgess's unfailing ability to entertain, the satirist's legitimate recourse to the time-honoured device of exaggeration.

Although Stinson did not share the warm enthusiasm as displayed by Auberon Waugh or A.S. Byatt, even he is likely to have accepted Geoffrey Aggeler's qualified appreciation of what Burgess achieved or failed to achieve with his third Enderby novel. New readers as well as Burgess aficionados will agree with Aggeler, the late doyen of Burgess criticism, in his overall assessment of *The Clockwork Testament*. As he convincingly argues in *Anthony Burgess: The Artist as Novelist*, thanks to being animated by the writer's 'fine rage and an unwearying wit', this less than forty-thousand-word novel is 'a superb little satire'.[71]

---

71 Geoffrey Aggeler, *Anthony Burgess: The Artist as Novelist* (Tuscaloosa, AL: University Alabama Press, 1979), p. 180.

The Clockwork Testament
or: Enderby's End

To Burt Lancaster
('... deserves to live, deserves to live.')

One

The first thing he saw on waking was his lower denture on the floor, its groove encrusted with dried Dentisement, or it might be Orastik, Mouthficks, Gripdent, or Bite (called *Bait* in Tangier, where he could be said to have a sort of permanent, that is to say, if you could talk of permanency these days in anything, so to speak, address), the fully teethed in my audience will hardly conceive of the variety of denture adhesives on the market. His tongue, at once sprung into life horribly with no prelude of decent morning sluggishness, probed the lower gum briskly and found a diminution of yesterday's soreness. Then it settled into the neutral schwa position to await further directives. So. The denture, incrustations picked loose, laved, recharged with goo of Firmchew – family size with NEW wintergreen flavour – could be jammed in without serious twinge. As well, since today students must be met and talked at.

He lay, naked for the central heat, on his belly. If the bed, which was circular in shape, were a clock, then he was registering twenty of two, as Americans put it, meaning twenty to two. If, that was, his upper part were the hour hand. If that was, twelve o'clock was where the bed touched the wall. The Great Bed of Ware of English legend had been round also, though much bigger, the radius being the length of a sleeper – say six feet. How many pairs of dirty (read Rabelaisian, rollicking) feet meeting at the center (re)? Circumference 2 pi r, was it? It didn't seem big enough somehow. But all the big things of European legend were smaller than you had been brought up to imagine. American scholars sorted that sort of thing out for you.

Anybody could eat whole mediaeval sheep, being no bigger than rabbit. Suits of armor (our) would accommodate twelve-year-old American girl. Not enough vitamins in roystering rollicking diet. Hell was originally a rubbish-dump outside Jerusalem.

He lay naked also on a fast-drying nocturnal ejaculation, wonderful for man of your age, Enderby. What had the dream been that had conduced to wetness? Being driven in a closed car, muffled to the ears, in black spectacles, funeral sombrero, very pimply guffawing lout driving. Driven into slum street where twelve-year-old girls, Puerto Rican mostly, were playing with a ball. Wait, no, two balls, naturally. The girls jeered, showed themselves knickerless, provoked. He, Enderby, had to go on sitting in black and back of car while guffawing driver got out and ministered very rapidly to them all, their number of course changing all the time. *Finnegans Wake*, ladies and gentlemen, is false to the arithmetic of true dreams, number in that book being an immutable rigidity while, as we know, it is a mutable fluidity in our regular dreaming experience. There are seven biscuits, which you call er cookies, on a plate. You take away, say, two and three remain. Or, of course, they could be what you call biscuits and we, I think, muffins. Principle is the same. I question that, said a sneering Christ of a student. Professor Enderby, asked a what Enderby took to be Polack, Nordic anyway, lacking eyelashes, please clarify your precise threshold of credibility.

This driver lout got through the lot, standing, with quick canine thrusts. Then Enderby was granted discharge and the entire scene, as in some story by that blind Argentinian he had been urged to read by somebody eager and halitotic in the Faculty Lounge, collapsed.

The bed he lay on, twenty of two, squinting down at his watch also on the floor, ten of eight of a New York February morning, was circular because of some philosophy of the regular tenant of the apartment, now on sabbatical and working on Thelma Garstang (1798–1842, bad poetess beaten to death by drunken husband, alleged anyway) in British Museum. The traditional quadrangular bed was male tyranny, or something. This regular tenant was, as well as being an academic, a woman novelist who wrote not very popular novels in which the male characters ended up being castrated. Then, it was implied, or so Enderby understood, not having read any of them, only having been told about them, they became considerate lovers eager for cunnilingus with their castratrices, but they were sneered at for being impotent. Well, he, unimpotent Enderby, temporary professor, would do nothing about cleaning that sperm-stain from her circular mattress, ridiculous idea, must have cost a fortune.

Enderby had slept, as now he always did, with his upper denture in. It was a sort of response to the castrating aura of the apartment. He had also found it necessary to be ready for the telephone to ring at all hours, an edentulous chumble getting responses of *Pardon me?* if the call were a polite one, but if it were insulting or obscene or both, provoking derision. Most of the Serious Calls came from what was known as the Coast and were for his landlady. She was connected with some religiolesbic movement there and she had neglected to send a circular letter about her sabbatical. The insults and obscenities were usually meant for Enderby. He had written a very unwise article for a magazine, in which he said that he thought little of black literature because it tended to tendentiousness and that the Amerindians had shown no evidence of talent for anything except scalping and very inferior folkcraft. One of his callers, who had once termed him a toothless cocksucker (that toothlessness had been right, anyway, at that time anyway), was always threatening to bring a tomahawk to 91st Street and Columbus Avenue, which was where Enderby lodged. Also students would ring anonymously at deliberately awkward hours to revile him for his various faults – chauvinism, or some such thing; ignorance of literary figures important to the young; failure to see merit in their own free verse and gutter vocabulary. They would revile him also in class, of course, but not so freely as on the telephone. Everybody felt naked these days without the mediacy of a mode of mechanical communication.

Eight of eight. The telephone rang. Enderby decided to give it the honour of full dentition, so he jammed in the encrusted lower denture. Try it out. Gum still sorish. But, of course, that was the hardened Gripdent or whatever it was. He had them all.

'Professor Enderby?'

'Speaking.'

'You don't know me, but this is just to inform you that both my husband and I consider that your film is filth.'

'It's not my film. I only wrote the –'

'You have a lot to answer for, my husband says. Don't you think there's enough juvenile crime in our streets without filth like yours abetting it?'

'But it's not filth and it's not my –'

'Obscene filth. Let me inform you that my husband is six feet three and broad in proportion –'

'Is he a Red Indian?'

'That's just the sort of cheap insult I would expect from a man capable of –'

'If you're going to send him round here, with or without toma-hawk –'

She had put down the receiver. What he had been going to say was that there was twenty-four-hour armed protection in the apart-ment lobby as well as many closed-circuit television screens. This, however, would not help him if the enemies were within the block itself. That he had enemies in the block he knew – a gat-toothed black writer and his wife; a single woman with dogs who had objected to his mentioning in his magazine article the abundance of cockroaches in this part of Manhattan as though it were a shameful family secret; a couple of fattish electronic guitarists who had smelt his loathing as they had gone up together once in the elevator. And there might also be others affronted by the film just this moment referred to.

Flashback. Into the bar-restaurant run by Enderby, exiled poet, in Tangier, film-men had one day come. Kasbah location work or something of the kind. One of the film-men, who had seemed and indeed proved to be big in his field, an American director considered for the brilliance of his visual invention quite as good as any direc-tor in Europe, said something about wanting to make, because of the visual possibilities, a shipwreck film. Enderby, behind bar and hence free to join in conversation without any imputation of inso-lence, having also British accent, said something about *The Wreck of the Deutschland*.

'Too many Kraut Kaput movies lately. Last days of Hitler, Joe Krankenhaus already working on Goebbels, then there was Visconti.'

'A ship,' said Enderby, 'called the Deutschland. Hopkins wrote it.'

'Al Hopkins?'

'G.M.,' Enderby said, adding, 'S.J.'

'Never heard of him. Why does he want all those initials?'

'Five Franciscan nuns,' Enderby said, 'exiled from Germany because of the Falk Laws. "On Saturday sailed from Bremen, American-outward-bound, take settler with seaman, tell men with women, two hundred souls in the round ..."'

'He knows it all, by God. When?'

'1875. December 7th.'

'Nuns,' mused the famed director. 'What were these laws?'

'"Rhine refused them. Thames would ruin them,"' Enderby said. '"Surf, snow, river, and earth,"' he said, '"Gnashed."'

'Totalitarian intolerance,' the director's assistant and friend said. 'Nuns beaten up in the streets. Habits torn off. Best done in flashback. The storm symbolic as well as real. What happens at the end?' he asked Enderby keenly.

'They all get wrecked in the Goodwin Sands. The Kentish Knock, to be precise. And then there's this final prayer. "Let him easter in us, be a dayspring to the dimness of us, be a crimson-cresseted east ..."'

'In movies,' the director said kindly, as to a child, 'you don't want too many words. You see that? It's what we call a visual medium. Two more double scatches on the racks.'

'I know all about that,' Enderby said with heat, pouring whisky sightlessly for these two men. 'When they did my *Pet Beast* it became nothing but visual clichés. In Rome it was. Cinecittà. The bastard. But he's dead now.'

'Who's dead?'

'Rawcliffe,' Enderby said. 'He used to own this place.' The two men stared at him. 'What I mean is,' Enderby said, 'that there was this film. Movie, you'd call it, ridiculous word. In Italian, *L'Animal Binato*. That was *Son of the Beast from Outer Space*. In English that is,' he explained.

'But that,' the director said, 'was a small masterpiece. Alberto Formica, dead now poor bastard, well ahead of his time. The clichés were deliberate, it summed up a whole era. So.' He looked at Enderby with new interest. 'What did you say your name was? Rawcliffe? I always thought Rawcliffe was dead.'

'Enderby,' Enderby said. 'Enderby the poet.'

'You did the script, you say?' the assistant and friend said.

'I wrote *The Pet Beast*.'

'Why,' the director said, taking out a visiting card from among embossed instruments of international credit, 'don't you write us a letter, the shipwreck story I mean, setting it all out?'

Enderby smiled knowingly, a poet but up to their little tricks. 'I give you a film script for nothing?' he said. 'I've heard of this letter business before.' The card read *Melvin Schaumwein, Chisel Productions*. 'If I do you a script I shall want paying for it.'

'How much?' said Mr Schaumwein.

Enderby smiled. 'A lot,' he said. The money part of his brain grew suddenly delirious, lifelong abstainer fed with sudden gin. He trembled as with the prospect of sexual outrage. 'A thousand dollars,' he said. They stared at him. 'There,' he said. And then: 'Somewhere in that region anyway. I'm not what you'd call a greedy man.'

'We might manage five hundred,' Schaumwein's assistant-friend said. 'On delivery, of course. Provided that it's what might be termed satisfactory.'

'Seven hundred and fifty,' Enderby said. 'I'm not what you'd call a greedy man.'

'It's not an original,' Mr Schaumwein said. 'You mentioned some guy called Hopkins that wrote the book. Who is he, where is he, who do I see about the rights?'

'Hopkins,' Enderby said, 'died in 1889. His poems were published in 1918. *The Wreck of the Deutschland* is out of copyright.'

'I think,' Mr Schaumwein said carefully, 'we'll have two more scatches on the racks.'

What, after Mr Schaumwein had gone back to the Kasbah and then presumably home to Chisel Productions, was to surprise Enderby was that the project was to be taken seriously presumably.

For a letter came from the friend-assistant, name revealed as Martin Droeshout (familiar vaguely to Enderby in some vague picture connection or other), confirming that, for $750.00, Enderby would deliver a treatment for a film tentatively entitled *The Wreck of the Deutschland*, based on a story by Hopkins, which story their researchers had not been able to bring to light despite prolonged research, had Enderby got the name right, but it didn't matter as subject was in public domain. Enderby presumed that the word *treatment* was another word for *shooting script* (a lot of film-men had been to his bar at one time or another, so the latter term was familiar to him). He had even looked at the shooting script of a film in which a heavy though not explicit sexual sequence had actually been shot, at midnight with spotlights and a humming generator truck, on the beach just near to his beach café-restaurant, *La Belle Mer*. So, while his boys snored or writhed sexually with each other during the siesta, he got down to typewriter – pecking out his cine-matization of a great poem, delighting in such curt visual directives as VLS, CU, and so on, though not always clearly understanding what they meant.

1. EXTERIOR NIGHT
Lightning lashes a rod on top of a church.

PRIEST'S VOICE:
Yes. Yes. Yes.

2. INTERIOR NIGHT A CHURCH
Thunder rolls. A priest on his knees at the altar looks up, sweating. It is Fr Hopkins, S.J.

FR HOPKINS, S.J.:
Thou hearest me truer than tongue confess
Thy terror, O Christ, O God.

3. EXTERIOR NIGHT A STARLIT SKY
The camera pans slowly across lovely-asunder starlight.

4. EXTERIOR NIGHT THE GROUNDS OF A
   THEOLOGICAL SEMINARY

Father Hopkins, S.J., looks up ecstatically at all the firefolk sitting in the air and then kisses his hand at them.

5. EXTERIOR SUNSET THE DAPPLED-WITH-DAMSON
   WEST

Father Hopkins, S.J., kisses his hand at it.

6. INTERIOR DAY A REFECTORY

The scene begins with a CU of Irish stew being placed on a table by an illgirt scullion. Then the camera pulls back to show priests talking vigorously.

PRIEST #1:
These Falk Laws in Germany are abominable and totally
sinful.

PRIEST #2:
I hear that a group of Franciscan nuns are sailing to America
next Saturday.

The voice of Father Hopkins, S.J. is heard from another part of the table.

HOPKINS (OS):
Glory be to God for dappled things,
For skies of couple-colour as a brinded cow ...

The priests look at each other.

7. THE SAME TWO SHOT

Father Hopkins is talking earnestly to a very beautiful fellow-priest who listens attentively.

HOPKINS:
Since, though he is under the world's splendour and wonder,
his mystery must be instressed, stressed …

FELLOW-PRIEST:
I quite understand.

The camera pans rapidly back to the other two priests, who look at each other.

PRIEST #1:
(*sotto voce*)
Jesus Christ.

It worried Enderby a little, as he proceeded with his film version of the first part of the poem, that Hopkins should appear to be a bit cracked. There was also a problem in forcing a relevance between the first part and the second. Enderby, serving one morning abstractedly sloe gin to two customers, hit on a solution. 'Sacrifice,' he said suddenly. The customers took their sloe gins away to a far table. The idea being that Hopkins wanted to be Christ but that the tall nun, Gertrude, kindly became Christ for him, and that her sort of crucifixion on the Kentish Knock (sounded, he thought gloomily, like some rural sexual aberration) might conceivably be thought of as helping to bring our King back, oh, upon English souls.

12. EXTERIOR DAY CU A SLOE
We see a lush-kept plush-capped sloe in a white well-kept priestly hand.

13. CU FATHER HOPKINS S.J.
Hopkins, in very large close-up, mouths the sloe to fleshburst. He shudders.

14. EXTERIOR DAY CALVARY
Christ is being nailed to the cross. Roman soldiers jeer.

15. RESUME 13.
Hopkins, still shuddering, looks down at the bitten sloe. The camera
tracks on to it into CU. It dissolves into:

16. INTERIOR DAY A CHURCH
The hands of a priest hold up the host, which looks a bit like the sloe.
It is, of course, Fr Hopkins, S.J., saying mass.

17. THE SAME CU
In CU, Father Hopkins murmurs ecstatically.

> HOPKINS:
> (*ecstatically*)
> Be adored among men, God, three-numbered form. Wring thy
> rebel, dogged in den, man's malice, with wrecking and storm.

18. EXTERIOR DAY A STORMY SEA
The *Deutschland*, American-outward-bound. Death on drum, and
storms bugle his fame.

The second part was easier, mostly a business of copy-
ing out Hopkins's own what might be thought of as prophetic
camera-directions:

45. EXTERIOR DAY THE SEA
Wiry and white-fiery and whirlwind-swivelled snow spins to the
widow-making unchilding unfathering deeps.

And so on. When it was finished it made, Enderby thought, a very
nice little script. It could be seen also as the tribute of one poet to
another. People would see the film and then go and read the poem.
They would see the poem as superior art to the film. He sent the
script off to Mr Schaumwein at Chisel Productions. He eventually
received a brief letter from Martin Droeshout saying that a lot of
it was very flowery, but that was put down to Enderby's being a
poet, which claim of Enderby had been substantiated by researchers.
However, they were going ahead, updating so as to make Germany

Nazi, and making the nun Gertrude a former love of Father Hopkins, both of them coming to realization that it was God they really loved but they would keep in touch. This meant re-write men, as Enderby would realize, but Enderby's name would appear among the credits.

Enderby's name did indeed eventually appear among the credits: *Developed out of an idea of*. Also he was invited to London to see a preview of *The Wreck of the Deutschland* (they couldn't think of a better title, any of them; there wasn't a better title). He was pretty shocked by a lot of it, especially the flashbacks and it was nearly all flashbacks, the only present-tense reality being the *Deutschland* on its way to be ground to bits on the Kentish Knock (which, some-body else at the preview said, to ecstatic laughter, sounded a little like a rural sexual aberration). For instance, Hopkins, who had been given quite arbitrarily the new name Tom, eventually Father Tom, was Irish, and the tall nun was played by a Swede, though that was really all right. These two had a great pink sexual encounter, but before either of them took vows, so that, Enderby supposed, was all right too. There were some over-explicit scenes of the nuns being violated by teenage storm-troopers. The tall nun Gertrude herself tore off her Franciscan habit to make bandages during the storm scenes, so that her end, in a posture of crucifixion on the Kentish Knock, was as near-nude as that of her Master. There was also an ambiguous moment when, storms bugling, though somewhat sub-dued, Death's fame in the background, she cried orgasmatically: 'O Christ, Christ, come quickly' – Hopkins's own words, so one could hardly complain. On the whole, not a bad film, with Hopkins getting two secondsworth of solo credit: *Based on the story by*. As was to be expected, it got a very restrictive showing rating, nobody under eighteen. 'Things have come to a pretty pass,' said Mr Shaumwein in a television interview, 'when a religious film is no longer regarded as good family viewing.'

So there it was then, except for complaints from the reaction-ary and puritanical, though not, as far as Enderby could tell, from Hopkins's fellow-Jesuits. *The Month*, which had originally refused the poem itself, made amends by finding the film adult and seri-ous. 'Mr Schaumwein very sensibly has eschewed the temptation to translate Hopkins's confused grammar and neologistic tortuosities into corresponding visual obscurities.' Enderby's association, however small, with a great demotic medium led to his being considered worthy by the University of Manhattan of being invited to come as a visiting professor for an academic year. The man who sent the invitation, the Chairman of the English Department, Alvin Kosciusko, said that Enderby's poems were not unknown there in the United States. Whatever anybody thought of them, there was no doubt that they were genuine Creative Writing. Enderby was therefore cordially invited to come and pass on some of his Creative Writing skill to Creative Writing students. His penchant for old-fashioned and traditional forms might act as a useful corrective to the cult of free form which, though still rightly flourishing, had led to some excesses. One postgraduate student had received a prize for a poem that turned out to be a passage from a vice-presidential speech copied out in reverse and then seasoned with mandatory obscenities. He had protested that it was as much Creative Writing as any of the shit that had been awarded prizes in previous years. Anyway, the whole business of giving prizes was reactionary. Subsidies were what was required.

Two

Naked as the day he was born though much hairier, Enderby prepared himself breakfast. One of the things he approved of about New York – a city otherwise dirty, rude, violent, and full of foreigners and mad people – was the wide variety of dyspeptic foods on sale in the supermarkets. In his view, if you did not get dyspepsia while or after eating, you had been cheated of essential nourishment. As for dealing with the dyspepsia, he had never in his life seen so many palliatives for it available – Sums and Windkill and Eupep and (magnificent proleptic onomatopoesis, the work of some high-paid Madison Avenue genius, sincerely admired by Enderby) Aaaarp. And so on. But the best of all he had discovered in a small shop specializing in Oriental medicines (sent thither by a Chinese waiter) – a powerful black viscidity that oozed sinisterly from a tube to bring wind up from Tartarean depths. When he went to buy it, the shopkeeper would, in his earthy Chinese manner, designate it with a remarkable phonic mime of the substance at work. Better than Aaaarp but not easily representable in any conventional alphabet. Enderby would nod kindly, pay, take, bid good day, go.

Enderby had become, so far as use of the culinary resources of the kitchen (at night the cockroaches' playground) were concerned, one hundred per cent Americanized. He would whip up a thick milk shake in the mixer, thaw then burn frozen waffles in the toaster, make soggy leopardine pancakes with Aunt Jemima's buckwheat pancake mixture (Aunt Jemima herself was on the packet, a comely Negress rejoicing in her bandanna'd servitude), fry Pepperidge Farm fat little sausages. His nakedness would be fat-splashed, but the fat easily washed off, unlike with clothes. And he would make tea, though not altogether in the American manner – five bags in a pint mug with ALABAMA gilded on it, boiling water, a long stewing, very sweet condensed milk added. He would eat his breakfast with H.P. steak sauce on one side of the plate, maple syrup on the other. The Americans went in for synchronic sweet and savoury, a sign of their salvation, unlike the timid Latin races. He would end his meal with a healthy slice of Sarah Lee orange cream cake, drink another pint of tea, then, after his black Chinese draught, be alertly ready for work. A mansized breakfast, as they said. There was never need for much lunch – some canned corned beef hash with a couple of fried eggs, say, and a pint of tea. A slice of banana cake. And then, this being America, a cup of coffee.

Heartburn was slow in coming this morning, which made Enderby, stickler for routine, uneasy. He noted also with rueful pride that, despite the emission of the night, he was bearing before him as he left the kitchen, where he had eaten as well as cooked, a sizeable horizontal ithyphallus lazily swinging towards the vertical. Something to do perhaps with excessive protein intake. He took it to a dirty towel in the bathroom, called those Puerto Rican bitches back from that dream, then gave it them all. The street was littered with them. The pimpled lout, astonished and fearful, ran round the corner. This meant that Enderby would have to drive the car away himself. He at once sold it for a trifling sum to a grey-haired black man who shuffled out of an open doorway, evening newspaper in his hand, and made his getaway, naked, on foot. Then dyspepsia struck, he took his black drops, released a savoury gale from as far down as the very caecum, and was ready for work, his own work, not the pseudo-work he would have to do in the afternoon with pseudo-students. For that he must shave, dress, wash, probably in that order. Take the subway, as they called it. Brave mean streets full of black and brown menace.

Enderby, still naked, sat at his landlady's desk in the bedroom. It was a small apartment, there was no study. He supposed he was lucky to have gotten (very American touch there: *gotten*) an apartment at all at the rent he was able, the salary not being overlarge, to pay. His landlady, a rabid ideological man-hater, had addressed one letter to him from her digs in Bayswater, confirming that he pay the black woman Priscilla to come and clean for him every Saturday, thus maintaining a continuity of her services useful for when his landlady should return to New York. Enderby was not sure what sex she thought he, Enderby, had, since there was a reference to not trying to flush sanitary pads down the toilet. The title professor, which she rightly addressed him by, was common, as the old grammars would put it. Perhaps she had read his poems and found a rich femininity in them; perhaps some kind man in the English Department had represented Enderby as an ageing but progressive spinster to her when she sought to let her apartment. Anyway, he had answered the letter promptly on his own portable typewriter, signing with a delicate hand, assuring her that sanitary pads would go out with the garbage and that Priscilla was being promptly paid and not over-worked (lazy black insolent bitch, thought Enderby, but evidently illiterate and not likely to blow the sex gaff in letter or transatlantic cable). So there it was. On the other hand, his landlady might learn in London from librarians or in communications from members of the Californian religiolesbic sorority that Enderby was really a (*sounded suspiciously like the voice of an MCP to me, toothless too, a TMCP, what little game are you playing, dear?*). But it was probably too late for her to do anything about it now. Couldn't evict him on grounds of his sex. The United Nations, conveniently here in New York, would, through an appropriate department, have something very sharp to say about that. So there it was, then. Enderby got down to work.

Back in Morocco, as previously in England, Enderby was used to working in the toilet, piling up drafts and even fair copies in the never-used bath. Here it would not do, since the bath-taps dripped and the toilet-seat was (probably by some previous Jewish-mother tenant who wished to discourage solitary pleasures among her men-folk) subtly notched. It was ungrateful to the bottom. Neither was there a writing table low enough. Nor would Priscilla understand. This eccentric country was great on conformity. Enderby now

wrote at the desk that had produced so many androphobic mistress
pieces. What he was writing was a long poem about St Augustine and
Pelagius, trying to sort out for himself and a couple of score readers
the whole worrying business of predestination and free will. He read
through what he had so far written, scratching and grunting, naked,
a horrible White Owl cigar in his mouth.

> He came out of the misty island, Morgan,
> Man of the sea, demure in Monk's sackcloth,
> Taking the long way to Rome, expecting –
> Expecting what? Oh, holiness quintessentialized,
> Holiness whole, the wholesome wholemeal of,
> Holiness as meat and drink and air, in the
> Chaste thrusts of marital love holiness, and
> Sanctitas sanctitas even snaking up from
> Cloacae and sewers, sanctitas the effluvium
> From his Holiness's arsehole.

Perhaps that was going a bit too far. Enderby poised a ballpoint,
dove, retracted. No, it was the right touch really. Let the *arsehole*
stay. Americans preferred *asshole* for some reason. This then very
British. But why not? Pelagius was British. Keep *arsehole* in.

> On the long road
> Trudging, dust, birdsong, dirty villages,
> Stops on the way at monasteries (weeviled bread,
> Eisel wine), always this thought: *Sanctitas.*
> What dost seek in Rome, brother? The home
> Of holiness, to lodge awhile in the
> Sanctuary of sanctity, my brothers, for here
> Peter died, seeing before he died
> The pagan world inverted to sanctitas, and
> The very flagged soil is rich with the bonemeal
> Of the martyrs. And the brothers would
> Look at each other, each thinking, some saying:
> Here cometh one that only islands breed.

What can flourish in that Ultima Thule save
Holiness, a bare garment for the wind to
Sing through? And not Favonius either but
Sour Boreas from the pole. Not the grape,
Not garlic not the olive, not the strong sun
Tickling the manhood in a man, be he
Monk or friar or dean or
Burly bishop, big ballocks swinging like twin censers.
Only holiness. God help him, God bless him for
We look upon British innocence.
And the British innocent, hurtful of no man,
Fond of dogs, a cat-stroker,
Trudged on south – vine, olive, garlic,
Brown tits jogging while brown feet
Danced in the grapepress and the
Baaark ballifoll goristafick

That last was inner Enderby demanding the stool. He took his poem
with him thither, frowning, sat reading.

Monstrous aphrodisiac danced in the heavens
Prrrrrrp faaaark
Wheep
Till at length he came to the outer suburbs and
Fell on his knees O *sancta urbs sancta sancta*
Meaning sancta suburbs and
Plomp

Enderby wiped himself with slow care and marched back, frowning,
reading. As he reached the telephone on the bed table the telephone
rang, so that he was able to pick it up at once, thus disconcerting the
voice on the other end, which had not expected such promptitude.

'Oh. Mr Enderby?' It was a woman's voice, being higher than a
man's. American female voices lacked feminine timbre as known in
the south of vine and garlic, were just higher because of accident of
larynx being smaller.

'Professor Enderby speaking.'

'Oh, hi. This is the Sperr Lansing Show. We wondered if you –'

'What? Who? What is this?'

'The Sperr Lansing Show. A talk show. Television. *The* talk show. Channel Fif –'

'Ah, I see,' Enderby said, with British heartiness. 'I've seen it, I think. She left it here, you see. Extra on the rent.'

'Who? What?'

'Oh, I see what you mean. Yes. A television. She's a great one for her rights. Ah yes, I've seen it a few times. A sort of thin man with a fat jackal. Both leer a good deal, but one supposes they have to.'

'No, no, you have the wrong show there, professor.' The title now seemed pretentious, also absurd, as when someone in a film is addressed as *professor*. 'What you mean is the Cannon Dickson Show. That's mostly show business personalities. The Sperr Lansing Show is, well, *different*.'

'I didn't really mean to insist, ha ha,' Enderby said, 'on the title of professor. Fancy dress, you know. A lot of nonsense really. And I really must apologize for ...' He was going to say *for being naked*: it was all this damned visual stuff. 'For my innocence. I mean my ignorance.'

'I guess I ought to introduce myself – we've already been talking for such a long time. I'm Midge Tauchnitz.'

'Enderby,' Enderby said. 'Sorry, that was ... So, eh?' "The strong spur, live and lancing like the blowpipe flame." I suppose that's where he got it from.'

'Pardon me?'

'Anyway, thank you for calling.'

'No, it doesn't go out live. Nothing these days goes out live.'

'I promise to watch it at the earliest opportunity. Thank you very much for suggesting ...'

'No, no, we want you to appear on it. We record at seven so you'd have to be here about six.'

'Why?' Enderby said in honest surprise. 'For God's sake why?'

'Oh, makeup and so on. It's on West 46th Street, between Fifth and ...'

'No, no, no. Why me?'

'Pardon me?'

'Me.'

'Oh.' The voice became teasing and girlish. 'Oh, come now, professor, that's playing it too cool. It's the movie. *The Deutschland*.'

'Ah. But I only wrote the – I mean, it was only my idea. That's what it says, anyway. Why don't you ask one of the others, the ones who really made it?'

'Well,' she said candidly. 'We tried to get hold of Bob Ponte, the script-writer but he's in Honolulu writing a script, and Mr Schaumwein is in Rome, and Millennium suggested we get on to you. So I phoned the university and they gave us your –'

'Hopkins,' Enderby said, in gloomy play. 'Did you try Hopkins?'

'No luck there either. Nobody knows where he is.'

'In the eschatological sense, I should think it's pretty certain that –'

'Pardon me?'

'But in the other it's no wonder. 1844 to 89,' he twinkled.

'Oh, I'll write that down. But it doesn't sound like a New York number –'

'No no no no no. A little joke. He's dead, you see.'

'Gee, I'm sorry, I didn't know. But you're okay? I mean, you'll be there?'

'If you really want me. But I still don't see –'

'You don't? You don't read the newspapers?'

'Never. And again never. A load of frivolity and lies. They've been attacking it, have they?'

'No. Some boys have been attacking some nuns. In Manhattanville. I'm shocked you didn't know. I assumed –'

'Nuns are always being attacked. Their purity is an affront to the dirty world.'

'Remember that. Remember to say that. But the point is that they said they wouldn't have done it if they hadn't seen the movie. That's why we're –'

'I see. I see. Always blame art, eh? Not original sin but art. I'll have my say, never fear.'

'You have the address?'

'You ignore art as so much unnecessary garbage or you blame it for your own crimes. That's the way of it. I'll get the bastards, all of them. I'm not having this sort of nonsense, do you hear?' There was silence at the other end. 'You never take art for what it is – beauty, ultimate meaning, form for its own sake, self-subsisting, oh no. It's always got to be either sneered at or attacked as evil. I'll have my bloody say. What's the name of the show again?' But she had rung off, silly bitch.

Enderby went snorting back to his poem. The stupid bastards.

But wherever he went in Rome, it was always the same –
Sin sin sin, no sanctity, the whole unholy
Grammar of sin, syntax, accidence, sin's
Entire lexicon set before him, sin.
Peacocks in the streets, gold dribbled over
In dark rooms, vomiting after
Banquets of ostrich bowels stuffed with saffron,
Minced pikeflesh and pounded larkbrain,
Served with a sauce headily fetid, and pocula
Of wine mixed with adder's blood to promote
Lust lust and again.
Pederasty, podorasty, sodomy, bestiality,
Degrees of family ripped apart like
Bodices in the unholy dance. And he said,
And Morgan said, whom the scholarly called PELAGIUS:
Why do ye this, my brothers and sisters?
Are ye not saved by Christ, are ye not
Sanctified by his sacrifice, oh why why why?
(Being British and innocent) and

What was the name of that show again? Art blamed as always. Art was neutral, neither teaching nor provoking, a static shimmer, he would tell the bastards. What was it again? And then he thought about this present poem (a draft of course, very much a draft) and wondered: *is it perhaps not didactic?* But how about *The Wreck of the Deutschland?* Hopkins was always having a go at the English, and the Welsh too, for not rushing to be converted back (the marvellous milk was Walsingham Way, once) to Catholicism. But somehow Hopkins was of the devil's party without knowing it (better remember not to say that on this Live Lancing Show, that was the name, something like it anyway, people were stupid, picked you up literally on that sort of thing. It was a kind of paganism with him: lush-kept plush-capped sloe, indeed, with God tacked on. The our-king-back-oh-upon-English-souls stuff was merely structural, something to bring the poem to an end. But how about this?

No, he decided. He was not preaching. Who the hell was he to preach? Out of the Church at sixteen, never been to mass in forty years. This was merely an imaginative inquiry into free will and predestination. Somewhat comforted, he read on, scratching, the White Owl, self-doused, relighted, hooting out foul smoke.

> They said to him cheerfully, looking up
> From picking a peahen bone or kissing the
> Nipple or nates of son, daughter, sister,
> Brother, aunt, ewe, teg: Why, stranger,
> Hast not heard the good news? That Christ
> Took away the burden of our sins on his
> Back broad to bear, and as we are saved
> Through him it matters little what we do?
> Since we are saved once for all, our being
> Saved will not be impaired or cancelled by
> Our present pleasures (which we propose to
> Renew tomorrow after a suitable and well-needed
> Rest). Alleluia alleluia to the Lord for he has
> Led us to two paradises, one to come and the other
> Here and now. Alleluia. And they fell to again,
> To nipple or nates or fish baked with datemince,
> Alleluia. And Morgan cried to the sky:
> How long O Lord wilt thou permit these
> Transgressions against thy holiness?
> Strike them strike them as thou once didst
> The salty cities of the plain, as through

Phinehas the son of Eleazar the son of Aaron
Thou didst strike down the traitor Zimri
And his foul whore of the Moabite temples of Cozbi.
Strike strike. But the Lord did nothing.

Here came the difficulties. This whole business of free will and pre-destination and original sin had to be done very dramatically. And yet there had to be a bit of sermonizing. How the hell? Enderby, who was not at present wearing his spectacles (ridiculous when one was otherwise naked, anyway he only needed them for distance really), gazing vaguely about the bedroom for an answer found none forthcoming. The bookshelves of his landlady sternly turned the backs, spines rather, of their contents towards him: not our business, we are concerned with the real issues of life, meaning women downtrodden by men, the economic oppression of the blacks, counter-culture, coming revolt, Reich, Fanon, third world. Then Enderby, squinting, could hardly believe what he saw. At the bedroom door a woman, girl, female anyway. Covering his genitals with his poem he said:

'What the devil? Who let you? Get out.'

'But I have an appointment with you at ten. It's ten after now. It was arranged. I'll wait in the – Unless – I mean, I didn't expect –'

She had not yet gone. Enderby, pumping vigorously at White Owl as if it would thus make him an enveloping cloud, turned his back to her, covered his bottom with his poem, then found his dressing-gown (Rawcliffe's really, bequeathed to him with his other effects) on a chair behind a rattan settee and near to the air-conditioner. He clothed himself in it. She was still there and talking.

'I mean, I don't mind if you don't –'

'I do mind,' Enderby said. And he flapped towards her on bare feet but in his gown. 'What is all this anyway?'

'For *Jesus*.'

'For *who*, for Christ's sake?' He was close to her now and saw that she was a nice little thing he supposed she could be called, with nicely sculpted little tits under a black sweater stained with, as he supposed, coke and pepsi and hamburger fat (*good food* was what these poor kids needed), long American legs in patched worker's pants.

Strange how one never bothered to take in the face here in America, the face didn't matter except on films, one never remembered the face and all the voices were the same. And then: 'They shouldn't have let you in, you know, just like that. You're supposed to be screened or something, and then they ring me up and ask if it's all right.'

'But he knows me, the man downstairs. He knows I'm one of your students.'

'Oh, are you?' said Enderby. 'I didn't quite – Yes,' peering at her, 'I suppose you could be. We'd better go into the sitting-room or whatever they call it.' And he pushed past her into the corridor to lead the way.

The room where he was supposed to *live*, that is, watch television, play protest songs on his landlady's record-player, look out of the window down on the street at acts of violence, was furnished mostly with barbaric nonsense – drums and shields and spears and very ill-woven garish rugs – and you were supposed to sit on *pouffes*. Enderby waved this girl to a *pouffe* with one hand and with the other indicated the television set, saying, puffing out White Owl smoke, 'I'm to be on that thing there.'

'Oh.'

'The Blowpipe Show or something. Can't think of the name off-hand. What did you say your name was?'

'Oh, *you know*. Lydia Tietjens.' And, as he sat on a neighbouring *pouffe*, she gave him a playful push, as at his rather nice eccentric foreign silliness.

'Ah yes, of course. Ford Madox Ford. Met him once. He had terrible halitosis, you know. Stood in his way. The Establishment rejected him. And it was because he'd had the guts to fight and get gassed, while the rest of the bastards stayed at home. I say, you're not recording that, are you?' For, he now saw, she had a small Japanese cassette machine and was holding it towards him, rather like a sides-woman with offertory-box.

'Just getting a level.' And then, after some whirring and clicking, Enderby heard an unfamiliar voice say: *rest of the bastards stayed at home I say you're not rec.*

'What did you say it was for?'

'For *Jesus*. Our magazine. Women for Jesus. *You know.*'

'Why just women for Jesus? I thought anyone could join.' And Enderby looked with fascination at the xeroxed thing she brought out what looked like a British respirator haversack – their magazine, typewritten, as he could see from the last page, with no margin justifying, and the front page just showing the name JESUS and a crude portrait of a beardless though plentifully haired messiah.

'But that's not him.'

'Right. Not *him*. What proof is there that it was a *him*?' Enderby breathed hard a few times and said: 'Would you like what we English call elevenses? Cakes and tea and things? I could cook you a steak if you liked. Or, wait, I have some stew left over from yesterday. It wouldn't take a minute to heat it up.' That was the trouble with all of them, poor kids. Half-starved, seeing visions, poisoned with cokes and hamburgers.

Three

'Do you believe in God?' she asked, a steak sandwich in one paw and the cassette thing in the other.

'Is that tea strong enough for you?' Enderby asked. 'It doesn't look potable to me. One bag indeed. Gnat piss,' he added. And then: 'Oh, God. Well, believing is neither here nor there, you know. I believe in God and so what? I don't believe in God and so what again? It doesn't affect his own position, does it?'

'Why do you say *his*?' she hizzed.

'Her, then. It. Doesn't matter really. A matter of tradition and convention and so on. Needs a new pronoun. Let's invent one, unique, just for – himherit. Ah, that's it, then. Nominative *heshit*. Accusative *himrit*. Genitive *hiserits*.'

'But you're still putting the masculine first. The *heshit* bit's all right, though. Appropriate.'

'I don't mind what goes first,' Enderby said. 'Would you like something by Sarah Lee? Please yourself then. All right. *Shehit. Herimit. Herisits*. It doesn't affect herisits position whether I believe or not.'

'But what happens when you die?'

'You're finished with,' Enderby said promptly. 'Done for. And even if you weren't – well, you die then, gasp your last, then you're sort of wandering, free of your body. You wander around and then you come into contact with a sort of big thing. What is this big thing? God, if you like. What's it, or shehit, like? I would say,' Enderby said thoughtfully, 'like a big symphony, the page of the score of infinite length, the number of instruments infinite but all bound into one big unity. This big symphony plays itself for ever and ever. And who listens to it? It listens to itself. Enjoys itself for ever and ever and ever. It doesn't give a bugger whether you hear it or not.'

'Like masturbation.'

'I thought it would come to that. I thought you'd have to bring sex into it sooner or later. Anyway, a kind of infinite Ninth Symphony. God as Eternal Beauty. God as Truth? Nonsense. God as Goodness. That means shehit has to be in some sort of ethical relationship with beings that are notGod. But God is removed, cut off, self-subsistent, not giving a damn.'

'But that's horrible. I couldn't live with a God like that.'

'You don't have to. Anyway, what have you or anybody else got to do with it? God doesn't have to be what people want shehit to be. I'm fed up with God,' Enderby said, 'so let's get on to something else.' And at once he got up painfully and noisily to find the whisky bottle, this being about the time for. 'I haven't got any glasses,' he said. 'Not clean ones, anyway. You'll have to have it from the bottle.'

'I don't want any.' She didn't want her tea either. Quite right: gnat piss. Enderby got down again. 'If there's no life after death,' she said, 'why does it matter about doing good in this world? I mean, if there's no reward or punishment in the next.'

'That's terrible,' Enderby sneered. 'Doing things because of what you're bloody well going to get out of it.' He took some whisky and did a conventional shudder. It raged briefly through the inner streets and then was transmuted into benevolent warmth in the citadel. Enderby smiled on the girl kindly and offered the bottle. She took it, raised it like a trumpet to the heavens, sucked in a millilitre or so. 'And, while we're at it,' he said, 'let's decide what we mean by good.'

'You decide. It's you who are being interviewed.'

'Well, there are some stupid bastards who can't understand how the commandant of a Nazi concentration camp could go home after torturing Jews all day and then weep tears of joy at a Schubert symphony on the radio. They say: here's a man dedicated to evil capable of enjoying the good. But what the imbecilic sods don't realize is that there are two kinds of good – one is neutral, outside ethics, purely aesthetic. You get it in music or in a sunset if you like that sort of thing or in a grilled steak or in an apple. If God's good, if God exists that is, God's probably good in that way. As I said.' He sipped from the bottle she had handed back. 'Before.'

'Or sex. Sex is as good whether – I mean, you don't have to be in what they used to call a state of grace to enjoy it.'

'That's good,' Enderby said warmly. 'That's right. Though you're still going on about sex. You mean lesbian sex, of course, in your case. Not that I have anything against it, naturally, except that I'm not permitted to experience it. The world's getting narrower all the time. All little sects doing what they call their own thing.'

'Why do you keep showing your balls all the time?' she said boldly. 'Don't you have underpants or anything?'

Enderby flushed very deeply all over. 'I had no intention,' he said. 'I can assure you. What I mean is, I'll put something on. I was not trying to provoke – I apologize,' he said, going off back to the bedroom. He came out again wearing nondescript trousers, something from an old suit, and a not overclean striped shirt. Also slippers. He said, 'There.' The hypocritical little bitch had been at the bottle in his brief absence. He could tell that from her slight slur. She said:

'Evil.'

'Who? Oh, evil.' And he sat down again. 'Evil is the destructive urge. Not to be confused with mere wrong. Wrong is what the government doesn't like. Sometimes a thing can be wrong and evil at the same time – murder, for instance. But then it can be right to murder. Like you people going round killing the Vietnamese and so on. Evil called right.'

'It wasn't right. Nobody said it was right.'

'The government did. Get this straight. Right and wrong are fluid and interchangeable. What's right one day can be wrong the next. And vice versa. It's right to like the Chinese now. Before you started playing ping pong with them it was wrong. A lot of evil nonsense. What you kids need is some good food (there you are, see: good in non-ethical sense) and an idea of what good and evil are about.'

'Well, go on, tell us.'

'Nobody,' said Enderby, having taken a swig, 'has any clear idea about good. Oh, giving money to the poor perhaps. Helping old ladies across the street. That sort of thing. Evil's different. Everybody knows evil. Brought up to it, you see. Original sin.'

'I don't believe in original sin.' She was taking the bottle quite manfully now. 'We're free.'

Enderby looked on her bitterly, also sweating. It was really too hot to wear anything indoors. Damned unchangeable central heating, controlled by some cold sadist somewhere in the basement. Bitterly because she'd hit on the damned problem that he had to present in the poem. She ought to go away now and let him get on with it. Still, his duty. One of his students. He was being paid. Those brown bastards in whose hands he had left *La Belle Mer* would be shovelling it all from till to pocket. Bad year we had, señor. Had to near shut up bloody shop. He said carefully:

'Well, yes. Freeish. *Wir sind ein wenig frei.* Wagner wrote that. Gave it to Hans Sachs in *Die Meistersinger.*' And then: 'No, to hell with it. Wholly free. Totally free to choose between good and evil. The other things don't matter – I mean free to drink a quart of whisky without vomiting and so on. Free to touch one's forehead with one's foot. And so forth.'

'I can do that,' she said. The latter. Doing it. That was the whisky, God help the ill-nourished child.

'But,' Enderby said, ignoring the acrobatics. She didn't seem to be bothering to use her cassette thing any more. Never mind. 'But we're disposed to do evil rather than good. History is the record of that. Given the choice, we're inclined to do the bad thing. That's all it means. We have to make a strong effort to do the good thing.'

'Examples of evil,' she said.

'Oh,' said Enderby. 'Killing for the sake of doing it. Torturing for pleasure – it always is that, though, isn't it? Defacing a work of art. Farting during a performance of a late Beethoven quartet. That must be evil because it's not wrong. I mean, there's no law against it.'

'We believe,' she said, sitting up seriously, checking the cassette machine and holding it out, 'that a time will come when evil will be no more. She'll come again, and that will be the end of evil.'

'Who's *she*?'

'Jesus, of course.'

Enderby breathed deeply several times. 'Look,' he said. 'If you get rid of evil you get rid of choice. You've got to have things to choose between, and that means good *and* evil. If you don't choose, you're not human any more. You're something else. Or you're dead.'

'You're sweating just terribly,' she said. 'There's no need to wear all that. Don't you have swimming trunks?'

'I don't swim,' Enderby said.

'It is hot,' she said. And she began to remove her coke-and-hamburger-stained sweater. Enderby gulped and gulped. He said:

'This is, you must admit, somewhat irregular. I mean, the professor and student relationship and all that sort of thing.'

'You exhibited yourself. That's somewhat irregular too.' By now she had taken off the sweater. She was, he supposed, decently dressed by beach standards, but there was a curious erotic difference between the two kinds of top worn. This was austere enough – no frills or representations of black hands feeling for the nipples. Still, it was *undress*. Beach dress was not that. He said:

'An interesting question when you come to think of it. If somebody's lying naked on the beach it's not erotic. Naked on the bed is different. Even more different on the floor.'

'The first one's functional,' she said. 'Like for a surgical operation. Nakedness is only erotic when it's obviously not for anything else.'

'You're quite a clever girl,' Enderby said. 'What kind of marks have I been giving you?'

'Two Cs. But I couldn't do the sestina. Very old-fashioned. And the other one was free verse. But you said it was really hexameters.'

'People often go into hexameters when they try to write free verse,' Enderby said. 'Walt Whitman, for instance.'

'I have to get A's. I just have to.' And then: 'It is hot.'

'Would you like some ice in that? I can get you some ice.'

'Have you a cold coke?'

'There you go again, with your bloody cokes and seven ups and so on. It's uncivilized,' Enderby raged. 'I'll get you some ice.' He went into the kitchen and looked at it gloomily. It was a bit dirty, really, the sink piled high. He didn't know how to use the washing-up machine. He crunched out ice-cubes by pulling a lever. Ice-cubes went tumbling into dirty water and old fat. He cleaned them on a dishrag. Then he put them into the GEORGIA tea mug and took them in. He gulped. He said: 'That's going too far, you know.' Topless waitresses, topless students. And then: 'I forgot to wash a glass for you. Scatch on the rocks,' he added, desperately facetious. He went back to the kitchen and at once the kitchen telephone rang.

'Enderby?' It was an English voice, male.

'Professor Enderby, yes.'

'Well, you're really in the shit now, aren't you, old boy?'

'Look, did you put her up to this? Who are you, anyway?'

'Ah, something going on there too, eh? This is Jim Bister from Washington. I saw you in Tangier, remember. Surrounded by all those bitsy booful brown boys.'

'Are you tight?'

'Not more than usual, old boy. Look, seriously. I was asked by my editor to get you to say something about this nun business.'

'What nun business? What editor? Who are you, anyway?' He was perhaps going too far in asking that last question again, but he objected to this assumption that British expatriates in America ought to be matey with each other, saying *in the shit* and so forth at the drop of a hat.

'I've said who I am. I thought you'd remember. I suppose you were half-pissed that time in Tangier. My newspaper is the *Evening Banner*, London if you've forgotten, what with your brandy and pederasty, and my editor wants to know what you –'

'What did you say then about pederasty? I thought I caught something about pederasty. Because if I did, by Jesus I'll be down there in Washington and I'll –'

'I didn't. Couldn't pronounce it even if I knew it. It's about this nun business in Ashton-under-Lyne, if you know where that is.'

'You've got that wrong. It's here.'

'No, that's a different one, old man. This one in Ashton-under-Lyne – that's in the North of England, Lancashire, in case you don't know – is manslaughter. Nunslaughter. Maybe murder. Haven't you heard?'

'What the hell's it to do with me anyway? Look, I distinctly heard you say pederasty –'

'Oh, balls to pederasty. Be serious for once. These kids who did it said they'd seen your film, the *Deutschland* thing. So now everybody's having a go at that. And one of the kids –'

'It's not mine, do you hear, and in any case no work of art has ever yet been responsible for –'

'Ah, call it a work of art, do you? That's interesting. And you'd call the book they made it from a work of art too, would you? Because one of the kids said he'd read the book as well as seen the film and it might have been the book that put the idea into his head. Any comments?'

'It's not a book, it's a poem. And I don't believe that it would be possible for a poem to – In any case, I think he's lying.'

'They've been reading it out in court. I've got some bits here. May have got a bit garbled over the telex, of course. Anyway, there's this: 'From life's dawn it is drawn down, Abel is Cain's brother and breasts they have sucked the same.' Apparently that started him dreaming at night. And there's something about 'the gnarls of the nails in thee, niche of the lance, his lovescape crucified.' Very showy type of writing, I must say. They're talking about the danger to susceptible young minds and banning it from the Ashton-under-Lyne bookshops.'

'I shouldn't imagine there's one bloody copy there. This is bloody ridiculous, of course. They're talking of banning the collected poems of a great English poet? A Jesuit priest, as well? God bloody almighty, they must all be out of their fucking minds.'

'There's this nun dead, anyhow. What are you going to do about it?'

'Me? I'm not going to do anything. Ask the buggers who made the film. They'll say what I say – that once you start admitting that a work of art can cause people to start committing crimes, then you're lost. Nothing's safe. Not even Shakespeare. Not even the Bible. Though the Bible's a lot of bloodthirsty balderdash that ought to be kept out of people's hands.'

'Can I quote you, old man?'

'You can do what the hell you like. Pederasty, indeed. I've got a naked girl in here now. Does that sound like pederasty, you stupid insulting bastard?' And he rang off, snorting. He went back, snorting, to his whisky and *pouffe*. The girl was not there. 'Where are you?' he cried, 'you and your bloody Jesus-was-a-woman nonsense. Do you know what they've done now? Do you know what they're trying to do to one of the greatest mystical poets that English poetry has ever known? Where are you?'

She was in his bedroom, he found to no surprise, lying on the circular bed, though still with her worker's pants on. 'Shall I take these off?' she said. Enderby, whisky bottle in hand, sat down heavily on a rattan chair not too far from the bed and looked at her, jaw dropped. He said:

'Why?'

'To lay me. That's what you want, isn't it? You don't get much of a chance, do you, you being old and ugly and a bit fat. Well, anyway, you can if you want.'

'Is this,' asked Enderby carefully, 'how you work for this bloody blasphemous Jesus of yours?'

'I've got to have an A.'

Enderby started to cry noisily. The girl, startled, got off the bed. She went out. Enderby continued crying, interrupting the spasm only to swig at the bottle. He heard her, presumably now sweatered again and clutching her cassette nonsense that was partially stuffed with his woolly voice, leaving the apartment swiftly on sneakered feet. Then she threw in her face, as it were, for him to look at now that her body had gone – a lost face with drowned hair of no particular colour, green eyes set wide apart like an animal's, a cheeseparing nose, a wide American mouth that was a false promise of generosity, the face of a girl who wanted an A. Enderby went on weeping and, while it went on, was presented intellectually with several bloody good reasons for weeping: his own decay, the daily nightmare of many parcels (too many cigarette-lighters that wouldn't work, too many old bills, unanswered letters, empty gin-bottles, single socks, physical organs, hairs in the nose and ears), everyone's desperate longing for a final refrigerated simplicity. He saw very clearly the creature that was weeping – a kind of Blake sylph, a desperately innocent observer buried under the burden of *extension*, in which dyspepsia and sore gums were hardly distinguishable from past sins and follies, the great bloody muckheap of multiplicity (make that the name of the conurbation in which I live) from which he wanted to escape but couldn't. I've got to have an A. The sheer horrible innocence of it. Who the hell didn't feel he'd got to have an A?

It was still only eleven-thirty. He went to the bathroom and, mixing shaving-cream with tears not yet dried, he shaved. He shaved bloodily and, in the manner of ageing men, left patches of stubble here and there. Then he shambled over to the desk and conjured Saint Augustine.

> He strode in out of Africa, wearing a
> Tattered royal robe of orchard moonlight
> Smelling of stolen apples but otherwise
> Ready to scorch, a punishing sun, saying:
> Where is this man of the northern sea, let me
> Chide him, let me do more if
> His heresy merits it, what is his heresy?
> And a hand-rubbing priest, olive-skinned,
> Garlic-breathed, looked up at the
> Great African solar face to whine:
> If it please you, the heresy is evidently a
> Heresy but there is as yet no name for it.
> And Augustine said: All things must have a name
> Otherwise, Proteus-like, they slither and slide
> From the grasp. A thing does not
> Exist until it has a name. Name it
> After this sea-man, call it after
> Pelagius. And lo the heresy existed.

What could be written some time, Enderby suddenly thought, was a saga of a man's teeth – the Odontiad. The idea came to him because of this image of the African bishop and saint and chider,

whose thirty-two wholesome and gleaming teeth he clearly saw,
flashing like two ivory blades (an upper teeth and a lower teeth) as
he gnashed out condemnatory silver Latin. The Odontiad, a poetic
record of dental decay in thirty-two books. The idea excited him so
much that he felt an untimely and certainly unearned gust of hunger.
He sharply down-sir-downed his growling stomach and went on
with his work.

Pelagius appeared, north-pale, cool as one of
Britain's summers, to say, in British Latin:
Christ redeemed us from the general sin, from
The Adamic inheritance, the sour apple
Stuck in the throat (and underneath his solar
Hide Augustine blushed). And thus, my lord,
Man was set free, no longer bounden
In sin's bond. He is free to choose
To sin or not to sin, he is in no wise
Predisposed, it is all a matter of ·
Human choice. And by his own effort, yea,
His own effort only, not some matter of God's
Grace arbitrarily and capriciously
Bestowed, he may reach heaven, he may indeed
Make his heaven. He is free to do so.
Do you deny his freedom? Do you deny
That God's incredible benison was to
Make man free, if he wished, to offend him?
That no greater love is conceivable
Than to let the creature free to hate
The creator and come to love the hard way
But always (mark this mark this) by his own
Will by his own free will?
Cool Britain thus spoke, a land where indeed a
Man groans not for the grace of rain, where
He can sow and reap, a green land, where
The God of unpredictable Africa is
A strange God

It was no use. He ached with hunger. He went rumbling to the kitchen and looked at his untidy store cupboards. Soon he sat down to a new-rinsed dish of yesterday's stew reheated (chuck-steak, onions, carrots, spuds, well-spiced with Lea and Perrin's and a generous drop or so of chili sauce) while there sang on the stove in deep though tepid fat a whole bag of ready-cut crinkled potato pieces and, in another pan, slices of spongy canned meat called Mensch or Munch or something. The kettle was on for tea.

To his surprise, Enderby felt, while sitting calm, relaxed, and in mildly pleasant anticipation of good things to come, a sudden spasm that was not quite dyspepsia. An obscene pain struck in the breastbone then climbed with some difficulty into the left clavicle and, from there, cascaded like a handful of heavy money down the left upper arm. He was appalled, outraged, what had he done to deserve – He caught an image of Henry James's face for some reason, similarly appalled though in a manner somehow patrician. Then nausea, sweating, and very cruel pain took over entirely. What the hell did one do now? The dish of half-eaten stew did not tell him, except not to finish it. What was that about the something-or-other distinguished thing? Ah yes, death. He was going to die. That was what it was.

He staggered moaning and cursing about the unfairness to the living-room (dying-room?). Death. It was very important to know what he was dying of. Was this what was called a heart attack? He sat on a comfortless chair and saw pain dripping on to the floor from his forehead. His shirt was soaked. It was so bloody hot. Breathing was very difficult. He tried to stop breathing, but his body, ill as it was, was not going to have that. Forced to take in a sharp lungful, he found the pain receding. Not death then. Not yet. A warning only. There was a statutory number of heart attacks before the ultimate, was there not? What he was being warned against he did not know? Smoking? Masturbation? Poetry?

He smelt smoke. Ah, was that also a symptom, a dysfunctioning of the olfactory system or something? But no, it was the damned food he had left sizzling. He tottered back into the kitchen and turned everything off. Didn't feel much like eating now.

Four

Enderby left the apartment and the apartment building itself with great caution, as though death, having promised some time to present himself in one form, might (with a dirtiness more appropriate to life) now present himself in another. Enderby was well wrapped against what he took to be the February cold. He had looked from his twelfth-floor window to see fur caps as if this were Moscow, though also sun and wind-scoured sidewalks. Liverish weather, then. He was dressed in his old beret, woollen gloves, and a kind of sculpted Edwardian overcoat bequeathed by his old enemy Rawcliffe. Rawcliffe was long-dead. He had died bloodily, fecally, messily, and now, to quote his own poem, practically his only own poem, his salts drained into alien soil. He had got death over with, then. He was, in a sense, lucky.

Perhaps posthumous life was better than the real thing. Oh God yes, I remember Enderby, what a man. Eater, drinker, wencher, and such foreign adventures. You could go on living without all the trouble of still being alive. Your character got blurred and mingled with those of other dead men, wittier, handsomer, themselves more vital now that they were dead. And there was one's work, good or bad but still a death-cheater. *Aere perennius*, and it was no vain boast even for the lousiest sonneteer that the Muse had ever farted on to. It wasn't death that was the trouble, of course, it was dying.

Enderby also carried, or was part carried by, a very special stick or cane. It was a swordstick, also formerly Rawcliffe's property.

Enderby had gathered that it was illegal to go around with it in America, a concealed weapon, but that was the worst bloody hypocrisy he had ever met in this hypocritical country where everybody had a gun. He had not had cause to use the sword part of the stick, but it was a comfort to have in the foul streets that, like pustular bandages, wrapped the running sore of his university around. For corruption of the best was always the worst, lilies that fester, etc. What had been a centre of incorrupt learning was now a whorehouse of progressive intellectual abdication. The kids had to have what they wanted, this being a so-called democracy: courses in soul-cookery, whatever that was, and petromusicology, that being teenage garbage now treated as an art, and the history of black slavery, and innumerable branches of a subject called sociology. The past was spat upon and the future was ready to be spat upon too, since this would quickly enough turn itself into the past.

The elevator depressed Enderby to a vestibule with telescreens on the wall, each channel showing something different but always people unbent on violence or breaking-in, it being too early in the day and probably too cold. A Puerto Rican named Sancho sat, in the uniform designed by Ms Schwarz of the block police committee, nursing a sub-machine-gun. He greeted Enderby in Puerto Rican and Enderby responded in Tangerine. The point was: where was the capital of Spanish these days? Certainly not Madrid. And of English? Certainly not London. Enderby, British poet. That was exact but somehow ludicrous. Wordsworth, British poet. That was ludicrous in a different way. When Wordsworth wrote of a British shepherd, as he did somewhere, he meant a remote shadowy Celt. Enderby went out into the cold and walked carefully, leaning on his swordstick, towards Broadway. This afternoon he had two classes and he wondered if he was up to either of them. The first was really a formal lecture in which, heretically, he taught, told, gave out information. It was minor Elizabethan dramatists, a subject none of the regular English department was willing – or, so far as he could tell, qualified – to teach. This afternoon he was dealing with –

At the corner of 91st Street and Broadway he paused, appalled. He had forgotten. But it was as if he had never known. There was a blank in that part of his brain which was concerned with minor, or for that matter, major Elizabethan drama. Was this a consequence of that brief heart attack? He had no notes, scorned to use them. Nobody cared, anyway. It was something to get an A with. He walked into Broadway and towards the 96th Street subway entrance, conjuring minor Elizabethans desperately – men who all looked alike and died young, blackbearded ruffians with ruffs and earrings. He would have to get a book on – But there was no time. Wait. It was coming back. Dekker, Greene, Peele, Nashe. The Christian names had gone, but never mind. The plays they had written? *The Shoemaker's Holiday*, *Old Fortunatus*, *The Honest Whore*. Which one of those syphilitic scoundrels had written those, and what the hell were they about? Enderby could feel his heart preparing to stop beating, and this could not, obviously, be allowed. The other class he had was all right – Creative Writing – and he had some of the ghastly poems they had written in his inside jacket pocket. But this first one – Relax, relax. It was a question of not trying too hard, not getting uptight, keeping your cool, as they said – very vague terms.

Reaching the subway entrance, moving as ever cautiously among muttering or insolent or palpably drugged people whom it was best to think of as being there mainly to demonstrate the range of the pigmentation spectrum, he observed, with gloom, shock, pride, shame, horror, amusement, and kindred emotions, that *The Wreck of the Deutschland* was now showing at the Symphony movie house. The 96th Street subway entrance he had arrived at was actually at the corner of 93rd Street. To see the advertising material of the film better, he walked, with his stick's aid, towards the matrical or perhaps seniorsororal entrance, and was able to take in a known gaudy poster showing a near-naked nun facing, with carmined lips opened in orgasm, the rash-smart sloggering brine. Meanwhile, in one inset tableau, thugs wearing swastikas prepared to violate five of the coifed sisterhood, Gertrude, lily, conspicuous by her tallness among them, and, in another, Father Tom Hopkins S.J. desperately prayed, apparently having just got out of the bath to do so. Enderby felt his heart prepare, in the manner rather of a stomach, to react to all this, so he escaped into the dirty hell of the subway. A tall Negro with a poncho and a cowboy hat was just coming up, and he said no good to Enderby.

Hell, Enderby was thinking as he sat in one of the IRT coaches going uptownwards. Because we were too intellectual and clever and humanistic to believe in a hell didn't mean that a hell couldn't exist. If there were a God, he could easily be a God who relieved himself of the almost intolerable love he felt for the major part of his creation (on such planets, say, as Turulura 15a and Baa'rdnok and Juriat) by torturing for ever the inhabitants of 111/9 Tellus 1706defg. A touch of pepper sauce, his palate entitled to it. Or perhaps an experiment to see how much handing out of torture he himself could tolerate. He had, after all, a kind of duty to his own infinitely variable super-sensorium. Hamlet was right, naturally. Troubles the will and makes us rather. This little uptown ride, especially when the train stopped long and inexplicably between stations, was a fair miniature simulacrum of the ultimate misery – potential black and brown devils ready to rob, slice, and rape; the names of the devils blowpainted on bulkheads and seats, though never on advertisements (sacred scriptures of the infernal law) – JESUS 69, SATAN 127, REDBALL IS BACK.

Coming out of the subway, walking through the disfigured streets full of decayed and disaffected and dogmerds, he felt a sudden and inappropriate accession of wellbeing. It was as though that lunchtime spasm had cleared away black humours inaccessible to the Chinese black draught. Everything came back about minor Elizabethan drama, though in the form of a great cinema poster with a brooding Shakespeare in the middle. But the supporting cast was set neatly about: George Peele, carrying a copy of *The Old Wives' Tale* and singing in a fumetto about chopcherry chopcherry ripe within; poor cirrhotic Robert Greene conjuring Friars Bacon and Bungay; Tom Brightness-falls-from-the-air Nashe; others, including Dekker eating a pancake. That was all right, then. But wait – who were those other others? Anthony Munday, yes yes, a bad playbotcher but he certainly existed. Plowman? A play called *A Priest in a Whorehouse*? Deverish? *England's Might or The Triumphs of Gloriana*?

Treading through rack of crumpled protest handouts, desiccated leaves, beercans, admitted with reluctance by a black armed policeman, he made his familiar way to the officially desecrated chapel which now held partitioned classrooms. Heart thumping, though fairly healthily, he entered his own (he was no more than five minutes late) to find his twenty or so students waiting. There were Chinese, skullcapped Hebrews, a girl from the Coast who piquantly combined black and Japanese, a beerfat Irishman with red thatch, an exquisite Latin nymph, a cunning knowall of the Kickapoo nation. He stood looking vaguely at them all. They lounged and ate snacks and drank from cans and smoked pot and looked back at him. He didn't know whether to sit or not at the table on which someone had chalked ASSFUCK. A little indisposed today, ladies and gentlemen. But no, he would doggedly stand. He stood. That bright Elizabethan poster swiftly evanesced. He gaped. All was blank except for imagination, which was a scurrying colony of termites. He said:

'Today, ladies and gentlemen, continuing our necessarily superficial survey of the minor Elizabethan dramatists –'

The door opened and a boy and a girl, wan and breathless from swift fumbling in the corridor, entered, buttoning. They sat, looking up at him, panting.

'We come to –' But who the hell did we come to? They waited, he waited. He went to the blackboard and wiped off some elementary English grammar. The chalk in his grip trembled, broke in two. He wrote to his astonishment the name GERVASE WHITELADY. He added, in greater surprise and fear, the dates 1559–1591. He turned shaking to see that many of the students were taking the data down on bits of paper. He was committed now: this bloody man, not yet brought into existence, had to have existed. 'Gervase Whitelady.' he said, matter-of-factly, almost with a smear of the boredom proper to mention of a name nauseatingly well-known among scholars. 'Not a great name – a name, indeed, that some of you have probably never even heard of –' But the Kickapoo knowall had heard of it all right: he nodded with superior vigour. '– But we cannot afford to neglect his achievement, such as it was. Whitelady was the second son of Giles Whitelady, a scrivener. The family had settled in Pease Pottage, not far from the seaside town we now call Brighton, and were supporters of the

Moabite persuasion of crypto-reformed Christianity as far back as the time of Wyclif.' He looked at them all, incurious lot of young bastards. 'Any questions?' There were no questions. 'Very well, then.' The Kickapoo shot up a hand. 'Yes?'

'Is Whitelady the one who collaborated with – what was the name of the guy now – Fenprick? You know, they did this comedy together what the hell was the name of it?'

A very cunning young redskin sod, ought to be kept on his reservation. Enderby was not going to have this. 'Are you quite sure you mean Fenprick, er, er ...'

'Running Deer is the name, professor. It might have been Fencock. A lot of these British names sound crazy.'

Enderby looked long on him. 'The dates of Richard Fenpick,' he said – 'note that it is pick not prick, by the way, er, er –' Running Deer, indeed. He must sometime look through the admission cards they were supposed to hand in. 'His dates are 1574–1619. He could hardly have collaborated with er ...' He checked the name from the board. 'Er, Whitelady unless he had been a sort of infant prodigy, and I can assure you he was er not.' He now felt a hunger to say more about this Fenpick, whose career and even physical lineaments were being presented most lucidly to a wing of his brain which, he was sure, had been newly erected between the heart attack and now. 'What,' he said with large energy and confidence, 'we most certainly do know about er Fenpick is his instrumentality in bringing the Essex rebellion to a happy conclusion.' To his shock the hand of the girl who had just come in with that oversexed lout there, still panting, shot up. She cried:

'Happy for whom?'

'For er everybody concerned,' Enderby er affirmed. 'It had happened before in history, English naturally, as Whatsisname's own er conveniently or inconveniently dramatized.'

'Inconvenient for whom?'

'For er those concerned.'

'What she means is,' said the redthatched beerswollen Irish student, 'that the movie was on last night. The Late Late Date-with-the-Great Show. What Bette Davis called it was *Richard Two*.'

'*Elizabeth and Essex*,' the buttoned girl said. 'It failed and she had his head cut off but she cries because it's a Cruel Necessity.'

'What Professor Enderby was trying to say,' the Kickapoo said, 'was that the record is all a lie. There was really a King Robert the First on the British throne, disguised as the Queen.' Enderby looked bitterly at him, saying:

'Are you trying to take the – *Are you having a go?*'

'Pardon me?'

'The vital statistics,' a young Talmudist said, pencil poised at the ready. 'This Whitelady.'

'Who? Ah, yes.'

'The works.'

'The works,' Enderby said, with refocillated energy. 'Ah, yes. One long poem on a classical theme, the love of er Hostus for Primula. The title, I mean the hero and heroine are eponymous.' He clearly saw a first edition of the damned poem with titlepage a horrid mixture of typefaces, fat illdrawn nymphs on it, a round chop which said Bibliotheca Somethingorother. 'Specimen lines,' he continued boldly:

'Then as the moon engilds the Thalian fields
The nymph her er knotted maidenhead thus yields,
In joy the howlets owl it to the night,
In joy fair Cynthia augments her light,
The bubbling conies in their warrens er move
And simulate the transports of their love.'

'But that's beautiful,' said the beautiful Latin nymph, unfat, unilldrawn, unknotted.

'Crap,' the Talmudist offered. 'The transports of *whose* love?'

'Theirs, of course,' Enderby said. 'Primavera and the er her lover.'

'There were six plays,' the Kickapoo said, 'if I remember correctly.'

'Seven,' Enderby said, 'if you count the one long attributed to er Sidebottom –'

'Crazy British names.'

'But now pretty firmly established as mainly the work of er the man we're dealing with, with an act and a half by an unknown hand.'

'How can they tell?'

'Computer work,' Enderby said vaguely. 'Cybernetic wonders in Texas or some such place.' He saw now fairly clearly that he would have to be for the chop. Or no, no, I quit. This was intolerable.

'What plays?' the Chinese next to the Talmudist said, a small round cheerful boy, perhaps an assistant cook in his spare time or main time if this were his spare time.

'Yes,' with fine briskness. 'Take these down. *What do you lack, fair mistress?* A comedy, done by the Earl of Leicester's Men, 1588. *The Tragedy of Canicula*, Earl of Sussex's Men, the same year. A year later came *The History of Lambert Simnel*, performed at court for the Shrovetide Revels. And then there was, let me see –'

'Where can we get hold of them?' the melanonipponese said crossly. 'I mean, there's not much point in just having the titles.'

'Impossible,' prompt Enderby said. 'Long out of print. It's only important for your purpose that you know that Longbottom that is to say Whitelady actually existed –'

'But how do we know he did?' There were two very obdurate-strains in this mixed Coast girl.

'Records,' Enderby said. 'Look it all up in the appropriate books. Use your library, that's what it's for. One cannot exaggerate the importance of er his contribution to the medium, as an influence that is, the influence of his rhythm is quite apparent in the earlier plays of er –'

'Mangold Smotherwild,' the Kickapoo said, no longer sneeringly outside the creative process but almost sweatily in the middle of it. Enderby saw that he could always say that he had been trying out a new subject called Creative Literary History. They might even write articles about it: *The Use of the Fictive Alternative World in the Teaching of Literature.* Somebody called out: 'Specimen.'

'No trouble at all,' Enderby said. 'In the first scene of *Give you good den good my masters* you have a soliloquy by a minor character named Retchpork. It goes, as I remember, something like this:

So the world ticks, aye, like to a tocking clock
On th'wall of naked else infinitude,

Am I am hither come to lend an ear
To manners, modes and bawdries of this town
In hope to school myself in knavery.
Aye, 'tis a knavish world wherein the whore
And bawd and pickpurse, he of the quatertrey,
The coneycatcher, prigger, jack o' the trumps
Do profit mightily while the studious lamp
Affords but little glimmer to the starved
And studious partisan of learning's lore.
Therefore, I say, am I come hither, aye,
To be enrolled in knavish roguery.
But soft, who's this? Aye, marry, by my troth,
A subject apt for working on. Good den,
My master, prithee what o'clock hast thou,
You I would say, and *have* not *hast*, forgive
Such rustical familiarity
From one unlearn'd in all the lore polite
Of streets, piazzas and the panoply
Of populous cities –

'Something like that, anyway,' Enderby said. 'I could go on if you wished. But it's all a bit dull.'

'If it's all a bit dull,' the Irish one said, 'why do we have to have it?'

'I thought you said he was influential,' somebody else complained.

'Well, he was. Dully influential,' the Kickapoo said.

'Dead at thirty-two,' Enderby said, having checked with the blackboard data. 'Dead in a duel or perhaps of the French pox or of a surfeit of pickled herrings and onions in vinegar with crushed peppercorns and sour ale, or, of course, of the plague. It was a pretty bad year for the plague, I think, 1591.' He saw Whitelady peering beseechingly at him, a white face from the shades, begging for a good epitaph. 'He was nothing,' Enderby said brutally, the face flinching as though from blows, 'so you can forget about him. One of the unknown poets who never properly mastered their craft, spurned by the Muse.' The whole luggage of Elizabethan drama was now, unfantasticated by fictional additions, neatly stacked before him. He knew what was in it and what wasn't. This Whitelady wasn't there. And yet, as the mowing face and haunted eyes, watching his, showed, in a sense he was. 'The important thing,' Enderby pronounced, 'is to get yourself born. You're entitled to that. But you're not entitled to life. Because if you were entitled to life, then the life would have to be quantified. How many years? Seventy? Sixty? Shakespeare was dead at fifty-two. Keats was dead at twenty-six. Thomas Chatterton at seventeen. How much do you think you're entitled to, you?' he asked the Kickapoo.

'As much as I can get.'

'And that's a good answer,' Enderby said, meaning it, meaning it more than they, in their present stage of growth, could possibly mean it. He suddenly felt a tearful love and compassion for these poor orphans, manipulated by brutal statesmen and the makers of tooth-eroding sweet poisonous drinks and (his face blotted temporarily out that of anguished Whitelady) the bearded Southern colonel who made it a virtue to lick chickenfat off your fingers. Schmalz and Chutzpah. The names swam in, as from the Book of Deuteronomy. Who were they? Lawyers? He said: 'Life is sensation, which includes thought, and the sensation of having sensation, which ought to take care of all your stupid worries about identity. Christ, Whitelady has identity. But what he doesn't have and what he never had is the sensation of having sensations. Better and cleverer people than we are can be invented.' He saw how wrong he was about *aere perennius*. 'But what can't be invented is,' he said, directly addressing the couple who had come in late, 'what you two were doing outside in the corridor.'

The boy grew very red but the girl smirked.

'The touch of the skin of a young girl's breast. A lush-capped plush-kept sloe –'

'You got that the wrong way round,' the Kickapoo said.

'Yes yes,' Enderby said, tired. And then, in utter depression, he saw who Whitelady was. He winked at him with his right eye and Whitelady simultaneously winked back with his left.

Five

After the lesson on Whitelady (lose sensation, he kept thinking, and I become a fictional character) Enderby walked with care, aware of a sensation of lightness in his left breast as though his heart (not the real one, but the one of non-clinical traditional lore) had been removed. So sensation could lie, so whither did that lead you? His feet led him through a halfhearted student demonstration against or for the dismissal of somebody, a brave girl stripping in protest, giving blue breasts to the February post-meridian chill, to the long low building which was the English Department. Outside the office he shared with Assistant Professor Zeitgeist or some such name, there were black girl students evidently waiting for Professor Zeitgeist and beguiling their wait with loud manic music on a transistor radio. Enderby mildly said:

'Do switch that thing off, please. I have some work to do.'

'Well, you goan work some place else, man.'

'This is, after all, my office,' Enderby smiled, feeling palpitations drumming up. 'This is, after all, the English Department of a university.' And then: 'Shut that bloody thing off.'

'You goan fuck yoself, man.'

'You ain't nuttin but shiiit, man.'

Abdication. What did one do now – slap the black bitches? Remember the long servitude of their people and bow humbly? One of them was doing a little rutting on-the-spot dance to the noise. Enderby slapped the black bitch on the puss. No, he did not. He durst not. It would be on the front pages tomorrow. There would be a row in the United Nations. He would be knifed by the men they slept with. He said, smiling, rage boiling up to inner excoriation: 'Abdication of authority. Is that expression in your primer of Black English?'

'Pip pip old boy,' said the non-jigging one with very fair mock-British intonation. 'And all that sort of rot, man.'

'You go fuck yo own ass, man. You aint nuttin but shiiiiit.' Enderby had another weapon, not much used by him these days. He gathered all available wind and vented it from a square mouth.

Rarkberfvrishtkrahnbrrryburlgrong.

The effort nearly killed him. He staggered into his office, saw mail on his desk, took it and staggered out. The black girls, very ineptly, tried to give, in glee, his noise back to him. But their sense of body rhythm prevailed, turning it to oral tomtom music. The radio took four seconds off from discoursing on garbage of one sort to advertise garbage of another – male voice in terminal orgasm yelling sweet sweet sweet O Pan piercing sweet. Enderby went into the little lounge, empty save for shouting notices and a bearded man who looked knowingly at him. He opened his letters, chiefly injunctions to join things (BIOFEEDBACK BRETHREN GERONTOPHILIACS ANONYMOUS ROCK FOR CHRIST OUR SATAN THE THANATOLOGY MONTHLY), coming at length to a newspaper clipping sent, apparently out of enmity, by his publisher in London. It was from the *Daily Window* and was one of the regular hardhitting noholdsbarred nononsense manofthepeople responsibilityofagreatnationalorgan addresses to the reader written by a staffman named Belvedere Fellows, whose jowled fierce picture led, like a brave overage platoon officer, the heavy type of his heading. Enderby read: SINK THE DEUTSCHLAND! Enderby read:

My readers know I am a man that faces facts. My readers know that I will sit through any amount of filthy film rubbish in order to report back fairly and squarely to my readers about the dangers their children face in a medium that increasingly, in the name of the so-called Permissive Society, is giving itself over to nudity, sex, obscenity and pornography.

Well, I went to see *The Wreck of the Deutschland* and confess that I had to rush to the rails long before the end. I was
scuppered. Here all decent standards have finally gone Kaput.
Here is the old heave-ho with a vengeance.

But enough has been said already about the appalling scenes
of Nazi rape and the blasphemous nudity. We know the cul-
prits: their ears are deafened to the appeals of decency by the
crackle of the banknotes they are now so busily counting.
There are certain quiet scoundrels whose names do not reach
the public eye with the same tawdry glamour. Behind the film
image lies the idea, lies the writer, skulking behind the cigarette
smoke and whisky in his ivory tower.

I say now that they must take their share of the blame. I have
not read the book which the film is based on, nor would I want
to. I noted grimly however that there were no copies the other
day in my local library. My readers will be horrified however to
learn that he is a Roman Catholic priest. This is what the liberalism of that great and good man Pope John has been perverted
into.

I call now, equivocally and pragmatically, for a closer eye to
be kept on the filth that increasingly these days masquerades
as literature and even as poetry. The vocation of poet has traditionally been permitted to excuse too much – the lechery of
Dylan Thomas and the drunken bravoing of Brendan Behan
as well as the aesthetic perversions of Oscar Wilde. Is the final
excuse now to be sought in the so-called priestly vocation?
Perhaps Father Enderby of the Society of Jesus would like to
reply. I have no doubt he would find an attentive congregation.

Enderby looked up. The bearded man was still looking knowingly at
him. He said something. Enderby said: 'I beg your pardon?'

'I said: how are things in Jolly Old?'

Enderby could think of absolutely no reply. The two looked
at each other fixedly for a long time, and the bearded man's jaw
dropped progressively as if he were silently demonstrating an escalier of front vowels. Then Enderby sighed, got up and went out to

seek his Creative Writing class. Like a homer he tapped his way with
his swordstick through the dirty cold and student-knots to a building named for the inventor of a variety of canned soups, Warhall or
somebody. On the second floor, to which he clomb with slow care,
he found them, all ten, in a hot room with a long disfigured conference table. The Tietjens girl was there, drowned and sweatered. She
had apparently told them everything, for they looked strangely at
him. He sat down at the top or bottom of the table and pulled their
work out of his inside pocket. He saw that he had given Ms Tietjens
a D, so he ballpointed it into a rather arty A. The rest shall remain
as they are. Then he tapped his lower denture with the pen, plastic
to plastic: tck tck, tcktck tck, TCK. He looked at his students, a
mostly very untidy lot. They looked at him, lounging, smoking,
taking afternoon beverages. He said:

'The question of sartorial approach is relevant, I think. When
John Keats had difficulty with a poem he would wash and put on
a clean shirt. The stiff collar and bow tie and tails of the concert-
goer induce a tense attitude appropriate to the hearing of complex
music. The British colonial officer would dress for dinner, even in
the jungle, to encourage self-discipline. There is no essential virtue
in comfort. To be relaxed is good if it is part of a process of systole
and diastole. Relaxation comes between phases of tenseness. Art
is essentially tense. The trouble with your er art is that it is not
tense.'

They all looked at him, not tense. Many of their names he still
refused to take seriously – Chuck Szymanowski, for instance. His
sole black man was called Lloyd Utterage, a very reasonable name.
This man was very ugly, which was a pity and which Enderby
deeply regretted, but he had very beautiful clothes, mostly of
hot-coloured blanketing materials, topped with a cannibal-style
wire-wool hairshock. He was very tense, and this too Enderby naturally approved. But he was full of hate, and that was a bore. 'I
will not,' Enderby said, turning to him, 'read out all your poem,
which may be described as a sort of litany of anatomic vilification.
Two stanzas will perhaps suffice.' And he read them with detached
primness:

'It will be your balls next, whitey,
A loving snipping of the scrotum
With rather rusty nail-scissors,
And they tumble out then to be
Crunched underfoot crunch crunch.

It will be your prick next, whitey,
A loving chopping segmentally
With an already bloodstained meat hatchet,
And it will lie with the dog-turds
To be squashed squash squash.

One point,' he said. 'If the prick is to be chopped in segments it will not resemble a dog-turd. The writing of er verse does not excuse you from considerations of er …'

'He says it will lie with the dog-turds,' Ms Tietjens said. 'He doesn't say it will look like one.'

'Yes yes, Sylvia, but –'

'Lydia.'

'Of course, thinking of Ford. Sorry. But you see, the word *it* suggests that it's still a unity, not a number of chopped bits of er penis. Do you see my point?'

'Yeah,' Lloyd Utterage said, 'but it's not a point worth seeing. The point is the hate.'

'The poetry is in the pity,' said Enderby. 'Wilfred Owen. He was wrong, of course. It was the other way round. As I was saying, a unity and rather resembling a dog-turd. So the image is of this er prick indistinguishable from –'

'Like Lloyd said,' said a very spotty Jewish boy named Arnold Something, his hair too cannibalistically arranged, 'it's the hate that it's about. Poetry is made out of emotions,' he pronounced.

'Oh no,' Enderby said. 'Oh very much no. Oh very very very much no and no again. Poetry is made out of words.'

'It's the hate,' Lloyd Utterage said. 'It's the expression of the black experience.'

'Now,' Enderby said, 'we will try a little experiment. I take it that this term whitey is racialist and full of opprobrium and so on. Suppose now we substitute for it the word er *nigger* –' There was a general gasp of disbelief. 'I mean, if, as you said, the point is the hate, then the hate can best be expressed – and, indeed, in poetry must be expressed – as an emotion available to the generality of mankind. So instead of either *whitey* or *nigger* you could have, er, *bohunk* or, say, *kike*. But *kike* probably wouldn't do ...'

'You're telling me it wouldn't do,' Chuck Szymanowski said.

'Since the end-words are disyllabic or, er, yes trisyllabic but never monosyllabic. A matter of structure,' Enderby said. 'So listen. *It will be your balls next, nigger*, etc etc. *It will be your prick next, nigger*, and so on. Now it is the structure that interests me. It's not, of course, a very subtle or interesting structure, as er Lloyd here would be the first to admit, but it is the structure that has the vitality, not all this nonsense about hate and so on. I mean, imagine a period when this kind of race hate stupidity is all over, and yet the poem – *aere perennius*, you know – still by some accident survives. Well, it would be taken as a somewhat primitive but still quite engaging essay in vilification in terms of an anatomical catalogue, the structure objectifying and, as it were, cooling the hate. Comic too on the personal level, 'It will be your balls next, er Crassus or say Lycidas. Rather Catullan. You see.' He smiled at them. Now they were really learning something.

'You think,' Lloyd Utterage panted, 'you're going to get away with that, man?'

'Away with what?' Enderby asked in honest and rather hurt surprise.

'Look,' Ms Tietjens said kindly, 'he's British. He doesn't under-stand the ethnic agony.'

'That's rather a good phrase,' Enderby said. 'It doesn't mean anything, of course. Like saying potato agony. Oh I don't know, though. The meanings of imaginative language are not the same as those of the defilers of language. Your president, for instance. The black leaders. Lesbian power, if such a thing exists ...'

'He understands it,' said Lloyd Utterage. 'His people started it. Nigger-whippers despite their haw-haw-haw old top.'

'Now that's interesting,' Enderby said. 'You see how the whipping image immediately begat in your imagination the image of a top? You have the makings of a word-man. You'll be a poet some day when you've got over all this nonsense.' Then he began to repeat *nigger-whipper* swiftly and quietly like a tongue-twister. 'Prosodic analysis,' he said. 'Do any of you know anything about that? A British linguistic movement, I believe, so it may not have er gotten to you. *Nigger* and *whipper*, you see, have two vowels in common. Now note the opposition of the consonants: a rich nasal against a voiceless semi-vowel, a voiced stop against a voiceless. Suppose you tried *nigger-killer*. Not so effective. Why not? The g doesn't oppose well to the l. They're both voiced, you see, and so –'

'Maaaaaan,' drawled Lloyd Utterage, leaning back in simulated ease, smiling crocodilewise. 'You play your little games with yourself. All this shit about words. Closing your eyes to what's going on in the big big world.'

Enderby got angry. 'Don't call me *maaaaaan*,' he said. 'I've got a bloody name and I've got a bloody handle to it. And don't hand me any of that *shiiit*, to use your own term, about the importance of cutting the white man's balls off. All that's going to save your immortal soul, *maaaaaan*, if you have one, is words. Words words words, you bastard,' he crescendoed, perhaps going too far.

'I don't think you should have said that,' said a mousy girl called Ms Crooker or Kruger. 'Bastard, I mean.'

'Does he have the monopoly of abuse?' Enderby asked in heat. 'It's he who's doing the playing about, anyway, with his bloody castration fantasies. He wouldn't have the guts to cut the balls off a pig. Or he might have. If it were a very little pig and ten big fellow melanoids held it down for him. I say,' he then said, 'that's good. *Fellow melanoids*.'

'I'm getting out of here,' Lloyd Utterage said, rising.

'Oh no you're not,' Enderby cried. 'You're going to stay and suffer just like I am. Bloody cowardice.'

'There's no engagement,' Lloyd Utterage said. 'There's no common area of understanding.' But he sat down again.

'Oh yes there is,' Enderby said. 'I understand that you want to cut a white man's genital apparatus off. Well, come and try. But you'll get this sword in your black guts first.' And he drew an inch or so of steel.

'You shouldn't have said black guts,' Ms Flugel or Crookback said. It was as though she were Enderby's guide to polite New York usage.

'Well,' Enderby said, 'they are black. Is he going to deny that now?'

'I never denied anything, man.'

Suddenly the cannibal-haired kike or Jew, Arnold Something, began to laugh in a very high pitch. This started some of the others off: a bespectacled big sloppy student with a sloppy viking moustache, for instance, began to neigh. Lloyd Utterage sulked, as did Enderby. But then Enderby, trying, which was after all his job here, to be helpful, said, 'Greek *hystera*, meaning the womb. This shows, and this might possibly bring er here, our friend I mean, and myself into a common area of understanding, that etymology can get in the way of scientific progress, since Sigmund Freud's opponents in Vienna used etymology to confute his contention that hysteria, as now and here to be witnessed, could be found in the male as well as the female.' Little of this could be heard over the noise. At length it subsided, and the sloppy viking whose name was, Enderby thought and would now check from the papers before him and yes indeed it was, Sig Hamsun, said:

'And now how's about looking at my crap.'

That very nearly made the cannibal Jew Arnold begin again, but he was rebuked ironically by Lloyd Utterage, who said: 'This serious, man, yeah serious, didn't you know it was serious? Yeah serious, as you very well know.'

Hamsun's crap, Enderby now saw again, looking through it, was in no way sternly Nordic. To match its excretor it was rather sloppy and fungoid. Enderby recited it grimly however:

'And as the Manhattan dawn came up
Over the skyline we still lay

In each other's arms. Then you
Came awake and the Manhattan dawn
Was binocularly presented in your
Blue eyes and in your pink nipples
Monostomatic heaven ...'

'What does that word mean?' a Ms Hermsprong asked. 'Mono something.'

'It means,' Enderby said, 'that he had only one mouth.'

'Well, we all know he only has one mouth. Like everybody else.'

'Yes,' Enderby said, 'but she had two nipples, you see. The point is, I think, that he would have liked to have two mouths, you see. One for each nipple.'

'No,' Hamsun said. 'One mouth was enough.' He leered.

'Permit me,' Enderby said coldly, 'to tell you what your poem means. Such as it is.'

'I wrote it, right?'

'You could just about say that, I suppose. It means fundamentally – which means this is the irreducible minimum of meaning – play between unitary and binary, that is to say: 1 dawn, 2 eyes, 2 nipples, 1 mouth. There's also colour play, of course: pink dawn in blue sky, two pink dawns in two blue eyes, two pink nipples, one pink mouth (also two pink lips), one blue heaven in pink nipples and pink mouth. You see? Well then, now we come to the autobiographical element or, if you like, the personal content. It's a childhood reminiscence. The woman in it is your mother. You're greedy for her breasts, you want two mouths. Why should there be two of everything else, even the manifestly single city and single dawn, and only one sucking mouth? There.' He sat back in post-exegetical triumph that the twin simmering murder in Lloyd Utterage's eyes did something to qualify. Ms Tietjens said, in counter-triumph:

'If you want to know the truth, it was me.'

'You mean you wrote it? You mean he stole it? You mean –'

'I mean I'm the woman in the poem, complete with two nipples. As you can vouch for.'

'Look,' Enderby said.

'He wrote it about me.'

'What I mean is that I didn't bloody well ask to see them. Here, by the way, is your poem back. With an A on it. And a lousy poem it is, if I may say so. Coming into my apartment,' he told the class, 'and stripping off. Something to do with Jesus Christ being a woman. And you,' he accused, 'pretending to be lesbian.'

'I never said I was that. You make too many false assumptions.'

'Look,' Enderby said in great weariness and with crackling energy. 'All of you. A poem isn't important because of the biographical truth of the content.'

'Look,' countersaid the sloppy nordic, 'it was one way of keeping her there, can't you see that? She's there in that fucking poem for ever. Complete with pink nipples.'

'I'm not a thing to be kept,' Ms Tietjens said hotly. 'Can't you see that attitude makes some of us go the way we do?'

'The point is,' Enderby said, 'that there are certain terrible urgencies.' Lloyd Utterage guffaw-sneered in a way that Enderby could only think of as *niggerish*. It was in the act of the formulation of the term that he realized with great exactitude the impossibility of his position. There was no communication; he was too old-fashioned; he had always been too old-fashioned. 'The urgencies are not political or racial or social. They're, so to speak, semantic. Only the poetical inquiry can discover what language really is. And all you're doing is letting yourselves be ensnared into the irrelevancies of the slogan on the one hand and sanctified sensation on the other.' So. Identity? Unimportant. Sensation? Unimportant. What the hell was left? 'The urgent task is the task of conservation. To hold the complex totality of linguistic meaning within a shape you can isolate from the dirty world.'

'The complex what?' Ms Hermsprong asked. The rest of them looked at him as if he were, which he probably was, mad.

'Never mind,' Enderby said. 'You can't fight. You'll never prevail against the big bastards of computerized organizations that are kindly letting you enjoy the illusion of freedom. The people who write poems, even bad ones, are not the people who are going to rule. Sooner or later you're all going to go to jail. You have to learn to be alone, no sex, not even any books. All you'll have is language, the great conserver, and poetry, the great isolate shaper. Stock your minds with language, for Christ's sake. Learn how to write what's memorable. No, not write, compose in your head. The time will come when you won't even be allowed a stub of pencil and the back of an envelope.' He paused, looking down. He looked up at their pity and wonder and the black man's hatred. 'Try,' he said lamely, 'heroic couplets.'

The cannibal Arnold said: 'How long will you be staying?' Enderby grinned citrously. 'Not much longer, I suppose. I'm not doing any good, am I?' Nobody said anything. Hamsun did a slow and not ungraceful shrug. Chuck Szymanowski said:

'You're defeatist. You're anti-life. You're not helping any. The time will come later for all this artsy shmartsy crap. But it's not now.'

'If it's not now,' Enderby said, 'it's not ever.' He didn't trouble to get angry at the designation of high and neutral art as crap. 'You can't split life into diachronic segments.' He would write a letter of resignation when he got back to the apartment. No, he wouldn't even do that. Today was what? Friday the twenty-sixth. There would be a salary cheque for him on Monday. Grab that and go. He was, by God, after all, despite everything, free. Ms Cooper or Krugman said, kindly it seemed:

'What's your idea of a good poem?'

'Well,' Enderby said. 'Perhaps this:

Queen and huntress, chaste and fair,
Now the sun is gone to sleep,
Seated in thy silver chair,
State in wonted manner keep.
Hesperus entreats thy light,
Goddess excellently bright ...'

'Jesus,' Lloyd Utterage said with awe. 'Playing your little games, man.' And then, blood mixed somewhere down there in his larynx: 'You bastard. You misleading reactionary *evil* bastard.'

Six

Enderby saw, in gloomy clarity, going back to 96th Street on the IRT, that the area of freedom was very small. *Ein wenig frei* was about right. He was not free, for instance, not to be messily beaten up by the black gang Lloyd Utterage had, in sincere and breathy confidence with much African vowel-lengthening, promised to unleash on him during the weekend. He was not free not to feel excruciating stabs in his calves, something probably to do with the silting up of the arteries, which had now come upon him as he embraced the metal monkey-pole in the IRT train, all the seats having been taken by young black and brown thugs just out of school, who would by rights be forced to stand up for their elders. But he was free to leave America. A matter of booking on a plane to Madrid and then another to Tangier. Being free in this area, however, he decided not to make use of his freedom. Which meant he would not be free not to be messily beaten up etc etc. Which meant he was choosing to be messily ... etc. They would bruise and rend his body, but there would be a thin clear as it were refrigerated self deep within, unbruisable and unrendable and, as it were, free. Augustine of Hippo, whom he now saw blanketed and shockhaired like Lloyd Utterage, was waiting for him back in the apartment to sort out other aspects of freedom for him. But, wait ... he had to appear on a television talk-show some time this evening, didn't he? He must not forget that, he must keep track of the time. *Ein wenig frei* to speak out for Gerard Manley Hopkins, sufferer, mystic, artist, pre-Freudian.

As he let himself into the apartment, he was aware of the ghost of the cardiac attack, if that was what it was, earlier; not shooting but already shot, a sort of bruised line of trajectory. It was obvious that he was intended to be doing some urgent thinking about death. He gloomed at the mess of the kitchen, lusting for a pint of strong tea and a wedge of some creature of Sarah Lee. He gave way to the lust defiantly, grumbling round the sitting-room while the water boiled, searching for his ALABAMA mug. He found it eventually, full of warmish water that had once been ice. Soon he was able to sit on a *pouffe*, gorging sponge and orange cream out of one fist, the other holding the handle of the mug of mahogany tea like a weapon against Death, what time he looked at a children's cartoon programme on television. It was all talking animals in reds, blues, and yellows, but you could see the chained wit and liberalism of the creators escaping from odd holes in the fabric: that legalistic pig there was surely the vice-president? Might it be possible to get the story of Augustine and Pelagius across in cartoon-form?

Back in the study-bedroom with his draft, he saw how bad it was and how much work on it lay ahead. And yet he was supposed to start thinking of death. It was the leaving of things unfinished that was so intolerable. It was all very well for Jesus Christ, not himself a writer though no mean orator, to talk about thinking not of the morrow. If you'd started a long poem you had to think of the bloody morrow. You could better cope with the feckless Nazarene philosophy if you were like those scrounging dope-takers who littered the city. Sufficient unto the day is the evil thereof, as also the dope thereof.

Augustine said: If the Almighty is also Allknowing,
He knows the precise number of hairs that will fall to the floor
From your next barbering, which may also be your last.
He knows the number of drops of lentil soup
That will fall on your robe from your careless spooning
On August 5th, 425. He knows every sin
As yet uncommitted, can measure its purulence
On a precise scale of micropeccatins, a micropeccatin

Being, one might fancifully suppose,
The smallest unit of sinfulness. He knows
And knew when the very concept of man itched within him
The precise date of your dispatch, the precise
Allotment of paradisal or infernal space
Awaiting you. Would you diminish the Allknowing
By making man free? This is heresy.
But that God is merciful as well as allknowing
Has been long revealed: he is not himself bound
To fulfil foreknowledge. He scatters grace
Liberally and arbitrarily, so all men may hope,
Even you, man of the northern seas, may hope.
But Pelagius replied: Mercy is the word, mercy.
And a greater word is love. Out of his love
He makes man free to accept or reject him.
He could foreknow but refuses to foreknow
Any, even the most trivial, human act until
The act has been enacted, and then he knows.
So men are free, are touched by God's own freedom.
Christ with his blood washed out original sin,
So we are in no wise predisposed to sin
More than to do good: we are free, free,
Free to build our salvation. Halleluiah.
But the man of Hippo, with an African blast,
Blasted this man of the cool north ...

No no no, Enderby said to himself. It could not be done. This was not poetry. You could not make poetry out of raw doctrine. You had to find symbols, and he had no symbols. The poem could not be written. He was free. The paper chains rustled off. He stuffed them into the waste-basket. Free. Free to start writing the *Odontiad*. Hence bound to start writing the *Odontiad*. Hence not free.

He sighed bitterly and went to the bathroom to start tarting himself up for the television show. Clean and bleeding, he put on garments bequeathed to him by Rawcliffe and stood, at length, to review himself at length in the long wall-mirror near the bedroom door.

Seedy Edwardian, recaller of dead glories, finale of Elgar's First Symphony belting out Massive Hope for the Future. There was an empire in those days, and it was assumed that the centre of the English language was London. Wealthy Americans were still humble provincials. Ichabod. He put on the sculpted overcoat and his beret and, swordstick pathetic in his feeble grip, went out.

The subway had not yet erupted into violent nocturnal life. His fellow-passengers on the downtown express to Times Square were as dimly ruminant as he, perhaps recalling dimly the glories of other departed empires, Ottoman, Austro-Hungarian, Pharaonic. But one black youth in a rutilant combat jacket saw drug-induced empires within; under the *pax alucinatoria* the rhomboid and spiral became one. Enderby looked again at the torn-off corner of the abandoned poem on which he had written *Live Lancing Show 46th Street or somewhere like that.* He had time, also two ten-dollar bills in his pocket. He would go to the Blue Bar of the Algonquin Hotel, a once very literary place, and have a quiet gin or so. He felt all right. The black tea and Sarah Lee were worrying the heart combat troops: why was not the rutilant enemy scared?

He got out quite briskly at Times Square and walked down West 44th Street. In the lobby of the Algonquin there were, he saw, British periodicals on sale. He bought *The Times* and leafed through it standing. In a remote corner of it, he saw, a member of parliament was pleading for a special royal commission to clean up the Old Testament. Dangers even in great classics, provocation to idle and affluent youth etc. In the Blue Bar there were some conspiratorial and lecherous customers at tables, but seated on a bar-stool was a rather loud man whose voice Enderby seemed to recognize. Good God, it was Father Hopkins himself. No, the man who played him in the film. What was his name now?

'So I said to him *up yours*, that's what I said.'

'That's it, Mr O'Donnell.'

Coemgen (pronounced Kevin) O'Donnell, that was the man. Enderby had met him briefly at a little party after the London preview, when he had been affably drunk. No coincidence that he was here now: the Algonquin took in actors as much as writers.

Sitting at a stool two empty stools away from O'Donnell, Enderby asked politely for a pink gin. O'Donnell, hunched to the counter, heard the voice, swivelled gracelessly and said:

'You British?'

'Well, yes,' Enderby said. 'British-born but, like yourself I presume, living in exile. Look, we've already met.'

'Never seen you before in my life.' The voice was wholly American. 'Lots of guys like you, seen me on the movies, assume acquaintanceshhh. Ip. You British?'

'Well, yes. British-born but, like yourself I presume, living in ...'

'You said all that crap already, buster. All I asked was a straight queschhh. Okay, you're British. Needn't keep on about it. No need to eggs hhhibit the flag tattooed on your ass. And all that sort of. What? What?'

'The film,' Enderby said. 'The movie. *The Wreck of the Deutschland.*'

'I was in it. That was my movie.' He thrust his empty tumbler rudely towards the bartender. He was most unpriestlike in his dress, glistening cranberry suit, violet silk, shoes that Enderby took to be Gucci. The face was a rugged cornerboy's, apt for some slum baseball-with-the-kids Maynooth type priest, but hardly for the delicate intellectual unconscious pederast ah-my-dear Hopkins.

'The point is,' Enderby said, 'that I too was in it in a sense. It was my idea. My name was among the credits. Enderby,' he added, to no applause. 'Enderby,' to not even recognition. Coemgen O'Donnell said:

'Yeah. I guess it had to be somebody's idea. Everything is kind of built on the idea of some unknown guy. You seen the figures in this week's *Variety*? Sex and violence, always the answer. But the guy that wrote the book was not like the guy I played in the movie. No, sir. The original Father Hopkins was a fag.'

'A priest a fag?' the bartender said. 'You don't say.'

'There are priest fags,' O'Donnell said. 'Known several. Have it off with the altar boys. But in the movie he's normal. Has it off with a nun.' He nodded gravely at Enderby and said: 'You British?'

'Listen,' Enderby said, 'Gerard Manley Hopkins was not a homosexual. At least not consciously. Certainly not actively.

Sublimation into the love of Christ perhaps. A theory, no more. A possibility. Of no religious or literary interest, of course. A love of male beauty. *The Bugler's First Communion* and *The Loss of the Eurydice* and *Harry Ploughman*. Admiration for it. "Every inch a tar. Of the best we boast our sailors are." "Hard as hurdle arms with a broth of goldish flue." What's wrong with that, for Christ's sake?'

'Broth of goldfish my ass,' O'Donnell said. 'Has that guy from the front office come yet?' he asked the bartender.

'He'll come in here, Mr O'Donnell. He'll know where you are. If I was you, sir, I'd make that one the last. Until after the show, that is.'

'Show?' Enderby said. 'Are you by any chance on the –' He consulted the tear-off from his pocket. 'Live Lancing Show?'

'Hey, that's good. Sperr would like that. Not that it's live, old boy, old boy. Nothing's live, not any more.' And then: 'You British?'

'I've said already that I –'

'You a fag? Okay okay. That's not what I was going to ask. What I was going to ask was – What was I going to ask?' he asked the bartender.

'Search me, Mr O'Donnell.'

'I know. Something about a bugle-boy. What was that about a bugugle-boy?'

'*The Bugler's First Communion*?'

'That's it, I guess. Now this proves that he was a fag. You British? Yeah yeah, asked that already. That means you know the town of Oxford, where the college is, right? It was my father.'

'*What*?'

'Got that balled-up, I guess. Big army barracks there. Cow cow cow something.'

'Cowley?'

'Right, you'd know that, being British. Another scatch on the –'

'Sorry, Mr O'Donnell. You yourself give me strict instructions when you started.'

'Okay okay, gotta be with old Can Dix. Sending a limousine.'

'Who? What?'

'Sending a car round. This talk-show.'

'I,' Enderby said, 'am on the other one, the Spurling one. What,' he said with apprehension, 'are you going to tell them?'

'Listen, old boy old boy, not finished, had I, right? Right. It was my mother's father. British, with an Irish mother. Sent him off to be good Catholic. Right? One hell of a row, father was Protestant.'

'Yes,' Enderby said. '"Born, he tells me, of Irish / Mother to an English sire (he / Shares their best gifts surely, fall how things will)."'

'Not finished, had I, right?'

'Sorry.'

'No need to be sorry. Never regret anything, my what the hell do you call it slogan, right? Went over to Ireland with my mother's father's mother, he was my mother's father, you see that?'

'Right.'

'Married Irish, the British all got smothered up. Well, that was his story.'

'What was his story?'

'Had him down there in the what do you call it presbyt presbyt, his red pants off of him and gave him, you know, the stick. Met him again in Dublin when he was some sort of professor, reminded him of it. Made him very sick. Very sick already.'

'Oh God,' Enderby said.

O now well work that sealing sacred ointment!
O for now charms, arms, what bans off bad
And love locks ever in a lad!
Let me though see no more of him, and not disappointment
Those sweet hopes quell whose least me quickenings lift ...

'I can't believe it,' Enderby said. 'I won't.' He had intimations of a renewal of quasi-lethal pains ready to shoot from chest to clavicle to arm. No, he wouldn't have it. He frightened the promise away with a quick draught of gin. 'So,' he said. 'You're going to tell them all about it?'

'Not that,' O'Donnell said. 'Crack a few gags about nuns. I was with this dame in a taxi and she was a nun. She'd have nun of this and nun of that.'

'What a filthy unspeakable world,' Enderby said. 'What defilement, what horror.'

'You can say that again. Ah, Josh. It is Josh? Sure it's Josh. How are things, Josh? How's the kids and the missus? The old trouble-and-strife our British friend here would say.' His Cockney was tolerable. 'A cap of Rosy Lee and dahn wiv yer rahnd the ahzes.'

'Getting married next month,' this Josh said unelatedly. He looked Armenian to Enderby, hairy and with an ovine profile.

'Is that right, is that really right, well I sure am happy for you, Josh. Our friend here,' O'Donnell said, 'has been talking about our movie, *Kraut Soup*.' He stood up and appeared not merely sober but actually as though he had just downed a gill of vinegar. He was, after all, an actor. Could you then believe anything he said or did? But how did he know about the barracks at Cowley? 'What defilement, what horror,' he said, in exactly Enderby's accent and intonation.

'Is that right?' Josh said. 'We'd best be on our way, Mr O'Donnell. There may be a fight with the autograph hounds.'

'Say that story isn't true,' Enderby begged. 'It can't be true.'

'My granddaddy swore it was true. He always remembered the name. We had a Mrs Hopkins who cleaned for us. He had nothing against priests, he said. He was a real believer all his life.'

Though this child's drift / Seems by a divine doom channelled, nor do I cry / Disaster there …

'The car's waiting, Mr O'Donnell.'

'And he saw it wasn't real sexual excitement. Not like he'd seen in the barracks. It was all tied up with – Well, his hands were shaking with the joy of it, you know.' Low-latched in leaflight housel his too huge godhead. *Too huge*, my dear. 'Come on, Josh, let's go. He was only a kid but he saw that.' He nodded very soberly. 'So I had to do the part, I guess.' O'Donnell waved extravagantly to the bartender and guccied out, shepherded by Josh. Enderby had another pink gin, feeling pretty numb. What did it matter, anyway? It was the poetry that counted. I am gall, I am heartburn, God's most deep decree / Bitter would have me taste. And no bloody wonder.

The ways leading to the television place on 46th Street were warming up nicely with the threat of violence. Violence in itself is not bad, ladies and gentlemen. In a poem you would be entitled to exploit the fortuitous connotations – violins, viols, violets. We need violence sometimes. I feel very violent now. Beware of barbarism, violence for its own sake. It was a little old theatre encrusted with high-voltage light-bulbs. There was a crowd lining up outside, waiting to be the studio audience. They would see themselves waving to themselves tomorrow night, the past waving to the future. The young toughs in control wore uniform blazers, rutilant with a monogram SL, and they would not at first let him in by the stagedoor: you line up with the rest, buster. But then his British accent convinced them that he must be one of the performers. They let him in.

Seven

PARTIAL TRANSCRIPT OF SPERR LANSING SHOW B/3/57. RECORDED BUT NOT USED. RESERVE 2 (AUSTRALIAN TOUR) PUT OUT AS LAST MINUTE SUBSTITUTE.

SPERR: Thank you thank you (*no response to applause killer*) thank you thank you well this is what Id call a real dose of the (*laughter and applause*) I didnt say that I didnt say no I didnt. Seriously though (*laughter*) the rise in prices. I went to a new barber yesterday and before I even sat down he said thatll be one dollar fifty (*laughter*). Thats cheap I told him for a haircut (*laughter*). That he said is for the estimate (*laughter and applause*). Seriously though (*laughter*) the way they speak English in New York (*laughter*). I saw two men at Kennedy Airport the other day and one said to the other When are you leaving. The other said I am leaving in the Bronx (*laughter and applause*). I have a new tailor did I tell you or should I say I HAD a new tailor (*L*). I took the suit back and said this doesnt fit. Sure it doesnt fit he said. Youre not wearing it right (*L*). You have to stick out your left hip and your right shoulder and bend that knee a bit (*L and A*). Then it fits nice (*L*). So I did as he said (*visual. L and A*) and was walking along 46th Street when two doctors came by and I heard one say to the other Look at that poor feller a terrible case of deformity (*L*). Right says the other. The suit fits nice though (*L and prolonged A*). Seriously though clients and customers anybody here tonight from Minneapolis and St Paul (*A and jeers*). I thought not (*L*). That means I cant say I went out with a girl from up there (*L*). She was called the tail of two cities (*prolonged L and A. Sperr shouts over*). Be right back. A great guest list tonight folks desirable Ermine Elderley Jake Summers Prof (*Premature start commercial break*).

SPERR: So if you want to stay slim and feel overfed girls try it. My first guest tonight is a famous British poet at present visiting professor at ... University of Manhattan. Weve asked him to come and say something about a movie that was all his idea and is at present causing a riot in the movie houses of the civilised world. Ladies and gentlemen – Professor Fox Enderby. (*Applause card applause. Visual unrehearsed guest trips on wire. A and L*).

SPERR: Must say we all admire the suit Professor Enderby (*A*). A bit of Oldy England (*A*).

ENDERBY: (*Unintelligible*) right name.

SPERR: Oh I see just the initials. Pardon me. Well an O is zero right. And a zeros nothing right. So its just an F and an X. With nothing between. Like I said. F O X. (*prolonged A*).

ENDERBY: (*Unintell*).

SPERR: Are you married, professor? (*headshake no*) Do you have children? (*L*)

ENDERBY: A wise child knows his own (*?*)

SPERR: What I want to say is do you would you like children of yours to see a movie like Wreck of the Deutschland.

ENDERBY: Anybody can see what the hell they like for all I care. Anybodys children. Cluding (*?*) yours.

SPERR: I have a daughter of six. (*A*) You wouldnt object to her seeing a movie of nuns being er (*prolonged A*).

ENDERBY: Not the point. The point is to have a world in which nuns are not. Then it wouldnt be in films. Then thered be no danger of your daughter. Besides its adults only.

SPERR: Maybe. But there are disturbing reports of the young seeing the film and then committing atrocities (*A*).

ENDERBY: What the hell are they clapping for. Because of the atrocities. Would your six year old daughter go round raping nuns.

SPERR: No but shed be disturbed and maybe wake up crying with nightmares. (*A*) We like to protect our children professor (*very prol. A*).

ENDERBY: And wheres it got (?) you protecting them. More juvenile violence in America than anywhere else in the world. Not that I object to violence (*audience protest*). You cant change things without violence. You baggers (?) were violence when you broke away from us in 1776. Not blaming you for that of course. You wanted to do it and were term in to do it (??). You were wrong of course. Might still be a bit of law and order if you were still colonial territory. Not ready for self gov (*audience protest and some A*).

SPERR: Your attitude ties up with your dress professor (*prol. A*). I understand then that youre very patriotic. But youre not living in Britain are you.

ENDERBY: Cant stand the bloody place. Americanized. The past is the only place worth living in. Imaginary past. Lets get back to what we were talking about before you introduced irreverences (?).

SPERR: You did it not me (*A*).

ENDERBY: People always blame art literature drama for their own evil. Or other peoples. Art only imitates life. Evils already there. Original sin. Curious thing about America is that it was founded by people who believed original sin and also priesty nation (???) but then you had to watch for signs of gods grace and this was in commercial success making your own way building heaven on earth and so on this led to American plagiarism (?).

SPERR: What words that professor.

ENDERBY: A British monkey called Morgan in Greek Plage us (??????) taught no national pensity (?) to evil. Errorsy (?). Evils in everybody. Desire to kill rape destroy mindless violence ...

SPERR: I thought you said you liked violence (*prol A*).

ENDERBY: Never said that you silly bagger (?). Never said mindless MINDLESS violets. Constructive different.

SPERR: Oh I see sorry. Take a break now. Be right back. Dont go away (*prol A. MUSIC POMP CIRCUS DANCE (?)*). (*Commercial break*)

SPERR: Oh there you are. Hi. My next guest is also a professor youve met often on the show. Expert on human behaviour and author of many books such as er The Human Engine Waits will you please welcome back professor of psychology Stations of the Cross university Ribblesdale NY Man Balaglas. (*Applause card applause. Prof Balaglas*)

SPERR: Well hi. Its been quite some time professor.

ENDERBY: What did you say it was called.

BALAGLAS: What.

ENDERBY: This university where youre at. I didnt quite catch the.

BALAGLAS: Stations of the Cross.

ENDERBY: Catholic.

BALAGLAS: Theres Protestant there too. Jews. Fifth Day Adventists. What youd call ecommunionicle (?).

SPERR: And do you like violence too professor (*A and some L*).

ENDERBY: I never said I liked the bloody thing. Mindless I said.

BALAGLAS: Most emphatic no. The great scourge of our age and one of the most urgent of our needs is to laminate (?) it and that is what my own department along with others in other universities regards as research priority. (*Pause then some A*)

ENDERBY: Youll never get rid of it. Original sin.

BALAGLAS: I would there most emphatic disagree an urgent problem we have to make our cities places where people can walk at night without getting mugged and raped and killed all the time (*A*).

ENDERBY: (*Unintell*) all the time.

SPERR: And how can this be done professor.

BALAGLAS: Positive rain forcemeat (?). Instructive urge is not killed (kwelled?) by prison or punishment. Brainwashing that is to say negative through fear of pain already tried but is fundamentally inhuman (*e*?). We must so condition human mind that reward is expected for doing good not the other way about.

ENDERBY: What other way about.

SPERR: Like he said professor. Psychology.

ENDERBY: A lot of simple (sinful?) bloody nonsense. You take the filament of human choice out of ethnical decisions. Men should be free to choose good. But theres no choice if theres only good. Stands to region there has to be evil as well.

BALAGLAS: I emphatic disagree. What does inhabited or unconditioned human choice go for. For too much rape and mugging (*A*).

ENDERBY: In other words original sin. Which leads us to the stations of the cross.

BALAGLAS: Pardon me.

ENDERBY: Youre not Christian then.

BALAGLAS: An irreverent question. Were all in this together (*A*).

SPERR: You think its possible then professor that people can be made to be good by er positive er.

BALAGLAS: Right. Its happening already. Volunteers in our prisons. Also in our universities. Stations of the Cross is proud of its volunteer record.

SPERR: Well thats just (*interrup by loud A*).

ENDERBY: What you mean is that the community is more important than the individual.

BALAGLAS: Pardon me.

ENDERBY: Stop saying bloody pardon me all the time. What I said was that you think human beings should give up freedom to choose so that the community can be free of violence (*A*).

BALAGLAS: Right. Youve said it loud and clear professor. Bloody clear if I may borrow your own er locomotion (*???*). The individual has to sacrifice his freedom to some extent for the benefit of his fellow citizens. (*Prolong A*).

ENDERBY: Well I think its bloody monsters (*?*). Human beings are defined by freedom of choice. Once you have them doing what theyre told is good just because theyre going to get a lump of sugar instead of a kick up the ahss (*?!*) then ethnics no longer exists. The State could tell them it was good to go off and mug and rape and kill some other nation. Thats what its been doing. Look at your bloody war in ...

SPERR: Well be right back after this important message. Dont go away folks. Be right b (*prem start comm break*)

(*Music. Band on camera. Audience shots*)

SPERR: This is the Sperr Lansing Show. Be right back after this station break.

(*Station Break*)

SPERR: Were talking with two professors Professor Balaglas psychologist and Professor er Endivy British poet. Professor Balaglas ...

BALAGLAS: Call me Man. (*Pause then A*) Representative Man. (*P then A*)

ENDERBY: Whats that short for. I knew you werent a bloody Christian.

SPERR: Do you believe professor that movies and books and er art can influence young people to violence rape mugging and so on (*A*).

BALAGLAS: There is I would consider ample proof that the impressionable and not merely those in the younger age groups can be incited to antisocial behaviour by the artistic representation of er antisocial acts. There was the instance in township of Inversnaid NY not too far from Ribblesdale where as you know I am at present on the faculty of the university there of the young man who killed his uncle and said that seeing Sir Laurence Oliviers movie of Hamlet had influenced him to perform the crime.

ENDERBY: How old was he. I asked how old was.

BALAGLAS: About thirty. And very unbalanced.

ENDERBY: And had his uncle just married his mother (*L*). His mother. Not his uncles mother (*L*).

BALAGLAS: I dont recollect as much. It was just the killing of his uncle as in this movie. And also if I recollect rightly that also comes in the play on which the movie was based.

ENDERBY: Shakespeare.

SPERR: Thats right. And would you believe in the restricting of the viewing of professor.

ENDERBY: Of course not. Bloody ridiculous idea.

SPERR: I meant the other professor professor (*L and A*).

BALAGLAS: Well as we are committed to control of the violentment (?) and as works of art and movies and the like are part of it then for the sake of society there must be control. There are too many dirty books and movies and also violent ones (*A*).

ENDERBY: This is bloody teetotal Aryan (??) talk. You mean that kids wouldnt be allowed to see or read Hamlet because they might go and kill their uncles. Ive never in my life heard such bloody stupid actionary (?) talk. Why by Christ man

BALAGLAS: Thats right Man thats my name (*L and A*). Call me Man by all means but cut out the blasph (*very loud A*).

ENDERBY: But bagger (?) it man you idiot I mean that would mean that nobody could read anything not even Alice in Windowland (?) because it says Off with his Head and the Wizard of Oz because of the wicked witch is

BALAGLAS: I do not know what standards of etiquette prevail in your part of the world Professor Elderley but I do most strenuously object to being called idiot (*very loud A*).

SPERR: And at that opportune moment we take a break. Stay with us folks. (*A*).

(COMMERCIAL BREAK)

SPERR: Professor Balaglas made an interesting slip of the tongue folks which weve just been discussing during the break.

ENDERBY: I still say he was trying to be bloody insulting. A man cant help his age.

SPERR: Right. Because if a girls name was ever improper that is to say not appropriate to what she is then the name of my next guest must be. Beautiful charming talented and above all YOUNG star of such movies as The Leaden Echo Mortal Beauty Rockfire and just about to be released Manshape here she is folks Ermine Elderley. (*Very loud and sustained applause also male whistles as she comes on kisses Sperr and Prof Balaglas not Prof Enderby sits down*)

SPERR: Wow (*L and A*).

ENDERBY: I see so youre Elderley. I thought he was trying to take the (*unintell* piece? pass?)

ERMINE: Sure I am. How young do you like em (*L and A*).

ENDERBY: What I meant was (*not heard under L and A*)

SPERR: Ermine if I may call you Ermine

ERMINE: Just buy it for me sweetie (*L and A*). I apologize. You always have done before baby (*L and A*). Called me it I mean (*L and A*).

SPERR: How would you like to be raped (*very sust L with a lot of visual L L and again L*). I meant in a movie of course. Seriously (*L*).

ERMINE: Seriously yes. If I was playing that sort of part okay but I dont think I would oh I might if there was a kind of you know moral lesson and the guy gets his comeuppance after or before he really gets under way his teeth knocked out that sort of thing not shooting shootings too good. But I wouldnt have it if I was playing a nun like in this German movie. Thats irreligious.

ENDERBY: Look Im not trying to defend it. What she calls this German movie. As a matter of fact its not allowed to be shown in Germany.

SPERR: No Deutschland for Deutschland right (*L*).

ENDERBY: I have to make this clear dont I.

ERMINE: You should know brother (*L*).

ENDERBY: The film is very different from the poem.

SPERR: What poem is that.

ENDERBY: Why the poem its based on. By Gerald Mann Leigh

ERMINE: You mean no rape in the poem (*L*). Well what do they do in the poem pluck daffodils (*L*).

Enderby, sweating hard under the lights and the awareness of his unpopularity, looked at this hard woman who exhibited great sternly supported breasts to the very periphery of the areola and was dressed in a kind of succulent rutilant taffeta. The name, he was thinking: as artificial as the huge aureate wig. He said:
    'I grant its cleverness. The name, I mean. I should imagine your real name is something like let me see Irma Polansky. No, wait,

Edelmann, something like that.' She looked very bard back at him.

'Do you read much poetry, professor?' Sperr Lansing asked.

'Well, I guess I hardly have the time these days.' This Professor Balaglas flashed glasses in the lights. He had the soft face of a boy devoted to his mother and wore a hideous spotted bowtie. 'What with working on the problems that this kind of movie under present discussion gives rise to.' There was laughter. The audience was full of mouths, always as it were at the ready, lips parted in potential ecstasy. 'I have a collection of rock records like everybody else, of course. It's the job of poets to get close to the people. We shall be able to use poets in the new dispensation,' he promised. 'Rhymes are of considerable value in hypnopaedia or sleep-teaching. A great deal of the so-called poetry they write these days...'

'Who writes?' Enderby asked.

'I don't mean you, professor. I never read anything you wrote. You may be very clear and straightforward for all I know.' Laughter. 'I mean, you've been using very clear and straightforward language to me tonight.' Very great laughter.

'The point I was trying to make,' Enderby said. 'About her name, that is.' He shoulderjerked towards the star, 'There you see the poetic process exemplified in a small way. Ermine, suggesting opulence, wealth, softness, luxury. Elderley, the piquancy of contrast with her evident near-youth, no longer *very* young, of course, but it happens to everybody, and the denotation of the name. The small *frisson* of gerontophilia.'

Sperr Lansing did not seem to be greatly enjoying his job. He was a man adept at appearing to be on top of everything, ready with quip and *oeillade*, but the eyes now had become as glassy as those of a hung hare. 'Get on top of whom?' he tried, and then saw he was being betrayed into unbecoming lowness. There was, rightly, no audience laugh.

Miss Elderley cunningly got in with 'I used to know a poem about the wreck of something.' There were relieved sniggers.

'The Hesperus perhaps,' Professor Isinglass (?) brightly said.

'Naw, this went "The boy stood on the burning deck ..."'

A thing exquisitely coarse shot up from Enderby's school-days. It was neat, too. Dirty verse depended upon an almost Augustan neatness. '"The boy stood in the witness-box," he recited, '"Picking his nose like fury –"' There were loud cries of hey hey and Lansing picked up a packet of Shagbag or something from among the various commercial artefacts stowed behind the ashtray-and-waterbottle table. 'I think,' he cried, 'it's time we heard another important message. Girls,' he counter-recited, 'is your fried chicken greasy?'

'– "Little blocks, And aimed it at the jury."'

'Because if you want it to be crisp and dry as the bone within here's how to do it.' There were at once waving fat studio major-domos running around, and the monitor screens began to show hideous greasy fried chicken, oleic, aureate.

'All right all right,' Sperr Lansing was saying, 'it's going to be Jake Summers next. Look,' he said to Enderby, 'keep it clean, willya.'

'I was only trying to keep it vulgar,' Enderby said. 'It's evidently a vulgar sort of show.'

'It wasn't till you got on to it, buster,' Miss Elderley began. 'Well, damn it,' Enderby said, 'the amount of tit you're showing, if you don't mind my saying so, is hardly conducive to the maintenance of a high standard of intellectual discourse.'

'You leave my bosoms out of this –'

'There's only *one* bosom. A bosom is a dual entity.'

'I object to him using that word about me. I've met these bastards before –'

'I object to being called a bastard –'

'Either sex maniacs or fags –'

Sperr Lansing composed his face to beatific calm and told the camera and the audience: 'Welcome back, folks. Now here's the man who pays for a moon shot with every Broadway success he writes. Somebody once said that there were only two men of the theatre, Jake Speare and Jake Summers. Well, here's one of them.'

Underneath the applause and the shambling on of a small near-bald clerkly man in spectacles and sweatshirt, Enderby said to Miss Elderley:

'I suppose you wouldn't call that vulgar. Eh? Jakes Peare, indeed.
And I'll tell you another thing – I won't be called a bloody fag.'

'I didn't say that. I said the British are either fags or sex maniacs.
Keep it quiet, willya.'

For Sperr Lansing was now praising this Summers man lavishly to
his face. '– Five hundred and forty-five performances is what I have
written down here. To what do you attribute –'

Summers was wearily modest. 'Write well, I guess. Keep it clean,
I guess. When they do it, they do it offstage.' Applause and laughter.
'No, yah. Let them hear about sex and violence, I guess, not see it.'
(*A and L.*) 'Talking about poetry,' he said, 'I used to write it. Then I
meet this guy on his yacht and he says give it up, there's nothing in
it.' Applause.

Enderby saw the tortured ecstatic face of Father Hopkins on top
of the bugler and went mad. 'Filth,' he said, 'filth and vulgarity.'

'Aw, can it willya,' Miss Elderley said. Professor Glass said:

'It is not my place, not here and now that is, to proffer any
diagnosis of er Professor Endlessly's perpetual er manic state of
excitation. Facts must be faced, though. The world has changed.
England is no longer the centre of a world empire. The English
language has found its finest er flowering in what he called a colonial territory.'

'Attaboy,' Miss Elderley said. 'Wow.'

'Be fair, I guess,' Summers said. 'Those boys with guitars.' 'He
feels his manhood threatened,' Professor Elderglass went on. 'Note
how his dress proclaims an, er, long dead national virility. He thinks
man is being abolished. His kind of man.'

'Bankside,' Summers said. Everybody roared.

'Yes, the character or homunculus in your play. Man *qua* man.
Man in his humanity. Man as Thou not It. Man as a person not a
thing. These are not very helpful expressions, but they supply a clue.
What is being abolished is autonomous man, the inner man, the
homunculus, the possessing demon, the man defended by the litera-
tures of freedom and dignity.'

'That's it, you bastard,' Enderby said, 'you've summed it
all up.'

'His abolition has been long overdue. He has been constructed from our ignorance, and as our understanding increases, the very stuff of which he is composed vanishes. Science does not dehumanize man, it dehomunculises him, and it must do so if it is to prevent the abolition of the human species. Hamlet, in the play I have already mentioned, by your fellow-playwright, Mr Summers, said of man "How like a god." Pavlov said "How like a dog." But that was a step forward. Man is much more than a dog, but like a dog he is within range of a scientific analysis.'

'Look,' shouted Enderby over the applause, 'I won't have it, see. We're free and we're free to take our punishment. Like Hopkins. I suppose you'd watch him doing it with your bloody neat little bowtie on and say how like a dog. Well, he's been punished enough with this bloody film or movie as you'd call it, bloody childish. That's his hell. He was gall, he was heartburn.'

'He should have taken Windkill,' Jake Summers said and got roars. Enderby was very nearly sidetracked.

'Leave the commercials to me, Jake,' Lansing said, delighted. 'And talking about commercials it's time we took another –'

'Oh no it bloody well isn't,' Enderby shouted. 'You can keep your bloody homunculus, for that's all he is –'

'Pardon me, it's you who believe in the homunculus –'

'Man was always violent and always sinful and always will be.'

'And now he's got to change.'

'He won't change, not unless he becomes something else. Can't you see that that's where the drama of life is, the high purple, the tragic –'

'Oh my,' Jake Summers sighed histrionically and was at once loudly rewarded. 'No time for comedy,' he added and then was not clearly understood.

'The evolution of a culture,' Professor Lookingglass said, 'is a gigantic exercise in self-control. It is often said that a scientific view of man leads to wounded vanity, a sense of hopelessness, and nostalgia –'

'Nostalgia means homesickness,' Enderby cried. 'And we're all homesick. Homesick for sin and colour and drunkenness –'

'Ah, so that's what it is,' Miss Elderley said. 'You're stoned.'

'Homesick for the past.' Enderby could feel himself ready to weep. But then fire possessed him just as Sperr Lansing said, 'And now we let our sponsor get a word in –' Enderby stood and declaimed:

'For how to the heart's cheering
The down-dugged ground-hugged grey
Hovers off, the jay-blue heavens appearing
Of pied and peeled May!'

'Fellers,' Sperr Lansing said, 'do you ever feel, you know, not up to it?' He held in his hands a product called, apparently, Mansex. 'Well, just watch this.' Then he turned on Enderby, as did everybody, including the sweating studio major-domos. The band, which appeared to have a whole Wagnerian brass section as well as innumerable saxophones and a drummer in charge sitting high on a throne, gave out very piercingly and thuddingly.

'Blue-beating and hoary-glow height; or night, still higher,
With belled fire and the moth-soft Milky Way,
What by your measure is the heaven of desire,
The treasure never eyesight got, nor was ever guessed what for
    the hearing?'

SPERR: Well I dont think it can. Youd better get on to Harry right away.

ENDERBY: Fucking home uncle us (????) indeed. Ill give you fucking home uncle us (?????). Degradation of humanity. No, but it was not these the jading and jar of the cart (?) times tasking it is fathers (?) that asking for ease of the sodden with its sorrowing hart (art?) not danger electrical horror then further it finds the appealing of the passion is tenderer (?) in prayer apart other I gather in measure her minds burden in winds (????????)

Eight

'And I'll tell you another thing,' said the man in the bar. 'Your Queen of England. She owns half of Manhattan.'

'That's a lie,' Enderby said. 'Not that I give a bugger either way.'

It was a small dark and dirty bar not far from the television theatre whence Enderby had been not exactly ejected but as it were ushered with some measure of acrimony. The programme that had been recorded could not, it was felt, go out. The audience had been told too and had been angry until told that they were going to do it all over again but without Enderby.

'What's the matter with you then?' this man asked. 'You not patriotic?' He had a face round and shiny as an apple but somehow unwholesome, as though a worm was burrowing within. 'Your Winston Churchill was a great man, wasn't he? He wanted to fight the commies.'

'He was half American,' Enderby said, then sipped at his sweetish whisky sour.

'Ain't nothing wrong with that. You trying to say there's something wrong with that?'

'After six years of fighting the bloody Germans,' Enderby said, 'we were supposed to spend another six or sixty years fighting the bloody Russians. And he always had these big cigars when the rest of us couldn't get a single solitary fag.'

'What's that about fags?'

'Cigarettes,' Enderby explained. 'While you've a lucifer to light your fag, smile, boys, that's the style.'

'My mother was German. That makes me half German. You trying to say there's something wrong with that?' And then: 'You one of these religious guys? What's that you was saying about Lucifer?'

'The light-bringer. Hence a match. For lighting a fag.'

'I'd set a light to them. I'd burn the bastards. It's fags that pretends the downfall. The Sin of Sodom. You ever read that book?'

'I don't think so.'

'Jack,' this man called to the bartender, 'do you have that book?'

'Gave it back to Shorty.'

'There,' the man said. 'But there's plenty around. Where you going now?'

'No more money,' Enderby said. 'Just one subway token.'

'Right. And your Queen of England owns half the real estate in Queens. That's why they call it Queens, I guess.'

Enderby walked slowly, not too displeased, towards the Times Square subway hellmouth. He had told the bastards anyway. Not apparently as many as he had expected to tell, but these matters could not always be approached quantitatively. He passed a great lighted pancake house and hungered as he did. No, watch diet, live. A whining vast black came out at him and whined for a coin. Enderby was able sincerely to say that he had no money, only a subway token. Well gimme that mane. I kin sell that for thirty cents. But how do I get home? That ain't ma problem mane. Enderby shook his head compassionately. Two other blacks and a white man, dispossessed or alienated, had made a little street band for their own apparent pleasure: guitar, flageolet, tambourine. Music of the people. Was that a possible approach?

An ole Sain Gus he said yo born in sin
Cos when Eve ate de apple she let de serpent in

He shook his head sadly and went down below, wondering not for the first time whether it was really necessary to be so punctilious about setting the turnstile working with a token in the slot, since so many black and brown youths merely used, without official protest, the exit gate as an entrance. There were a lot of noisy ethnic people, as they were stupidly called, around, but Enderby did not fear. Nor was it just a matter of his being illegally armed. It was a matter of being *integer vitae* and also of having committed himself to a world in which pure and simple aggression was to be accepted as part of the human fabric. Die with Beethoven's Ninth howling and crashing away or live in a safe world of silly clockwork music?

He got into a train, thinking, and then realized his mistake. This was not the uptown express to 96th Street but the uptown local. Never mind. He was interested to see that, among the few passengers, all harmless, there was a nun. She was a nun of a kind not to be seen in backward Europe or North Africa, since she wore the new reformed habit, fruit of ill-thought-out Catholic liberalism. There had been a nun in a class he had taught the previous semester, though it had been a long time before he realized it, since she wore a striped sailor sweater and bell-bottomed trousers. When he discovered her name was Sister Agnes, he had wondered if she were part of some religious mission to seawomen. But then she left the class, being apparently put off by Enderby's occasional blasphemies. This nun on the train was dressed in a short skirt that revealed veal-to-the-heel legs in what looked like lisle stockings, a modest tippet, a rather heavy pectoral cross, and the wimple of her order. She had a round shining Irish face with a dab of lipstick. Of the world and yet not of it. She had a Bloomingdale's shopping-bag on her lap. She smiled at some small inner vision, perhaps of the kettle on the hob singing peace into her breast, a doorstep spiced veal sandwich waiting for her supper. Enderby looked kindly at her.

The two brown louts who got on, quickening Enderby's heart, spoke not Spanish but Portuguese. Brazilians, a new spice for the ethnic stew, plenty of Indian blood there. Enderby at once feared for the nun, but she seemed protected either by her reformed uniform or their own superstition. They leered instead towards a blonde lay girl reading some thick college tome, probably on what was called sociology, further up the car. CRISTO 99. JISM 292. They wore long flared pants with goldish studs stretching on the outer seams from waist to instep. Their jackets were of a bolero type, blazoned with symbols of destruction and death: thunderbolt, rawhead, fasces, unionjack, swastika. One of them wore a *Gott Mit Uns* belt. They stood, two brown left hands gently frotting the metal monkey-pole. They spoke to each other. Enderby hungrily hearkened.

'*E conta o que ele fez com ela e tern fotografia e tudo.*'

'*Um velho lélé da cuca.*'

They were apparently talking about literature. At the next stop they grinned at everybody, leered at the girl with the tome, mock-genuflected at the nun, then got off. '*Boa noite,*' Enderby said, having once had a regular drunk from Santander in his Tangier bar, one much given in his cups to protesting the deuterocaroline dowry. Now there was a kind of quiet general exhalation. At the next stop but one three nice WASP boys, as Enderby took them to be, got on. In the eyes of two of them was the very green of the ocean between Plymouth and Plymouth Rock. The other had warm tea-hued pupils. They were chubbyfaced and wore toggled duffle-jackets. Their hair belonged to some middle crinal zone between aseptic nord and latinindian jetwalled lousehouse. Without words and almost with the seriousness of asylum nurses they at once set upon an unsavoury-looking matron who began to cry out Mediterranean vocables of distress. Staggering but laughing, they had her staggering upright, held from the back by the tea-eyed one, while her skirt was yanked up to disclose sensible thick navy-blue knickers. One drew nail-scissors and began delicately to slice at them. Oh my God, Enderby prayed. Gerontal violation. The nun, who had lapsed back into her dream of supper, was quicker than Enderby. She staggered on to them, the train jolting much, hitting with her Bloomingdale's bag. Delighted, the nail-scissored one turned on her, while the knicker-ripping was completed by hand by the others. Enderby was, in the desperate resigned second before his own intervention, interested to see the reading girl go on reading and even turn a page, while an old man slept uneasily and two black boys chewed and watched as if this were television. Enderby tottered to the train's rocking, was now there with his stick. How much better to be out of it, the kettle on the hob, a spiced veal sandwich. Delighted, the nail-scissored one turned on him, dropping his nun to the deck to pray or something. And yet God has not said a word, nor they either. Yet noises were corning out, even out of Enderby, such as yaaark and grerrr and gheee.

'Scrot,' one of them said. 'Balzac.' Educated then. You did not educate people out of aggression, great liberal fallacy that. The one with scissors was trying to stab at Enderby's crotch. The other two had left the matron to moan and stagger and were grinning at the prospect of doing in an old man. Enderby lunged out at random with his stick and, as he had expected, it was at once grasped by, strangely, two left hands. Enderby pulled back. The sword emerged, half then wholly naked. They had not expected this. It flashed Elizabethanly in the swaying train, hard to keep upright, they all had legs bowed to it like sailors. Whitelady looked down amazed at Enderby from an EMPLOY A VETERAN advertisement. LOPEZ 95 MARLOWE 93 BONNY SWEET ROBIN 1601. Enderby at once pinked one of them in the throat and red spurted. 'Glory be to God,' the nun prayed, getting up from the deck. Spot-of-blood-and-foam dapple Bloom lights the orchard apple. Enderby tried a more ambitious thrust in some belly or other. It hit a belt. He tried underarm pricking on one who raised a fist wrapped round an object dull and hard. He drew out a sword-tip on which red rode and danced. And thicket and thorp are merry With silver-surféd cherry. The train danced clumsily to its next stop. There was a lot of loud language now: fuckabastardyafuckingpiggetyafuckingballs. One of the boys, the throat-pinked one who now gave out blood like a pelican, led the way out. Enderby thrust towards his backside and then felt pity. Enough was enough. He lunged halfheartedly instead at the one who had not yet received gladial attention. Ow ouch. Nothing really: plenty of flesh there: a fleshy-bottomed race. They were all out now, the oxter-pierced one bleeding quite nastily, all crying bitterly and fiercely fuckfuckassbastardcuntingfuckbastardfuckingpig and so on. The door closed and their faces were execrating holes out there on the platform. The human condition. No art without aggression. Then they were execrating briefly out of the past into the future. Enderby, winded and dangerously palpitant, picked up his hollow stick from the deck, not without falling on his face first. He found his seat and, with great difficulty, threaded the trembling bloody metal back in.

The matron sat very still, handbag on lap, blue at the lips, seeing visions that made her cry out. The reading girl turned another page. The old man slept uneasily. The two black boys, seated tailorwise, made fencing gestures wow sssh zheeeph and so on at each other. The nun, still standing, said:

'That's a terrible weapon you have there.'

'Look,' Enderby panted, 'that was my stop. I've gone past my bloody stop.'

'You can ride back from the next one.'

'But I've no money.' And then: 'Are you all right now? Is she all right now?' They were all all right now except for the shock.

'You can get on without a token,' the nun said. 'A lot of them do it.' And then: 'You shouldn't be carrying a thing like that around with you. It's against the law.'

'Entitled self-protection. Bugger the law.'

'Are you an Englishman?' Nodnod. Nod. 'I thought so from your way of swearing. Are you a Protestant?' Shakeshake. 'I said to myself you had a Catholic face.'

'Aren't you,' Enderby said, 'frightened? Travelling like this. A lot of thugs and rapists and.'

'I trust in Almighty God.'

'He wasn't all that bloody quick in. Coming to your. Help.'

'Are you all right now? You look very pale.'

'Heart,' Enderby said. 'Heart.'

'I'll say a decade of the rosary for you.'

'You have your supper first. A nice veal sandwich. A cup of.'

'What a strange thing to say. I can't stand veal.'

Enderby got shakily off at the next stop but would not take a free ride back to 96th Street. Timorousness? No he did not think it was that. It was rather something to do with vital integrity, not lowering oneself, wearing a suit evocative of an age of decency when gentlemen thrashed niggers but paid their bills. So he walked as far as the Symphony movie house and thought it might be a good plan to sit there, resting in the dark, judging once more, if he had the strength, certain ethical aspects of *The Wreck of the Deutschland*, and then go home calmly and starving to bed. But, of course, approaching the paybox, he realized once more he had no money. He said, to the bored chewing black bespectacled girl behind the grille:

'Look, I just want to go in for a minute. I was involved in the making of this er movie, you see. Something I have to check. Business not pleasure.' She did not seem to care. She waved him towards the cavern of the antechamber, see man in charge, man. But there was no one around who cared much. It was past the hour for anyone to care much. Enderby entered tempestuous darkness: the breakers were rolling on the beam of the Deutschland with ruinous shock. And canvas and compass, the whorl and the wheel idle for ever to waft her or wind her with, these she endured. There did not seem to be, now he could see better, many audiences taking it all in. An old man slept uneasily. Some blacks chortled inexplicably at the sight of one stirring from the rigging to save the wild womankind below, with a rope's end round the man, handy and brave. Some fine swooping camerawork showed him being pitched to his death at a blow, for all his dreadnought breast and braids of thew. Cut to night roaring, with the heart-break hearing a heart-broke rabble, the woman's wailing, the crying of child without check. Then a lioness arose breasting the babble. Gertrude, lily, Fransiscan robe already rent, spoke of courage, God. Then came the flashback – Deutschland, double a desperate name. Beautifully contrived colour-contrasts: black uniforms, white nun-flesh, red yelling gob, blood, a patch of yellow convent-garden daffodils crushed under blackbooted foot. Hitler appeared briefly, roaring something (beast of the waste wood) to black approbation in the audience.

Away in the loveable west, on a pastoral forehead of Wales, Father Tom Hopkins S.J. seemed mystically or ESPishly aware of something terrible going on out there somewhere. Putting down his breviary, he dreamed back to boy-and-girl love. A student in Germany, Gertrude not yet coifed, passion amid *Vogelgesang* in Schwarzwald. Rather touching, really, but far too naked. Song of Hitlerjugend marching in the distance. Bad times coming for us all. Ja ja, Tom. It all seemed pretty harmless, Enderby thought. It aroused desire to see off the Nazis, no more, but that had already been done, Enderby vaguely assisting. And so he left. He walked down chill blowing

Broadway as far as 91st Street, then crossed towards Columbus Avenue. At this point.

At this point it happened again. Pain was pumped rapidly into his chest and he stopped breathing. The surplus of pain overflowed into the left shoulder and went rattling down the arm to the elbow. At the same time both legs went suddenly dead and the tough met-alled stick was not enough to sustain him. He went over gently on to the sidewalk and lay, writhing, trying to deal with the pain and the inability to breathe like a pair of messages that both had to be answered at once. Pain passed and breath shot in with the hiss of an airtight can being opened. But still he lay, now feeling the cold. A few people passed by, naturally ignoring him, some junky, a man knifed, dangerous to be involved. And they were right, of course, in a world that thought the worst of involvement. Why did you help him, mister? Got scared, did you? Let's see what you got in your pockets. What's this? A stomach tablet? That's a laaaugh. Soon he was able to get up. Blood and a kind of healthy pain were flowing into his legs. He felt all right, even gently elated. After all, he knew now where he stood. There was no need to plan anything long, that *Odontiad*, for instance. A loosening artistic obligation. There was only the obligation of setting things in order. He might live a long time yet, but time would be doled out to him in very small denom-inations, like pocket-money. On the other hand, there was no need to work at living a long time. He had not done too badly. He was fifty-six, already had done four years better than Shakespeare. As for poor Gervase Whitelady. Kindly he suddenly decided to allow Whitelady to live till 1637, which meant he could benefit from the critical acumen of Ben Jonson.

He got to the apartment block without difficulty. Mr Audley, the black guard, sat in his chair in the warmth of the foyer, while the many telescreens showed dull programmes: people muffled up hur-rying round the corner, the basement empty, the main porch newly free of entering Enderby. They nodded at each other, Enderby was allowed in, he took the elevator to his floor, he entered his apartment. Thanked, so to speak, be Almighty God. He drew his bloody sword and executed a courtly flourish with it at the mess in the kitchen.

Then he cleaned off the blood with a dishrag. His stomach, crassly ignoring the day's circulatory warnings, growled at him, knowing it was in the kitchen, messy or not.

There was an episode, Enderby remembered, in Galsworthy's terrible Forsyte or Forsyth epic, in which some old scoundrel of the dynasty faced ruin and determined to kill himself like a gentleman by eating a damn good dinner. In full fig, by George. By George, they had got him an oyster. By George, he had forgotten to put his teeth in, and here was a brace of mutton chops grilled to a turn. A rather repulsive story, but it did not debar Galsworthy from getting the Order of Merit and the Nobel Prize. Enderby had never got or gotten anything, not even the Heinemann Award for Poetry, but he did not give a bugger. He did not now propose to eat himself to death, in a subforsytian manner befitting his station, but rather just not to give a bugger. To take a fairly substantial supper with, since time might be short, a few unwonted luxuries added. Such as that French chocolate ice cream that was ironhard in the deep freeze. And that small tin of pâté mixed in the great culminatory stew he envisaged after, for tidiness's sake, finishing off his Sarah Lee collection and eating the potato pieces and spongemeat that waited for a second chance, nestling ready in their fat. And to get through the mixed pickles and Major Grey's chutney. He had always hated waste.

Nine

Enderby's supper was interrupted by two telephone calls. During the stew course (two cans of corned beef, frozen onion-rings, canned carrots, a large Chunky turkey soup, pâté, a dollop of whisky, Lea and Perrin's, pickled cauliflowers, the remains of the spongemeat, and the crinkle-cut potato-bits) Ms Tietjens sobbed to him briefly without preamble: I'm sick, I tell ya, I'm all knotted up inside, I'm sick, sick, there's something wrong with me, I tell ya; and Lloyd Utterage confirmed the impending fulfilment of his threat, so that Enderby was constrained to tell him to come along and welcome, black bastard, and have an already bloody sword stuck into his black guts. Enderby placidly ended his meal with the French ice cream (brought to near melting in a saucepan over a brisk flame) with raspberry jam spread liberally over, spooning the treat in on rich tea biscuits he ate as he spooned. Then he had some strong tea (six Lipton's bags in the pint ALABAMA mug) and lighted up a White Owl. He felt pretty good, as they said in American fiction, though distended. All he needed now, as again they would say in American fiction, and he laughed at the conceit, was a woman.

A woman came while he was making himself more tea. He was surprised to hear the doorbell ring with no anterior warning on the intercommunication system from the black guard below. Every visitor was supposed to be screened, frisked, reported to the intended visited before actually appearing. The woman at the door was young and very attractive in a reactionary way, being dressed in a bourgeois grey costume with a sort of nutria or coypu or something coat swinging open over it. She wore over decently arranged chastaigne hair a little pillbox hat of the same fur. She was carrying a handful of slim volumes. She said:

'Mr Enderby?'

'Or Professor, according to the nature of. How did you get here? You're not supposed just to come up, you know, without a premonition.'

'A what?'

'A forewarning from the gunman.'

'Oh. Well, I said it was a late visit from one of your students and that you were expecting me. It is all right, isn't it?'

'Are you one of my students?' Enderby asked. 'I don't seem to –'

'I am in a sense. I've studied your work. I'm Dr Greaving.'

'Doctor?'

'From Goldengrove College.'

'Oh very well then, perhaps you'd better. That is to say.'

And he motioned courtlily that she should enter. She entered, sniffing. 'Just been cooking,' Enderby said. 'My supper, that is to say. Can I perhaps offer?'

In the sitting-room there was a small table. Dr Greaving put down her books on it and at once sat on the straightbacked uncomfortable chair nearby.

'Whisky or something like that?'

'Water.' Now in, she had become vaguely hostile. She looked up thinly at him.

'Oh, very well. Water.' And Enderby went to get it. He let the faucet run but the stream did not noticeably cool. He brought back some warmish water and put the glass down with care next to the slim volumes. He saw they were of his own work. British editions, American not existing. 'Oh,' he said. 'How did you manage to get hold of those?'

'Paid for them. Ordered them through a Canadian bookseller. When I was in Montreal.' Enderby now noticed that she had taken out of her handbag a small automatic pistol, a lady killer.

'Oh,' he said. 'Now perhaps you'll understand why they're so keen down below on checking visitors and so on. Why have you brought that? It seems, to say the least, unnecessary.' He marvelled at himself saying this. (Cinna the poet: tear him for his bad verses?)

'You deserve,' she said, 'to be punished. Incidentally, my name is *not* Doctor Greaving. But what I said about being a student of your work is true.'

'Are you Canadian?' Enderby asked.

'You seem to be a big man for irrelevancies. One thing you're a big man in.' She drank some water, keeping her eyes on him. The eyes were of a kind of triple sec colour. 'You'd better bring a chair.'

'There's one in the kitchen,' Enderby said with relief. 'I'll just go and –'

'Oh no. No dashing into the kitchen to the telephone. If you tried that anyway I'd come and shoot you in the back. Get that chair over there.' It was not really a chair. It was a sort of very frail Indian-style coffee-table. Enderby said:

'It's really a sort of very frail. It belongs to my landlady. I might ...' He was really, to his surprise, quite enjoying this. It seemed quite certain to him now that he was not going to die of cancer of the lung.

'Bring it. Sit on it.' He did. He sat on its edge, pity to damage so frail a thing, horrible though he had always thought it. He said:

'Now what I can do for you, Miss er?'

'I'm not,' she said, 'going to tolerate any more of this persecution. And it's Mrs, as you perfectly well know. Not that I'm living with him any more, but that's another irrelevance. I'm not going to have you,' she said, 'getting into my brain.'

Enderby gaped. 'How?' he said. 'What?'

'I know them by heart,' she said, 'a great number of them. Well, I don't want it any more. I want to be free. I want to get on with my own things, can't you see that, you bastard?' She pointed the little gun very steadily at Enderby.

'I don't understand,' Enderby said. 'You've read my things, you say. That's what they're for, to be read. But there's no er compulsion to read them, you know.'

'There's a lot of things there's no compulsion for. Like going to the movies to see a movie that turns out to be corruptive. But then you're corrupted, just the same. You never know in advance.' As this seemed to her ears apparently, as certainly to his, to be a piece of neutral or even friendly expository talk, she added sharply, with a gun gesture, 'You bastard.'

'Well, what do you want me to do?' Enderby asked. 'Unwrite the damned things?' And then, this just striking him, 'You're mad, you know, you must be. Sane readers of my poems don't –'

'That's what they all say. That's what *he* said, till I stopped him.'

'How did you stop him?' Enderby asked, fascinated.

'Another irrelevance. Don't you bastards ever think of your responsibility?'

'To our art,' Enderby said. 'Oh my God,' he added in quite impersonal distress, 'do you mean there's to be no more art? Aye, by Saint Anne,' he added, seeing that *mad* was a very difficult term to define, 'and ginger shall be hot in the –'

'There you go again. Decent people suffer and you sit on your fat ass talking about *art*.'

'That's just low abuse,' he frowned. 'Besides, I don't think you could call this really sitting.' She had, he could see, beneath the peel of the mad hate, a sweet face, a Catholic face, ruined, God help the girl, ruined. 'No, no,' he said in haste. 'Relevance is what is called for. I see that.' And then: 'Look. If you shoot me, it won't make any difference, will it? It won't destroy the words I wrote.' And then: 'What intrigues me, if that doesn't sound too irrelevant a term, is how you got to know them in the first place. My poems, I mean. I mean, not many people do. And here you are, young as I see, also beautiful if I may say that without sounding frivolous or irrelevant, knowing them. If you do know them, that is, of course, I mean,' he ended cunningly.

'Oh, I know them all right,' she cried scornfully. 'I see lines set up at eyelevel in the subway. There's one in fifteen-foot-high Gothic letters just by the Port Authority. They get sort of stitched into that Times Square news ticker thing.'

'Interesting,' Enderby said.

'There you go,' she gun-pointed. '*Interesting*. So tied up in yourself and your so-called work you're just *interested*. *Interested* in how it happened, and all that crap about youth and beauty and the other irrelevancies.'

'They're not irrelevant,' Enderby said sharply. 'I won't have that.
Beauty and youth are the only things worth having. Dust hath closed
Helen's eye. And they go. And here you are, saying they don't
matter. Silly bitch,' he attempted, not sure whether that would pull
the trigger.

'That bastard introduced me to them, if you must know,' she said,
not listening. 'It started off when we were on our honeymoon and
it was in the morning and he giggled and said The marriage contract
was designed in spite of what the notaries think to be by only one
pen signed and that is mine and full of ink. But he didn't, oh no, just
giggled.'

'A mere *jeu d'esprit*,' Enderby mumbled regretfully, remembering
his own honeymoon when he didn't either, just giggled.

'That's how that bastard started me off. Anything to make me
suffer, bastard as he was.'

'That doesn't sound like a North American idiom,' Enderby said
in wonder. 'That's more the way they speak where I come from.'

'Yes. Possession, isn't it? Takeover. *Bastard*.'

'Well, blame him, not me. I mean, damn it, it could have been
William Shakespeare, couldn't it? Or Robert Bridges, bloody fool,
not worthy of him. *And thy loved legacy, Gerard, hath lain Coy in
my breast*. Bloody evil idiot. Or Geoffrey Grigson.'

'Shakespeare's dead,' she said reasonably. 'So may the other two
be, whoever they are. But you're alive. You're here. I've waited a
long time for this.'

'How did you know I was here?'

'Irrelevant irrelevant. It was announced, if you must know, after
a talk-show this evening that you were going to be on tomorrow
night.'

'Recorded it too early. Take too much for granted. I'm not. It's all
been changed now.'

'And I called them and they said you wouldn't be on and they'd
never have you on. But they gave me your address.'

'The swine. They're not supposed to. Address a private thing.
Sheer bloody vindictiveness.' He fumed briefly. She smiled thinly in
scorn and said:

'Self self self. Self and art. You bastard.'

'Oh,' Enderby said, 'get the bloody shooting over with. We've all got to die sometime. You too. They'll send you to the chair, or whatever barbarity they have now. I don't believe in capital punishment. I cancelled this long poem about Pelagius. I won't write the Odontiad. I've nothing on hand. Come on, get it over.'

'Oh no. Oh no. Oh no. What you're going to do is grovel. And after that I may or I may not –'

'May not what?'

'You're not going to have a nice easy martyrdom. I know men. You'll be glad to grovel.'

'Grovel grovel grovel,' Enderby growled like a tom-turkey. 'Artists are expected to grovel, aren't they? While the charlatans and the plagiarists and the corrupters and the defilers and the politicians have their arseholes licked. What do you want me to do – *eat* the bloody things? I've just had supper, remember. And,' cunningly, 'you won't want to turn me into Jesus Christ, will you?'

'Blasphemous bastard.'

'And, moreover, if I may say so, I don't see how you're going to *make* me grovel. Your only alternative is to use that bloody thing there. Well, I don't mind dying.'

'Of course you don't. Enderby flopped over his slim volumes, blood coming out of his mouth. Not that that would ever get into books. I'd make sure of that. There are no martyrs these days. Except blacks.'

'All right, then. I'm going to get up now, this bloody table's uncomfortable anyway, and walk into that kitchen there, and get the block guard on the blower, tell him to bring the cops along.' *Cops* was the only possible word, a *thriller* word. Okay buster you call the cops.

She kept shaking her head all the time. 'Glad to grovel, glad to. I've seen it before. With him. I have six rounds in here. I'm a good shot, my father taught me, my father, worth ten of you, you bastard. I can nip at bits of you. Nip nip nip. Make you deaf. Make you noseless. Give you a fucking anatomical excuse for being sexless.'

'Where did you get that idea from? Who taught you that? Who's been talking –'

'Irrelevant.'

'Look,' Enderby said, wondering whether, to be on the safe side, to make a good act of contrition or not. 'I'm getting up.'

He got up. 'That's better. And I'm going to go, as I said I would, to –'

'You won't make it, friend. Your anklebone will be shattered.'

He realized bitterly that he did not want his anklebone shattered. Good clean death, yes. Altogether different, by George. 'Well, then,' he said. And then: 'They'll come up, in. Pistol-shots. Break the door down.'

'Do you honestly believe that, you innocent bastard of an idiot? This is not safe little England. Do you honestly think that anyone would care?' She shook her head at his lack of cisatlantic sophistication. 'Listen, idiot. Listen, bastard.'

Enderby listened. Of course, yes. You got used to it in time. In time it was just a decoration of the silence. Silence in a baroque frame. I say, that's good, I could use that. He heard the whining of police cars and the scream of ambulances. And then, from the west, bang bang. 'Yes, of course.'

'But,' she said, 'we'll make sure, won't we? Go over there and turn on the TV. Turn it on *loud*. Keep going round the dial till I tell you to stop.' Enderby moved with nonchalance, but only to sit down on a *pouffe*. Much much better. He said, with nonchalance:

'You do it. Play Russian roulette with it. That's Nabokov,' he said in haste, 'not me. *Pale Fire*,' he clarified.

'Bastard,' she said. But she got up and walked towards him, pointing her little gun. It was a nice little weapon from the look of it. She had delightful legs, Enderby saw regretfully, and seemed to be wearing stockings, not those pantee-hose abominations. Suspenders, what they called garters here, and then knickers. He was surprised to find himself, under the thick hot Edwardian trousers, responding solidly to the very terms. Camiknicks. Beyond his *pouffe*, she moved sidelong to the television set. She then switched on and turned the dial click click click with her left hand, looking towards Enderby and pointing her weapon. Enderby sat on his *pouffe* calmly, hands about his knees. She had been drawn now into a harmless area of entertainment. It was sound she was choosing, she would be in charge of the visual part. A new kind of art really, pop and audience participation and so on, gestures of creative impotence. There was a swift diachronic kaleidoscope of images and a quite interesting synthetic statement: That's it I guess its quality for you and for your so send fifteen dollars only its Butch you love isn't it I guess so emphatic denial issued by. Then she came to a palpable war-film and, eyes uninterested still, turned up the noise of bombardment. Enderby said:

'That's much too loud. The neighbours will complain.'

'What?' She hadn't heard him. 'Now,' coming towards him, pointing. Enderby could see, in black and white, brave GIs in foxholes. Then grenades were thrown lavishly by the undersized enemy. 'Take your clothes off.'

'*What?*'

'Everything off. I want to see you in your horrible potbellied hairy filthy nakedness.'

'How do you know it's …' And then: 'Why?'

'Degradation. The first phase.'

'No. Ow.' She had fired the little gun but it had not hit Enderby. It had merely whistled past him at very nearly earlevel. He saw her there, a kind of numinous blue smoke before her, and smelt what seemed rather appetizing smoked bacon. And thus he faced the breakfast of his death. He turned his head to see that the spine of a large illustrated volume on his landlady's shelves now looked disfigured. It was called *Woman's Bondage*. He had dipped into it once, a very humourless book, not about sex after all. She had timed the firing very felicitously, as though she knew the war-film by heart. A village had gone up very loudly into the air. But now there was a love-scene between a GI and a woman in a nurse's uniform, her hair crisp in a wartime style.

'Go on. Take them off.'

Enderby was wearing neither jacket nor tie. It was, of course, very hot. He was, God knew, often enough naked in here, but he was damned if he was going to be told to be naked.

'Go on. Now.' And she prepared to aim.

'It is, after all, quite … I mean, I meant to do this anyway. I normally do, you see. But I'm doing it because I want to. Do you understand that?'

'Go on.'

Enderby took off his waistcoat and then his shirt. He smelt his axillary fear very clearly.

'Go on.'

'Oh dear,' Enderby said with mock humorous exasperation. 'You are a hard little taskmistress.'

'I've not even started yet. Go on.'

In socks and underpants Enderby said: 'Will that do?'

'Argh. Disgusting.'

'Well, if I'm disgusting why do you want to.'

'Go on. To the horrible disgusting limit.'

'No. Ow.'

There was an ugly violet glass vase on the mantelpiece. She hit it very neatly as thunderous strafing was resumed on the screen. But at once a commercial break broke in. In unnatural high colour a smirking naked-shouldered woman made love to her slowly floating hair. Weave a circle round him, girls. No, not that. They wouldn't have the bloody sense. Sighing, Enderby stripped down to the limit. His phallus too palpably announced its interest in that camiknick business. He was, as they had so often told him in critical reviews, very much a belated man of the thirties. Sonnet-form and so on. The television screen homed in on fried chicken. Enderby hid the thing with his hands.

'Disgusting.'

'Well, it was your idea, not mine.'

'Now,' she ordered. 'You're going to piss on your own poems.'

'*I'm going to what*?'

'Urinate. Micturate. Squirt your own filthy water on your own filthy poems. *Go on*.'

'They're not filthy. They're clean. What stupid fucking irony. All the genuinely filthy pseudo-art and not-art that's about, and you pick on honest and clean and craftsmanlike endeavour –'

The weapon (in thrillerish locution: Enderby saw the word in botched print at the very moment of firing) spoke again. That frail

Indian-type table thing proved itself very frail, tumbling over as though fist-hit in aesthetic viciousness. Enderby's phallus rose a few more notches. He said: 'That's three. That means only three left.'

'It's enough. Next time I promise it's going to be some of that ugly filthy fat hairy blubbery bloated ...' She spoke out of smoke.

Enderby took up the top book with his right hand, his left hand still serving pudeur. It was *Fish and Heroes*, he saw tenderly. He couldn't open it one-handed, so he turned his bottom towards her and gave both hands to leafing the few but thickish leaves. By God what a genius he had then.

> *Wachet auf!* A fretful dunghill cock
> Flinted the noisy beacons through the shires.
> A martin's nest clogged the cathedral clock.
> Still, it was morning. Birds could not be liars ...

And what would Luther have done in these circumstances? He was a great one for farting and shitting, but only on the Fiend. Piss on that Bible, Luther. Unthinkable. But then (O my God, poem there to be written. Meaning have to live?) he might have thought: only a copy, the Book subsists above the single copy, I must live, spread the Word, the mature man gives in occasionally to the foolish, evil, mad. Luther lifted up his great skirts, disclosing a fierce red thursday, and pissed vigorously on a mere mess of Gothic print. Here stand I, I can in no wise do otherwise. Enderby said loudly:

'No!'

'I can see what you're looking at,' she said. 'That sonnet about the Reformation.' She knew the bloody book so well, it seemed such a pity. The television film showed a whining GI, cap tucked in epaulette, whining: 'Can't we talk this thing over, Mary?'

'Oh, all right then,' Enderby said wearily. And he turned his nozzle, with some slight muscular effort, on to the page. 'See,' he said. 'I'm doing my best. But nothing will come. It stands to reason nothing will come. *Stand*, blast you, is the operative word.'

And then, Luther throwing, but it was an inkpot, they showed you the inkstained wall in Wittenberg, Enderby threw the book, which fluttered vogelwise, towards her. Instinctively she shot at it. He had known, somehow, she would. He strode, heavily naked, balls aswing, weapon pointing, through the smoke and the echo of noise. And yet God has not said a word. She aimed straight at him, saying, 'If you think you're going to be a fucking martyr for art –'

'Said that already,' Enderby said, and he grasped her wrist at the very instant of her firing vaguely at the ceiling. The noise and smell were surely excessive. He had that damned gun now, a dainty hot little engine. She clawed at his buttocks as he went to the window partly open for the heat. Threw the bloody thing out. 'There,' he said. Luther, he remembered for some reason, had married a nun. Christ's lily and beast of the waste wood. This girl now beat at him with teeny fists. Enderby had had a good supper. He saw the two of them in the little mirror above a bookshelf devoted to psychology deeply Jewish and anguished. He had his glasses on, he observed, would not indeed have been able to observe otherwise, otherwise, of course, naked. He gave her a push somewhere around the midriff. She ended up crying on a *pouffe*.

'Bastard bastard.'

Enderby took off his glasses and placed them carefully on top of the television set which, well into the noise of impending victory, he clicked off. 'You and your bloody guns,' he said. 'Get you into a bloody mediaeval monastery full of great ballocky monks, that would teach you. Flabby, indeed. Blubber, for Christ's sake. Silenus, Falstaff.' This was for his own benefit. 'Think of those, blast you.' His heart seemed to be pumping away very healthily. Noise of impending victory. Not with a whimper but ... 'Blaming me, indeed. Blaming poor dead Hopkins. As though I held the nuns down for them.'

'Go away. Get away from me.'

'I live here,' Enderby said. 'Sort of.' And then he pulled, two-handed, at the hems. Cry, clutching heaven by the. That was just to get a rhyme with *Thames*. Rhine refused them Thames would ruin them. Francis Thompson a far inferior poet. Hopkins appeared an instant, open-mouthed, clearly seen moaning at another's sin, though in the dark of the confessional. 'You did it,' Enderby said.

'So fagged, so fashed, indeed. Get away for a bit, can't you?' Hopkins became a pale daguerrotype, then was washed completely out. The skirt was elasticated at the waist and pulled down with little difficulty. In joy, Enderby saw the tops of stockings, suspenders, peach knickers.

'You filthy fucking –'

'Oh, this is all too American,' Enderby said. 'Sex and violence. What angel of regeneration sent you here?' For there was no question of mumbling and begging now. *Enderbius triumphans, exultans.*

Ten

This third heart attack, if that was what it had really been, did not seem to be really all that bad – a mere sketch to remind him of its shape. But he knew its shape intimately already, that of a Spenglerian parabola. Yet another interpretation seemed, as he sat in the toilet and excreted as quietly as he could, there being a guest in the apartment, possible, though he was fain to reject it. An inner hand showing in delicate deadly gesture the impending chop or noose. He was glad in a way that she had taken possession of the circular bed, no room for him, since bed was a place where people frequently died, sometimes in their sleep. She lay naked on her back, telling, say, ten-twenty with her arms and seven-thirty with her legs, her delicate snoring indicating that it was a fine February night and all was well. She had left her home in Poughkeepsie, it appeared, and was obviously welcome to stay here with Enderby so long as she did not go out to buy another gun. She at least knew his work. Anyway, there was no question of thinking in terms of a nice long future. These heart attacks had been as good to Enderby as a *like* and *you know* harangue from one of his students. But he did not really want the chop to come tonight and in his sleep. He fancied doing some more vigorous death-dodging in the light. There was this to be said for New York: it was not dull.

Wiped and having flushed, Enderby went out to the kitchen to make tea. There would be a hell of a row tomorrow, today that was, when that dusky bitch Priscilla came to do the chores (How come an educated man like you live in such Gadarene filth? She was, after all, a Bible scholar); but there always was a hell of a row. This time there would probably be something about fornication and cozbi as well as dirt. Enderby ate pensively a little cold left-over stew while he waited for the water to boil: quite delicious, really. He seemed to have lost a fair amount of protein in the last few hours, perhaps cholesterol too. When the tea had sufficiently brewed or drawn (five bags only; not overtempt providence) and had been sharply sweetened and embrowned, he took it into the living-room. He piled *pouffe* on *pouffe* to make himself comfortable in order to watch for the dawn to come up. He switched on the television set, which gave him a silly film apt for these small hours. It was a college musical of the thirties (*How come that such a scholar / Can put up with such squalor? / Just gimme hafe a dollar / And I'll make it spick and span, man.* There was a coincidence!) but it was made piquant with girls in peach-looking camiknicks with metallic hairdos. Enderby did some random leafing through the slim volumes she had brought for him to defile. God, what a genius, etc. The film, with interludes of advertising suspiciously cheap albums of popular music, went harmlessly on while he sipped his tea and browsed.

> You went that way as you always said you would,
> Contending over the cheerful cups that good
> Was in the here-and-now, in, in fact, the cheerful
> Cups and not in some remotish sphere full
> Of twangling saints, the-pie-in-the-sky-when-you-die
> Of Engels as much as angels, whereupon I ...

He could not well remember having written that. Besides, the type was blurring. He saw without surprise that the film had changed to one, in very good colour too, about Augustine and Pelagius. Thank God. The thing had been at last artistically dealt with. No need after all for him to worry about finding an appropriate poetic form.

35. (SAY) EXTERIOR DAY A ROAD
A man is vigorously whipping his donkey, which brays in great pain. His wife comes along to tell him to desist.

WIFE:

Desist, desist. The poor creature meant no harm, Fabricius.

MAN:

Farted in my face, didn't it? A great noseful of foul air.
(*he continues beating*)

WIFE:

Foul, you say? She eats only sweet grass and fresh-smelling
herbs, while you – you guzzle sour horsemeat and get drunk
on cheap wine.

MAN:

Oh, I do, do I? Take that, you slut.
(*he beats her till she bleeds*)

36. THE SAME TWO SHOT

Pelagius and Obtrincius are watching. The noise and the cries are
pitiable.

OBTRINCIUS:

What think you of that, O man of the northern seas? Evil,
yes? It comes of the primal fetor of Adam which imbrues the
world.

PELAGIUS:

Ah no, my dear friend. Adam's sin was his own sin. It was not
inherited by the generality of mankind.

OBTRINCIUS:

But this is surely foul heresy! Why was Christ crucified except
to pay, in Godflesh whose value is incomputable, for the
Adamic sin we all carry? Have a care, my friend. There may be
a bishop about listening.

> PELAGIUS:

Ah no, he came to show us the way. To teach us love. *Be ye perfect*, he said. He taught us that we are perfectible. That what you call evil is no more than ignorance of the way. Hi, you, my friend.

37. RESUME 35.

The man Fabricius has now turned on his son who, having apparently intervened to save his mother from the vicious blows, is bloody and bowed. The mother weeps bloodily. The ass looks on, sore but impassive, also bloody.

> MAN:
> (*temporarily desisting*)

Huh? You address me, sir?

38. RESUME 36.

> PELAGIUS:
> (*cheerfully*)

Yes, my good man and brother in Christ.

He moves out of the shot and into:

39. TWO SHOT: MAN AND PELAGIUS

> PELAGIUS:

Ah, my poor friend, you have much to learn. Sweet reason has temporarily deserted you. Take breath and then blow out your anger with it. It is a mere ghost, a phantasm, totally insubstantial.

> MAN:

You use fine words, sir. But try using sweet reason to stop a donkey farting in your nose.

PELAGIUS:

You should keep your nose away from the, er, animal's poste-
rior. Sweet reason must surely tell you that.

MAN:

Oh, well, mayhap you're right, sir. Anger wastes time and uses
up energy. Come, wife. Come, son. I will be reasonable, God
forgive me.
    (*sketching a blessing, Pelagius moves out of shot*)
Sweet reason, my ass.

40. EXTERIOR DAY ROME: A SCENE OF UNBRIDLED
    REVELRY
LS of a sort of carnival. Instruments of the fifth century AD are blar-
ing and thumping, while unbridled revellers frisk about, kissing and
drinking and lifting kirtles.

41. THE SAME GROUP SHOT
A group of gorgers are greasily fingering smoking haunches and
swineshanks, stuffing it in, occasionally vomiting it out.

PELAGIUS (OS):

My friends!

They all look, in the same direction, open mouths exhibiting half-
chewed greasy protein.

42. THEIR POV: PELAGIUS
He stands with pilgrim's staff, looking with calm sorrow.

PELAGIUS:

Does not reason tell you that such excess is unreasonable? It
coarsens the soul and harms the body.
    (*Noise of lavish vomiting*)
There, you see what I mean.

43. PELAGIUS'S POV

The gorgers look somewhat abashed, but a bold fat bald one speaks up baldly and boldly.

> FAT GORGER:
>
> We cannot help it, man of God, whoever you are, a stranger by your manner of speech. The seven deadly sins, of which gluttony, as thou mayhap knowest, is one, are the seven worms in the apple we ate at the great original feast which still goes on, and of which Adam and Eve are the host and the hostess.

> ANOTHER GORGER:
>
> (*much thinner, as with a worm, or even seven, inside him*)
>
> Aye, he speaketh truly, monk, whoever thou art. We are born into sin through none of our willing, and has not Christ atoned for our sins, past, future, and to come?

44. RESUME 42.

> PELAGIUS:
>
> (*very loudly*)

No He Has Not.

45. A GROUP OF FORNICATORS

Mitred bishops, bearded, venerable, lusty, look up from clipping their well-favoured whores. They look at each other, frown.

46. INTERIOR NIGHT THE HOUSE OF FLACCUS

The bishop Augustine sits at the end of dinner with his friend Flaccus, a public administrator. There are other guests, including Bishop Tarminius – one of the bishops who frowned in Scene 45.

> FLACCUS:
>
> (*while a slave proffers a dish*)
>
> Perhaps an apple, my lord bishop?

AUGUSTINE:
(*shuddering*)
Ah no, Flaccus my friend. If you only knew what part apples
have played in my life ...

TARMINIUS:
And one apple in the life of all mankind.

AUGUSTINE:
(*looking at him for an instant, then nodding gravely*)
Yes, Tarminius, very true. But oh, the moonwashed apples of
wonder in the neighbour orchard. I did not steal the apples
because I needed them. Indeed, my father's apples were far
better, sweeter, rosier. I stole them because I wished to steal. To
sin. It was my sin I loved, God help me.

FLACCUS:
Aye, it is in all of us. Baptism is but a token of extinguishing
the fire ...

AUGUSTINE:
Burning burning burning burning ...

FLACCUS:
But Christ paid, atoned, still makes the impact of our daily sin
on the godhead less acute.

AUGUSTINE:
Beware of theology, Flaccus. These deep matters have driven
mad many a young brain.

TARMINIUS:
You speak very true, Augustine. There is a man from Britain in
our midst – didst know that?

AUGUSTINE:

There are many from Britain in our midst – that misty northern island where the damp clogs men's brains. They are harmless enough. They blink in our southern light. They go down with the sun.

(*laughter*)

TARMINIUS:

I refer to one, Augustine, who seems not to be harmless, whose gaze is very steady, who is impervious to sun-stroke. His name is Pelagius.

FLACCUS:

(*frowning*)

Pelagius? That is not a British name.

TARMINIUS:

His true name is Morgan which, in their tongue, means man of the sea. Pelagius, in Greek, means exactly the –

AUGUSTINE:

(*testily*)

Yes yes, Tarminius. I think we all know what it means. Hm. I have heard a little about this man – a wandering friar, is he not? He has been exhorting the people to be kind to their wives and asses and warning of the dangers of gluttony. Also, I understand –

(*he looks sternly at Tarminius, who looks sheepish rather than shepherdish*)

Fornication. I see no harm in such simple homiletic teaching. A puritanical lot, our brothers of the north.

TARMINIUS:

But, Augustine, he is doing more. He is denying Original Sin, the redemptive virtues of God's grace, even, it would seem, our salvation in Christ. He seems to be saying that man does not need help from heaven. That man can better himself by his own efforts alone. That the City of God can be realized as the City of Man.

AUGUSTINE:
(*astounded*)
But – this – is – heresy! Oh my God – the poor lost British soul …

There is a sudden spurt of flame which ruddies the scene. All look to its source. The camera whip-pans to the spit, where flames are fierce. A toothless scullion grins, touching a forelock in apology.

SCULLION:
Sorry, my lords, sir, gentlemen. A bit of fat in the fire.

47. GROUP SHOT
Augustine, Tarminius, Flaccus look very grim.

AUGUSTINE:
Fat in the fire, indeed.

48. INTERIOR DAY A HOVEL
Pelagius is talking gently and wisely to a group of poor men, artisans, layabouts, who listen attentively. A pretty girl named Atricia sits at his feet and looks up in worship.

PELAGIUS:
In my land the weather is always gentle, rather misty, never lacking rain. The earth is fertile, and by our own efforts we are able to bring forth fair crops. The sheep munch good fat grass. There are no devilish droughts, there is no searing sun. It is no land for praying in panic – not like the arid Africa of our friend the Bishop Augustine.

ATRICIA:

Oh, how I should love to see it. Could one be happy there without fear, without constant fear?

PELAGIUS:

Fear of what, my dear child?

ATRICIA:

Fear of having to suffer for one's happiness?

PELAGIUS:

Ah yes, Atricia. In Britain we have no vision of hellfire, nor do we need to invoke heaven to make life's torments bearable. It is a gentle easy land, it is a kind of heaven in itself.

A LAYABOUT:

But you said something about making a heaven there. And now you say it is a heaven already.

PELAGIUS:

A *kind* of heaven I said, friend. We have many advantages. But we are not so foolish as to think we are living in the garden of Eden. No, our paradise is still to be built – a paradise of fair cities, of beauty and reason. We are free to cooperate with our neighbours, which is another way of saying *to be good*. No sense of inherited sin holds us in hopeless sloth.

ATRICIA:

I can see it now – that misty island of romance. Oh, I should so love to breathe its air, smell its soil …

PELAGIUS:

And why should you not, my dear? What the heart of man conceives may ever be realized. I was just saying the other day –

There is a noise of entering feet. They all look up. They are obscured somewhat by the gross shadow of those entering.

A VOICE (OS):

Is your name Pelagius?

PELAGIUS:

Why, yes –

49. PELAGIUS'S POV
Two gross authoritative men in imperial uniform stand in the way of the sunlight. They look sternly at the assembly.

FIRST MAN:

You are to come with us. At once.

50. PELAGIUS AND ATRICIA
She clings to him in fear. He comforts her with a patting hand.

PELAGIUS:
(*smiling*)
You appear to be men of authority. It would be useless for me to ask why or where.

51. TWO SHOT
The two authoritative men look at him in burly contempt.

SECOND MAN:

Quite quite useless.

52. INTERIOR DAY A CONVOCATION OF BISHOPS
Augustine speaks while the camera pans along a line of grave bishops. Pelagius is out of shot.

AUGUSTINE:
Quite quite useless to deny that you have been spreading heresy.

53. THE SAME PELAGIUS
Pelagius is sitting on a kind of creepystool, humble and tranquil during his episcopal investigation.

PELAGIUS:
I do not deny that I have been spreading gospel, but that it is heresy I do most emphatically deny.

54. GROUP SHOT
A number of beetlebrowed bishops beetle at him.

AUGUSTINE (OS):
Heresy! heresy! *heresy*!

55. RESUME 52.
Augustine strides up and down the line of bishops. His mitre frequently goes awry with the passion of his utterance, but he straightens it ever and anon.

AUGUSTINE:
Yes, sir. You deny that man was born in evil and lives in evil. That he needs God's grace before he may be good. The very cornerstone of our faith is *original sin*. That is doctrine.

56. RESUME 54.
The bishops nod vigorously.

BISHOPS:
Originalsinriginalsinrignlsn.

57. PELAGIUS
He gets up lithely from his creepystool.

PELAGIUS:

Man is neither good nor evil. Man is rational.

58. AUGUSTINE
In CU the writhing mouth, richbearded, of Augustine sneers.

AUGUSTINE:

Rational.

59. EXTERIOR DAY A SCENE OF RIOT
The Goths have arrived and are busily at their work of destruction. They pillage, burn, kill in sport, rape. A statue of Jesus Christ goes tumbling and breaking, pulverising itself on harmless screaming citizens. The Goths, laughing, nail an old man to a cross. Some come out of a church, bearing a holy chalice. One micturates into it. Then a pretty girl is made to drink ugh of the ugh.

60. EXTERIOR NIGHTFALL A WINDY HILL
Augustine and Pelagius stand together on the hill, looking grimly down.

AUGUSTINE:

Rational, eh, my son?

PELAGIUS:
(*hardly perturbed*)

It is the growing pains of history. Man will learn, man *must* learn, man *wants* to learn.

AUGUSTINE:

Ah, you and your British innocence ...

61. THEIR POV
A view of the burning city. Cheers and dirty songs. Screams.

AUGUSTINE (OS):

Evil evil evil – the whole of history is written in blood. There is, believe me, much much more blood to come. Evil is only beginning to manifest itself in the history of our Christian west. Man is bad bad bad, and is damned for his badness, unless God, in his infinite mercy, grants him grace. And God foresees all, foresees the evil, foredamns, forepunishes.

62. RESUME 60.

Augustine takes Pelagius by the shoulders and shakes him. But Pelagius gently and humorously removes the shaking hands. He laughs.

PELAGIUS:

Man is free. Free to choose. Unforeordained to go either to heaven or to hell, despite the Almighty's allforeknowingness. Free free *free*.

63. THE BURNING CITY

A vicious scene of mixed rape and torture and cannibalism. The song of a drunk is heard.

DRUNK (OS):
(*singing*)

Free free free,
We be free to be free …

64. GROUP SHOT

The drunk, surrounded by dead-drunks and genuine corpses, spills pilfered wine, singing.

DRUNK:

Free to be scotfree,
But
Not free to be not free,
Free free fr

There is a tremendous earthquake. A tear in the shape of a Spenglerian tragic parabola lightnings across the screen.

AND NOW THIS IMPORTANT WORD FROM OUR SPONSOR

FRSHNBKKKKGGGGRHNKSPLURTSCHGROGGLEWOK

Eleven

This, children, is New York. A vicious but beautiful city, totally representative of the human condition or, for any embryonic existentialists among you, *la condition humaine*. What's that when it's at home, you vulgarly ask, Felicia? You will find out, God help you, soon enough, child. It is named New York in honour of the Duke of York who became King James II of Great Britain, a foolish and bigoted monarch who tried to reimpose Catholicism on a happily Protestant nation and, as was inevitable, ignominiously failed. No, Adrian, this is no longer a British city: it is part of a great free complex or federation of states that are welded together under a most un-British constitution: rational, frenchified, certainly republican. They revolted against the British king to whom they had once owed allegiance and tribute. No, Charles, that was a *Protestant* king and also bigoted and foolish. Let us swoop a little lower: How beautiful those exalted towers in the Manhattan dawn now we have descended to clear air under the enveloping blanket, Wilfrid. The jagged teeth of a monostomatic monster? One way of looking at it, Edwina.

We are here, under the aegis of Educational Time Trips, Inc., to seek out our poet. This is a great city for poets, though there are few like ours. We swim aerially over the island a little way, north of the midtown area, nearer to the Hudson than to the East River. He is round here somewhere. Yes, Morgana, we will have to *peek* a little. Through the dawn windows of 91st Street, as they call it (a rational city, a *numerical* city). Avert your eyes, Felicia; what they are doing is entirely their own affair. Here, dear dear, a young man is murdering his bedmate in postcoital tristity. Those two middleaged men are actually *dancing*: it would seem somewhat early for that. A tired girl eats an insubstantial breakfast at a kitchen table. A man in undress and blue spectacles peers at the obituary page of the New York Times. Look at the squalor of the bedroom of that scholarly-seeming youth, cans and bottles and untidy stacks of an obviously filthy periodical. Here another murder, there a robbery, and now – the contortions in the name of pleasure, God help us.

That is interesting, that round bed. Do you see the round bed, Felicia, Andrea? Very unusual, a round bed. And on the round bed a skeletal lady sleeps alone, telling (if that tangent touches at twelve) the right time. Astonishing! Eight-ten, if her lower limbs are the hour-hand. But here. And now. Look look. We have found him! Gather round, children, and see. Mr Enderby, temporary professor as we are told he is in this fashed fag-end of his days, asleep naked in a nest of *pouffes*. Ugly, hairy, fat; ah yes, he always was. The television set, to which he is not listening, discourses the morning news, which is all bad. He seems, dear dear, to have been somewhat incontinent in his sleep. Gracious, the weaknesses of the great!

And now – a little surprise for you. A black woman, key in hand, of pious face but ugly gait, waddles in, sees him, is disgusted, holds up her key in pious deprecation of his besmirched nudity. But, soft. She goes closer, looks closer, touches. She holds up both her hands in expression of a quite different emotion, runs out of the room with open mouth, strange words emanating therefrom. So we now know, and it is a sort of satisfaction, for *nunc dimittis* is the sweetest of canticles. Remember us in the roads, the heaven-haven of the Reward. Let him easter in us, be a dayspring to the dimness of us, be a crimson-cresseted east. No, hardly that, I go too far perhaps. Is there anything of his own that will serve? Yes, Edmund?

> The work ends when the work ends,
> Not before, and rarely after.
> And that explains, my foes and friends,
> This spiteful burst of ribald laughter.

Stop giggling, will you, all of you? You are both foolish and too clever for words, Edmund, with your stupid and irreverent and *meaningless* doggerel improvisation. You will all smile on the other sides of your faces when I get you back to civilization. All right, all right, I am aware that I involuntarily rhymed. Come on, out of it. Another instalment of the human condition is beginning. Out of it: *he* is well out of it, you say, Andrea? But no: he is in it, we are all and always in it. Do not think that anyone can escape it merely by ... I will not utter the word: it is quite irrelevant. Out of it, indeed; he is not out of it at all.

Rome, July 1973.

Appendix 1: 'French Overture'

Editor's note: Burgess wrote this prologue to *The Clockwork Testament* in the expectation that it would appear in the French edition, *Le Testament de l'Orange*, translated by Georges Belmont and Hortense Chabrier, and published by Robert Laffont in 1975. For reasons which remain unclear, it was not included in the Laffont edition, but it did appear in the German translation, *Das Uhrwerk-Testament*, by Walter Brumm. A carbon copy of the typescript is in the archive of the Burgess Foundation in Manchester. The original English text has not previously been published.

'La vie de poète,' Enderby smiled nervously. 'Si vous er comprenez. Par exemple. C'est à er dire.' His audience, which was very small, was very stony. It consisted of about thirty Frenchmen and Frenchwomen, mostly the latter. They sat under a great creaking three-bladed fan turned up to full for the fierce Casablanca heat. The room was hideously crammed with throw-out ornaments of the Third Empire period, literally or rather actually throw-outs, since *literally* (meaning in terms of the actual letter of the bequest) they were the posthumous gift of a certain Achille Crébillon, formerly a resident of Casablanca but dead twenty years ago in Grenoble, surrounded by ghastly gilt cherubim and ormolu clocks, all of which he had willed to this sort of Colonial Literary Society, Enderby supposed you could call it. 'Pour mon part,' Enderby said, 'c'est à dire si vous comprenez, quant à ma position, je suis poète anglaise, c'est à dire anglaise. Je toujours oublie,' he confided, 'que le mot *poète* signifie quelque chose de masculin bien que ça ait – ' (he was proud of getting the subjunctive in there) ' – er un forme ou une forme – je toujours oublie les gendres de votre belle mais tout a fait exaspérante langue – féminin ou féminine, si vous comprenez.' The audience remained for the most part stony, but there were kind of baroque ripples of discontent across some of the refined but liverish Gallic faces. An elderly lady made a noise probably idiosyncratically borborygmal but sounding, as with inbuilt nostalgia, like the whistle of a French train:

'Fôôôôôme.'

Enderby sweated. Somewhat fiercely he said:

'Poète anglaise, comme j'ai déjà ah dit. Je demeure a Tangier. Je suis le patron d'un petit restaurant sur la plage qu'on appelle *La Belle Mer* – paronomastique, si cette espèce de chose vous intéresse. Nous avons tous, si vous comprenez, de belles-mères. La mer même, l'Eglise, l'Etat. Moi, j'avais une belle-mère tout à fait horrible.' He couldn't for the life of him think why the hell he was telling them all this. 'C'est à dire, une vraie belle-mère irlandaise. Elle buvait du thé très fort – l'équivalent de six ou sept sacs de thé à une une une – ' He kept his lips in the fish-position, enjoying distractedly the small sensual thrill or what was their bloody word ah yes *frisson* of the vowel, trying to work out (but why the hell was he telling them all this?) '– une une quart-litre d'eau bouillante. C'est très important,' he said, with a disproportionate passion, 'que l'eau avec laquelle on prépare le thé soit tout à fait bouillante. Les Français,' he put in, indiscreetly, 'ne savent de rien de cette chose, c'est à dire comme faire du thé.'

This was taken not quite so badly as, considering the fuss these French bastards usually made about gastronomic matters, Enderby had a right to expect. A lot of them looked at each other and shrugged Frenchly. Tea, after all, was to them a very barbarous taste, like Shakespeare.

'Anyway,' he said, 'elle est morte, ah oui, morte.' They seemed to look at him now with suspicion. 'Mais,' he added hastily, 'c'était une morte naturalle, si vous comprenez – le coeur, je suppose: elle était très grosse et bouffait trop.' A couple of old ladies, *veuves* he supposed them to be, since they were in black and bright lipstick, whispered to each other and seemed to be ready to gather their bags and parasols and so on together preparatorily to leaving, fed up with Enderby already. 'Je ne l'ai pas tuée,' Enderby told them fiercely, and that seemed to fix them back on their horrible hot gilt plush chairs. 'Elle méritait le matricide, si ça c'est le mot juste et le gendre n'importe en ce cas.' Why not? It mattered in every other bloody case. 'Néanmoins, elle est morte des choses naturelles, comme le coeur, si vous comprenez.' He beamed at them nervously, actually seeing the sweat on his nose-tip, and nodded in a reassuring way.

An elderly man on the back row, in colonial white, panama in hand as an auxiliary fan, said something long and rapid in enviable French and Enderby caught the word *poésie*.

'Coming to that,' Enderby said. 'Revenons,' he translated wittily, 'à nos moutons. Poète, moi, comme j'ai déjà dit, anglaise, si vous n'y avez pas d'objection, et exilé, ah oui. Au sol, au milieu des huées, comme votre grand poète Baudelaire je pense a dit.' There were the beginnings of tremors of disquiet among some of the elderly, who probably still thought of *Fleurs du Mal* as dirty and banned and so on. 'Mais c'est d'un poète anglaise dont je vous voudrais parler un petit pois, c'est a dire peu,' he said in some haste. 'Grand influence sur tous les poètes anglaise modernes.' As frequently happened on such occasions, he had completely forgotten the name of the great poet in question. 'Poète tout à fait révolutionnaire. Innovateur. Créateur d'une tout à fait nouvelle c'est à dire nouveau système prosodique.' The bloody name still hadn't arrived. 'Est-ce qu'il y a,' he now asked cunningly 'quelqu'un entre vous, mesdames et messieurs, qui er connaît le nom de ce grand poète anglaise que j'ai dans la tête à présent?'

There were a lot of shrugs now. They didn't like being sent back to the lycée or whatever the bloody fools called it. A young spotty woman, someone's unmarriageable daughter, said timidly:

'Thé Est-ce Elle y ôte?'

Enderby understood that quite clearly. 'Ah non,' he smiled, 'pas le grand Monsieur Eliot. Mort aussi,' he admitted, 'et grand innovateur et chrétien et tout ça. Mais le poète dont je vais traiter était prêtre, était jésuite, était mystique et tout ça.' He had better give up this bloody *tout ça* business. At that moment the face of his poet appeared before him, wan and holy and somehow blown about by the wind of the ceiling fan, shaking his head at the *tout ça*, a not very pertinent, indeed a frivolous, term in this context of religious mysticism and jesuitry and all that. Enderby now remembered his name and told it to his audience.

'Gerard Manley Hopkins,' he said. And, for good measure, 'Né mille neuf cent quarante-quatre. Mort mille neuf cent quatre-vent-neuf.' Nobody was impressed by these statistics. Nobody had heard of Hopkins. It was a very sticky wicket. Bravely however he opened his shoulders and struck out.

'Notre language,' he said, 'c'est à dire l'anglais. C'est une language de grands *bangs*.' He cracked his fist on the little table with gilt sphinx legs to show them what he meant. 'Vous comprenez? *Bang bang bang*.' He nearly broke the bloody thing. 'Naturellement, notre poésie est faite de ces grands *bangs bangs bangs*.' A very intellectual-looking Frenchman seemed delicately to sneer, confirmation of the barbarity of the English et tout ça. This made Enderby bang even more. 'Par exemple,' he cried. 'Dans un vers de poésie anglaise on ne compte pas point guère mie combien de syllables il y a or y a t'il or whatever the bloody hell the correct phrase is. On compte seulement le nombre de –' He couldn't remember the French word, if there was one, for *stress*. 'Par exemple,' he tried in some desperation, 'un vers de William Shakespeare. *To be or not to be that is the question.* To *bang* or *bang* to *bang bang* is the *bang*tion. Vous voyez donc? Vous comprenez donc? Il y a cinq *bangs*. *Bang – bang – bang – bang – bang*.' A very tremulous old *veuve* seemed ready to cry. 'Alors,' cried Enderby, not giving a damn now, and bugger this table of which a sphinx-leg already seemed ready to be detached. 'Si vous avez ces cinq *bangs* vous pouvez avoir combien de syllables sans *bang* que vous voulez. Par exemple. To *bang* on in intrepid *bang*ulation *bang*ulously *bangs* unelephantinely the *bang*operables. Une question d'accentuation,' he said somewhat coldly and, he thought, Gallically, having remembered the Gallic word for *stress*, 'une question d'accents prosodiques qui viennent dans le vers –' He pounced on them with the learned term he had long had waiting. '– Isochroniquement. Ça.' Nobody seemed to be particularly impressed. 'Comme dans la musique,' he offered, more subdued. 'Dans un mesure de la musique, tant de petites notes que vous voulez, autant qu'il y ait le *bang bang* isochronique tout le temps.' Nobody seemed to understand, even care. 'Sprung rhythm,' Enderby said, 'l'invention d'Hopkins. Quant à la votre poésie,' Enderby sweated. A man looked at his watch and then shook his wrist at ear-level. 'Votre poésie est faite de syllables. Il faut compter le numéro de syllables. Comme le latin.' Nobody seemed interested in this statement of the self-evident. And then somebody yawned. A dapper man on the front row, with very small and dapper feet in three-toned small dapper shoes, yawned. Enderby decided, or something, perhaps the spirit of English poesy, decided for him, to get mad. He hurled it at them now. 'Votre poésie,' he hurled, 'manque de l'accentuation. Manque de la masculinité. Manque du grand *bang bang bang bang bang.*'

He was in trouble now. A gross man with many chins gave it to him strong and sesquipedalian. All of his words, except his contemptuously cited *bang bang bang*, seemed of Greek derivation. *La politique* seemed to be coming into it. Naturally. These Spaniards and Italians and French couldn't discuss anything, not even prosody, without making it political. A reactionary bastard this one seemed to be. Enderby cried aloud:

'Gerard Manley Hopkins, prêtre, mystique, jésuite. Hopkins devrait être canonisé. Lisez son *Wreck of the Deutschland* – l'esprit tout à fait chrétien, l'amour du bon Dieu. Et tout ça,' he added lamely. The trouble with French was that it wasn't a religious language. 'Vous ne savez rien de ce poète anglaise, parmi les plus grands, ignorants que vous êtes. Vous,' he cried at a deep-toned woman with a moustache who was just getting up, apparently to denounce him, 'qu'est-ce vous savez de la plus grande littérature du monde entier? Vous, avec votre Racine et Corneille et tout ça, toujours comptant le numéro des syllables sur les doigts. Oui oui, vraiment, je sais bien que vous avez des alexandriens, avec douze syllables et quelquefois treize pour chaque bloody vers, et c'est bien dommage que vous n'avez pas douze, ou bien treize, doigts sur les deux mains. Eh bien, vous servez-vous des doigts des pieds alors, bâtards. Ici à Casablanca vous étiez gonflés de l'eau de Vichy, traîtres.' He had seen the film with Humphrey

Bogart and Ingrid Bergman and the pianistic negro et tout ça. The noise in the little lecture-room was now very considerable. Enderby thought he had better get out. They obviously didn't give a damn about Gerard Manley Hopkins, 1844–1889. The chairman, an Anglo-Frenchman whose mission was to promote good cultural relations between the French and British exiles of Morocco, also thought Enderby had better get out. He was very peeved. He more or less pulled Enderby out. A man with a pointed beard was fish-mouthing something at Enderby, shaking his fist and using the word *perfide*. 'Ah, vous,' Enderby cried back, leaving. 'Allez vous pédiquer dans un très sale pissoir, bâtard que vous êtes. Et ta soeur,' he said to another loud man. One old *veuve* was weeping quite bitterly about something, perhaps for the foul streets of Paris, full of argot evoked by now fluent Enderby. 'Nous vous avons battus,' he called finally. 'A Waterloo et tout ça. Si nous avions eu pris la Corse, comme James Boswell a raccomandé au gouvernement britannique, votre Napoléon aurait été un Anglais, alors mettez ça dans vos pipes et fumez-la.' By this time he was out, having however been spitefully daggered in the leg by a kind of spiky Laocoon in brass, much punished by subtropical humidity, that stood on a table by the door.

On a sidewalk café the Anglo-Frenchman bitterly said, clutching his glass of Ricard as if to crunch it, 'Why the hell did you come here?'

'Eh? You asked me, didn't you? Before I picked up the plane en route to New York. It was your idea.'

'No no no, that was all my fault. I meant, why did you come to Morocco?'

'Why did you, for that matter?' And, with a truculent arm-swing, Enderby downed certain centilitres of his British-type beer. 'Oh, never mind. I came to kill Rawcliffe but he died first and left me his beach restaurant. Simple as that.'

'Rawcliffe was all right. Rawcliffe was very helpful. You've undone ten years of good work, do you know that?' His name was Briand-Vavasour, or some such phony name. He was a bit too neat, not sweaty, youngish, greyish. Enderby knew he should never have trusted him.

'Bloody French,' Enderby said. 'They ought to know about Hopkins. And if they don't know, they should be willing to learn. Ineducable sods.'

'And how do you think you're going to get on in New York, what with this chauvinism and wanting to kill people all the time?'

'I never wanted to kill anybody,' Enderby said, somewhat wounded. 'Except my stepmother, and that bloody Rawcliffe who stole a poem of mine and made a film out of it, and the woman I married, forgotten her name, and –'

'Intolerant swine,' hissed Briand-Vavasour rather theatrically, but it all fitted in here, Muslims and yashmaks and beggars and assassins and so on.

'You've got to be intolerant,' Enderby said, 'when it's a matter of art.' The word rang hollowly on that colonial sidewalk, palm-lined. 'Art,' he repeated, and a donkey brayed afar, some of these black bastards probably torturing it. 'I'll tell those bloody American bastards all about art,' he promised.

Appendix 2: 'American Policies in Vietnam'

A letter published in *The Times* (London), 2 February 1967, p. 13.

Sir,—

Mr. Kingsley Amis and others claim (January 21) that they speak for a large body of opinion in their 'unequivocal support' for American policies in Vietnam.

We, the undersigned, without organization or secretariat, knowing that we too speak for a large body of opinion, wish to state that we deplore the idea of 'unequivocal support' for American policy with its implication that it is improper to criticize the conduct of the war; that we do not believe that the 'lesser issues' in Vietnam can be simply 'cleared away' so that such 'unequivocal support' is possible; and that considering the available information on this atrocious war, we do not believe that the policies of America and her allies are likely to bring about the peace which is earnestly desired by all. We firmly believe that the time has come to question the entrenched assumptions of the American Government and her allies, for we can see no possibility of peace in Vietnam with the current escalation of military involvement. On the contrary, we believe that for thinking people not to question these assumptions is to cause increasing devastation to the Vietnamese people and all combatants, and to bring ever nearer the prospect of global war.

Yours faithfully,

BRIGID BROPHY   B.S. JOHNSON
ANTHONY BURGESS   JULIAN MITCHELL
IVY COMPTON-BURNETT   JOHN MORTIMER
LEN DEIGHTON   ALAN SILLITOE
GILLIAN FREEMAN   WILLIAM TREVOR

Appendix 3: Outlines of three novels by Anthony Burgess

Editor's note: These novel outlines were written by Anthony Burgess and sent by Thomas P. Collins to Robert Gottlieb, an editor at the New York publishing house Alfred A. Knopf, on 18 September 1972. A lucrative three-novel book deal, to be agented by Collins, is mentioned in the correspondence between Burgess and Collins, now at the Burgess Foundation in Manchester (IABF). Burgess did not complete any of these books, although his novel *Man of Nazareth*, rather different from the work proposed here, appeared in 1979.

THE TRUE PATTON PAPERS

This is, as I see it, a very concise novel, totally unwindy, well-written but admitting no literary flourishes, dealing with the imaginary career of General Patton from D-Day until an unspecified time when he plants the flag of the United States on the Kremlin. Fantastic, yes, but told chiefly in highly plausible documents – newspaper reports and editorials, private letters, war office communications and so on – so that the logic of the process is more compelling than the hardly believable fantasy. The work begins with Patton's making a somewhat different speech at Marple, Cheshire, from the indiscreet one which earned him such opprobrium (he spoke of England and the USA dominating a future world, but made no mention of Russia). I wish to see him in a position – probably the one that General Bradley actually held – which puts him in virtual control of the entire liberation of Europe. With the active encouragement of the American President and the British Premier, and with the connivance of a dithering Eisenhower, Patton drives to Berlin and then beyond. Versed in all the strategies of the past and capable of making a Napoleonic identification, Patton nevertheless avoids Napoleon's logistic errors and penetrates a weakened Russia. Official propaganda has little difficulty in identifying the new drive against tyranny – with the one that has just ended – one is a logical extension of the other. Patton is in fact fulfilling Churchill's own mad dream.

The consequences of the act are not spelled out, but the implications are there. We have a vision of a post-war Europe very different from the one we have known – the post-war America as well. More than the record of the 'crusade', however, will be the portrait of Patton himself – tyranny-hating, bound to certain dangerous quixotic ideas, brilliant in the field, a huge personality – bigger, perhaps, than the historical reality.

One cannot ignore the cinematic possibilities here – with George C. Scott repeating his success.

THE RHAPSODY MAN

I propose a not over-long novel based on the career and personality of George Gershwin. The book begins in Carnegie Hall with my hero playing the solo part in a piano concerto he has written. He is aware of the smell of burning rubber – Gershwin's own first symptom of the cerebral tumour that killed him – but, apart from the tendency to hallucinate slightly, he is well enough to play his own work. The performance – the themes of the work, the sound of the orchestra, the individual instrumentalists – build up a reminiscent fantasy in which the composer recalls his past – popular successes in the theatre, his Jewish family background, his studies under Ravel in Paris. There is also the malaise springing from awareness of failure to do what he wished to do – become a genuinely great American composer, as great as Debussy or Mahler, instead of a melody-spinner with a gift for colour and form. The elements of American art have somehow not conduced to greatness. American music has been strongest in its expression of alienation – negro spiritual, jazz, Jewish schmalz. The Gershwin character never found his own identity and hence that of his art. The work ends, applause is overwhelming, but the composer is aware of impending death and his own failure. If he could live longer?

The book should also be a kaleidoscope of American theatre life in the twenties and thirties, with specially written lyrics and one or two music-type illustrations. It should be rich though brief. It should be a portrait of America as well as of an American artist. It should be a diagnosis of American sickness. It should be a muted celebration of American achievement. It should be highly entertaining as well as thoughtful and moving.

FIFTH GOSPEL (tentative title)

A re-telling of the synoptic gospels by a simple Hebrew youth whose search for reality has led him to drugs. He follows Christ around like a rather remote dog, kicked and rejected by the disciples. He tells the gospel story in his own peculiar language, which has Semitic roots in it (cf. *A Clockwork Orange*). His own somewhat clouded vision presents us with the facts of Christ's life that we already know, but they are very personally interpreted. This Christ, indeed, could be the founder of a new diabolism. The narrator is not really concerned with the *moral* nature of the kingdom of Christ's preaching: that it should be ultimately real, that it should offer rewards for adhering to its God (or devil) is enough. The whole book should, on one level, suggest the fragility of all historical documentation – since it has to come through frail human observers. On the other, it should raise the question of the importance of the moral aspects (are they really all that important?) of revealed religions. If Christ were an emissary of the Devil, and rose on the third day, would we still have to believe in him? What, anyway, are the differences between God and the Devil?

The author feels that these three projects represent, however arbitrarily, a kind of American trilogy. They are intended to appeal to a wider audience than the author has previously sought – nothing hermetic about them, no tortuous syntax or wanton wordplay, but, if possible, a certain connotative richness behind the comparative simplicities of the prose.

Appendix 4: Reader's report on *The Clockwork Testament* by Vilém Flusser, 29 August 1973

Editor's note: The writer and philosopher Vilém Flusser (1920–1991) wrote this report for the publishing house Editions Mame in Paris. The French translation of the novel was published by Editions Laffont in 1974. A copy of Flusser's report, which had presumably been sent to Burgess, is in the IABF archive in Manchester. Originally written in the author's own, somewhat Frenchified, English.

The Clockwork Testament, or Enderby's End, or Death in New York by Anthony Burgess.

The manuscript (of which p. 52 is missing and some pages are almost unreadable) can be read on various levels, which are curiously enough, rather unrelated, between each other. I shall shortly describe three of them:

A: what might be called the *'narrative' level*: A British poet is invited to New York to give lectures on English literature. He is Catholic, his poetry is of the 'philosophical' kind and he is deeply committed to a disciplined elaboration of beautiful language. In New York he is engulfed by brutal vulgarity, shallow political commitment, commercial Kitsch, a pleasureless sexuality and, what is worse to him, desacralization of poetry, in three different surroundings: his class (where he gives a lecture on Renaissance English poets invented by him to a group of alienated pseudo-intellectual youths, where he criticizes and gives grades to silly, pornographic and cheaply political poems made by his students, and where a girl wants to prostitute herself to him to obtain grade A), the subway (where a group of hoodlums are about to violate an elderly woman, whilst some passengers watch as if it were a TV show, and a nun prays, and he himself draws a sword hidden in his walking stick to fight the hoodlums), and in a TV program (to which he is invited because a film based on a poem of his is said to have provoked violence, and where he meets a hypocritical Catholic teacher, a silly and vulgarly efficient animator, and a hard, pitiless and glamorous movie star). He has three heart attacks and dies of the last after having made love to a woman who came to his apartment to kill him in revenge to the effect his poetry had on her.

B: What might be called the *'linguistic'* level: There is the obvious shock between the American and British use of the English language. There is the shock between the philosophical (and theological) and the brutally vulgar language. There is the shock between the language of poetry and the commercial and cheap political jargon. And there is the shock between the traditional discursive speech and the language of film scripts and TV programs. (There is a very funny transcription of a TV interview, where, for instance, 'ethical' becomes 'ethnical', and 'predestination' becomes 'priesty nation'.)

C: What might be called the *'message'* level: The dialectics between determination and freedom ('original sin' and 'choice between good and evil') is the constant theme that runs through the manuscript. The dialectics is never resolved, but is shown in various contexts. It is personified in St. Augustine and Pelagius, and the author seems to side with Pelagius (curiously one reason seems to be that Pelagius is British). The author seems to suggest that the deep-lying reason for the barbarous state of political and aesthetic affairs which he diagnosticizes is the fact that people are no longer aware of this dialectics. His manuscript aims at provoking such an awareness, because to him the impossibility to solve the contradiction between determination and freedom *is* the human condition, if we take this contradiction in its religious connotations (i.e. Catholic connotations).

Appreciation: The manuscript reads very well, because it has suspense, it has drama, it poses important questions, and is at times very funny. It is written with skill and it addresses itself to a great range of readers (from the 'high-brow' to the 'middle-brow'). It should sell well, because it is written by a well-known name, and it has sex, violence, and religion in it. In my opinion it does not raise the truly important questions about the problems it deals with (neither in the realm of politics, nor the arts, nor philosophy, nor religion). It leaves me unsatisfied (which might be due to the fact that human condition is unsatisfactory), but it also leaves me rather unconcerned (which might be due to the commercial skill it betrays, which means that the manuscript is part of the universe the author apparently criticizes with such violence). In other words: I do not think the manuscript is a true 'meta-discourse' of the theme it handles. But my opinion does not invalidate the interest of the manuscript: an intelligent, even fascinating description of one aspect of the world we have to live in. No doubt: the manuscript should be published in my opinion.

Appendix 5: 'The Nature of Violence'

Editor's note: In 1973, Burgess wrote a short essay on 'The Nature of Violence' in pursuance of a contract between himself and the Research Foundation of the City University of New York. This essay, the original of which is held in the Archive of the International Anthony Burgess Foundation in Manchester, is here published for the first time.

Violence – the term is compelling and curiously seductive: it rings with viola and smells of violets. At the present time the reality exercises many minds, usually of those to whom the concept has a strongly intellectual appeal. The violent merely proceed with their violence, as they always have, as they always will.

It is believed that there is more violence about than ever there was in the past (a past that books teach us must have been very violent). Because there are more people about than there were in the past, there must inevitably be more violence, but there ought also to be more charity and tranquillity about as well. These concepts are, however, less seductive and less newsworthy.

Human beings are essentially violent creatures, and it would seem to follow that, as we accept our humanity, we must also accept the fact of our innate violence. Violence is not necessarily a reprehensible thing. Corrupt and evil systems of government are frequently changed through violence. The free peoples of the world, in the period beginning 1936, used systematic violence to dethrone, or attempt to dethrone, various tyrannies. The forms of violence that the democracies used to batter Nazi Germany and Imperialist Japan into submission were of an ingenuity and a lethality unmatched by the totalitarian regimes. On the intellectual and creative planes, which may just be termed metaphorical areas, violence has always been taken for granted as a means of establishing new ideas and new art-forms. Even the individual act of artistic creation seems to depend on doing violence to a natural form: the sculptor deforms stone with chisel and hammer; the carpenter depends on the butchering of trees: the builders of new cities proceed in an orgy of creative violence.

It is not violence in itself, then, that one is disposed to condemn, but rather the use of violence less as a means than as an end, the employ-ment of aggressive urges to promote personal or collective fulfilment. This makes the gratuitous act of aggression take on the quality of an impersonal sexual act, in which raw libido is unseasoned by affection and careless of its biological sanctions. Impersonal copulation and hurtful aggression are seen to be cognates; being cognate, they are frequently combined. Rape is the mode of aggression most regularly condemned by law and private morality; it is also the mode which, especially to the intellectual, exerts most fascination. Day-dreams of rape are common, and in these day-dreams the dreamer figures frequently as both aggressor and victim at the same time, especially if the dreamer is a woman.

Rape and mayhem in the streets of towns and cities seem to have become part of the mythology, because of the reality, of our age, but our age can claim no monopoly of public aggression of this kind. In Shakespeare's London riot was so common that it was as thoughtlessly stamped on as it was thoughtlessly fomented. In 1595, an outbreak of riot by apprentices – the pretext was the rising price of butter – was answered summarily with a hanging of the miscrents on the spot. This proved to be discouraging. Our present-day substitute for summary judgement and execution is an armed police force readier to shoot than to pursue and ask questions. When the aggressiveness of the police enters the mythology of barbarism, then lay barbarism becomes the more glorified: the situation of cops-versus-robbers takes on the lineaments of some great cosmic yin-yang opposition. In England the police are not armed. Interestingly, there is less street barbarism than in the United States. Ulster is different, of course.

A growing concern has been with the increasing representation of acts of barbarism, or of just aggression, not really distinguishable from barbarism in most instances, in popular entertainment. It is assumed that to show gratuitous violence in art is to encourage it in life, though no firm evidence has ever been brought forward in support of the assumption. The materials of art are anterior to art itself; the artist cannot be held responsible for the existence of those materials. If I depict murder or rape in a story, play or film, I am showing what I know already to exist in the exterior world. Traditionally, fiction has always made powerful use of such materials, and our own age seems to exhibit a certain tasteful reticence in comparison with some past eras. The decadent drama of the decadent Roman Empire, apart from presenting real copulation on the stage, regularly used condemned criminals for execution scenes in which there was no pretence. Shakespeare's *Titus Andronicus* contains rape, mutilation, massacre and cannibalism. He may have gone too far, but he was merely pushing the Senecan tradition of the tragedy of blood to its logical limits. Even in the mature *King Lear*, where the sophisticated language abets the horror, he was not averse to the pulling out of eyes on the stage. *Straw Dogs* does not go so far as Elizabethan Senecanism, whose products are regarded as literary glories.

It is no accident, of course, that pointless, and even mindless, aggression is to be associated with youth (or with soldiers, who, at whatever age, remain a kind of youth). My own novel, *A Clockwork Orange*, is about youthful barbarism, though it is chiefly about bland governmental barbarism, and it is natural for youth, which lacks responsibility and purpose but does not lack either raw libido or energy, to provide us with the best contemporary images of barbarism in action. Gang-rape, vandalism, beating up the ancientry – phenomena of our age, as of Shakespeare's – spring not from social or familial deprivation, not from lack of occupation or a frustrated creative urge, but from energy which takes the easy way of expression – in joyful destruction, whether of property or of persons. Little can be done about it except in the way of summary punition. It does not represent an intellectual problem. It tends to find more positive channels of expression as maturity approaches – and this, incidentally, is what is dramatised in the final chapter of *A Clockwork Orange* as published in the British Commonwealth. America, more fascinated by barbarism than England appears to be, has a truncated version which no pressures of mine can hope to see superseded by the version which I wrote. The thing for us to remember is that man is a violent animal, that violence is not reprehensible in itself, and that barbarism is a wasteful allotrope of it which demands not sympathy or understanding (appropriate to a disease: barbarism is not a disease) but suppression. We first have to learn to suppress it in ourselves. It is not 'out there' but very much 'in here'.

Notes

26   **Burt Lancaster**: American actor, producer, celebrated film-star (1913–94). He played the part of Moses in the British-Italian television mini-series scripted by Burgess, *Moses the Lawgiver* (1974).

26   **deserves to live, deserves to live**: quoted from the 'Aeolus' episode of James Joyce's *Ulysses* where the words are spoken by the character J.J. O'Molloy, a lawyer, in reference to the Mosaic *lex talionis* (U7.771, ed. by H.W. Gabler, W. Steppe and C. Melchior, New York: Vintage/Random House, 1986, p. 115).

27   **Tangier**: a city in north-western Morocco, near the Strait of Gibraltar. It is here that Enderby inherited, in the second instalment of the tetralogy named after him (*Enderby Outside*, 1968), a seaside bar called *La Belle Mer* from fellow poet Rawcliffe, Enderby's erstwhile rival and enemy turned deathbed friend. The broken English spoken by Enderby's local employees is a constant source of parody in the earlier novel.

27   **schwa**: the central vowel sound /ə/, typically occurring in weakly stressed syllables, as in the final syllable of 'sofa' and the first syllable of 'along' (*OED*).

27   **The Great Bed of Ware**: a piece of Renaissance furniture named after the Hertfordshire town where it was made in the late sixteenth century to serve as a customer lure in the White Hare Inn. It was later acquired by the Victoria and

Albert Museum in London, where it has been on display since 1931. Richly ornamented and of massive dimensions allowing several persons to sleep or enjoy marital (or extra-marital) bliss, the bed is of a rather conventional, rectangular shape. It is thus the oddity and the multiplicity of functions associated with the bed, rather than its shape, that is likely to have suggested the analogy with the prize possession of Enderby's landlady.

27   **center (re)**: a playful suggestion of Enderby's piqued uncertainty when it comes to differences between British and American spelling.

28   **roystering, rollicking diet**: a reference to Charles Dickens, *Nicholas Nickleby* (1839): 'Never were such jolly, roystering, rollicking, merry-making blades, as the jovial crew of Grogzwig' (Chapter 6; London: Dent, 1975, p. 69).

28   **twelve-year-old girls**: The oneiric scene here can also be read as a parodic allusion to the similarly abused young eponym of Vladimir Nabokov's novel *Lolita*, whose full first name Dolores is of Hispanic origins – as are the Puerto Rican girls in Enderby's dream. While Burgess recognised Nabokov as one of 'the greatest modern masters' of English, he did not think very highly of the Russian-American writer's best-known work, which he dismissed as an 'inferior novel'. See *Ninety-Nine Novels: The Best in English Since 1939* (London: Allison, Busby, 1984), p. 92.

28   **what you call biscuits**: in North America, 'a small round savoury cake of bread, similar to a scone in appearance, and typically made from a mixture of flour, fat, and a raising agent' (*OED*). These are called muffins in British English.

28   **blind Argentinian**: in all probability, Jorge Luis Borges, short-story writer, essayist, poet and translator, and a major figure in Spanish-language and world literature. Burgess recalls having met him at a 1976 conference on Shakespeare in Washington, DC (see *You've Had Your Time*, p. 336) and refers, in a remark to Graham Greene on seeing a volume of Borges's work on his fellow-writer's shelf, to Borges as

'the man who kindly calls himself the Argentine Burgess' (*Graham Greene: The Last Interview*, ed. by John R. Macarthur, Brooklyn and London: Melville House, 2019, p. 9). Paul Theroux quotes Borges to have paid the compliment to Burgess of being a very good writer and 'a generous man' (*The Old Patagonian Express*, Boston: Houghton Mifflin, 1997, p. 189).

28 **Thelma Garstang:** a fictitious name and character. The surname may have been suggested by Garstang, Lancashire, a small town near Blackpool, the latter featuring large in Burgess's late novel *The Pianoplayers*.

29 **edentulous:** 'toothless' (*OED*).

29 **tomahawk:** The absurd-sounding threat here is related to Burgess's personal recollections of a 'Cherokee Indian [who] keeps sending me long, frightening, anti-British letters threatening to come after me with a tomahawk' (quoted in Andrew Biswell, *The Real Life of Anthony Burgess*, London: Picador, 2005, p. 351).

29 **91st Street and Columbus Avenue:** a location close to where the Burgesses rented Adrienne Rich's apartment at 10–D, 670 West End Avenue, NY 10025. See Biswell, *The Real Life of Anthony Burgess*, p. 351.

30 **gat-toothed:** also gap-toothed, having the teeth set wide apart; today regarded as an Americanism but the first recorded use dates back to Chaucer (*OED*).

30 **cockroaches:** For Burgess's recollections of how the kitchen of his Manhattan lodgings was infested with 'cockroaches or *cucarachas*', and the response of the 'block committee' to his remarks on the phenomenon published in the *New York Times*, see *You've Had Your Time* (p. 270).

30 **Kasbah:** 'the Arab quarter surrounding a castle or fortress in a North African town' (*OED*).

30 ***The Wreck of the Deutschland:*** the title of a 35-stanza ode by Gerard Manley Hopkins. Composed in 1875–76 but published only posthumously in 1918. Burgess's essay 'The Ecstasy of Gerard Manley Hopkins' (1989) contains a

summary of his views on the poet's significance: Hopkins's uncompromising attitude to his art and his glorification of 'pied beauty', that is, 'the intense variety of the physical world' (*One Man's Chorus: The Uncollected Writings*, New York: Carroll, Graf, 1998, p. 334).

31   **Kraut Kaput**: 'Germans finished/defeated'; kraut is a slang term for Germans and Austrians derived from the German word 'Sauerkraut, a form of pickled, shredded cabbage, supposedly loved by the nation' (Jonathon Green, *Chambers Slang Dictionary*, Edinburgh: Chambers, 2009)

31   **Krankenhaus**: hospital (German). The name is possibly meant to suggest the standard representation of the pathological nature of Nazism in the real and fictitious films mentioned here.

31   **Last days of Hitler**: The British film *Hitler: The Last Ten Days* released in May 1973 with Alec Guinness in the role of the Führer may well be behind this fictional title. The film was based on Hugh Trevor-Roper's extensively researched and hugely influential book of the same title (1947).

31   **Visconti**: a reference to Luchino Visconti's *The Damned* (*La caduta degli dei*, 1969). The critically acclaimed film stirred up some controversy due to its provocative representation of homosexuality, paedophilia, rape and incest – topics recurring in Burgess's own novels, including *The Clockwork Testament*.

31   **Al Hopkins**: Albert Green Hopkins (1889–1932), pioneer of American country music.

31   **S.J.**: the Society of Jesus, also known as the Jesuit order, of which Hopkins was a member.

31   **Falk Laws**: Named after the German culture minister Albert Falk and enacted during the *Kulturkapf*, or war of cultures and religions, of the 1870s, the Falk Laws were meant to marginalise the Catholic Church in the Kingdom of Prussia and in the whole of Germany.

31   **On Saturday … in the round**: This is quoted from stanza 12 of Hopkins's 'The Wreck of the Deutschland' written 'to the

happy memory of five Franciscan Nuns, exiles by the Falk Laws, drowned between midnight and morning of December 7th 1875' when the steamer *Deutschland* ran aground on the shoal known as the Kentish Knock near the Godwin Sands east of the Thames Estuary. The poem bemoans the deaths of the Franciscan nuns on their way to self-imposed exile in America. In the work, the poet attempts to resolve his own conflicting emotions and theological dilemmas concerning his dual calling as Catholic priest and visionary poet in a predominantly Protestant and pragmatic country. In the novel the poem serves as the basis of a popular but controversial film based on Enderby's Hopkins-inspired 'idea', involving Enderby in conflicts analogous to those that Burgess himself was involved in following the release of Stanley Kubrick's film adaptation of his novel *A Clockwork Orange*.

31   **1875. December 7th**: the day the steamer *Deutschland* ran aground.

31   **Rhine refused them ... Gnashed**: quoted from stanza 21 of 'The Wreck of the Deutschland'.

31   **Let him easter in us ... crimson-cresseted east**: quoted from stanza 35 of 'The Wreck of the Deutschland'. Such peculiarities of Hopkins's poetry can be seen here as the free conversion of one word class into another ('easter' treated as a verb) or the use of idiosyncratic compounds meant to convey the sense of 'inscape' and 'instress' akin to what Hopkins's Oxford tutor Walter Pater meant by 'moment' or James Joyce by 'epiphany'. Both Hopkins and Joyce feature large in Burgess's experimental writing and aesthetic creed.

31   *Pet Beast*: Enderby's long philosophical poem the composition, interpretation and publication history of which take up much of the first two parts of the Enderby quartet. The poem, whose central idea is stolen by the rival poet Rawcliffe who cashes in on the film adaptation of the work, is a fusion of Cretan mythology and Biblical story to treat the complex relationship of original sin, civilisation and freedom of choice. The complete text of this poem does not

appear anywhere in the Enderby novels but a three-page version is included in the posthumously published volume *Anthony Burgess, Collected Poems*, ed. by Jonathan Mann (Manchester: Carcanet, 2020, pp. 303–5).

31   **Cinecittà:** Cinecittà Studios or Cinema City Studios (Italian) is a large film-making complex in Rome. Although the set of studios, the largest of its kind in Europe, was founded by Mussolini in 1937, it is famous for some of the finest, and in their spirit usually progressive, art-films shot there in the postwar period. The celebrated arthouse film *L'Animal Binato*, based on Rawcliffe's stolen 'idea' derived from Enderby's long poem *The Pet Beast*, is made in Cinecittà according to the narrative of *Inside Mr Enderby*. Burgess writes about his involvement with the Italian film industry in *You've Had Your Time* (pp. 260, 291–2).

31   **Rawcliffe:** the guilt-ridden poet who bequeathed his seaside bar in Tangier to Enderby as belated compensation of sorts for his having defrauded Enderby of his prime intellectual property, *The Pet Beast*.

31   *L'Animal Binato*: quoted from Dante, *Purgatorio*, Canto 32:46: '*Così dintorno a l'albero robusto / gridaron li altri; e l'animal binato / "Sì si conserva il seme d'ogne giusto"*' (So, round the robust tree, the others shouted; and the two-natured animal: 'Thus is the seed of every righteous man preserved.')

32   **Alberto Formica:** the Italian director whose name has pride of place on the credit list of the film *L'Animal Binato*. As 'formica' is 'a hard, durable plastic laminate used as a decorative surfacing material' (*OED*), this is a tongue-in-cheek allusion to film-director Stanley Kubrick's surname, which also refers to a hard object used by builders.

32   **Schaumwein:** 'sparkling wine' (German). The name of the fictional director may also be an allusion to Stanley Kubrick, director of the film *A Clockwork Orange*. *Schaum*, a German word meaning 'froth' or 'foam', refers to a light and soft substance in its characteristics the opposite of (a cubic) *brick*, something hard and heavy.

32   **1918**: Hopkins's collected poems were published posthumously under the title *Poems* in that year by his lifelong friend, Robert Bridges.

32   **out of copyright**: Under the legislation in effect at the time (the Copyright Act of 1956), copyright expired fifty years after the end of the year in which the original copyright-holder died. (The 1995 Duration of Copyright and Rights in Performance Regulations extended the duration of copyright to seventy years.)

33   **Martin Droeshout**: an English engraver of Flemish origin, who made the portrait of Shakespeare for the cover of the First Folio edition of the great dramatist's plays. In the section titled 'The Muse' of the fourth and last Enderby instalment, an eerily animated 'reproduction of the Droeshout portrait of Shakespeare' appears to the horror of the time-travelling character Paley (Burgess, *Enderby's Dark Lady*, London: Hutchinson, 1984, p. 155). It is a telling detail that Enderby, who teaches Elizabethan drama at the 'University of Manhattan', should not remember such a widely known snippet of Shakespeareana – an oddity explained by a later turn in the narrative of *The Clockwork Testament*.

33   **VLS, CU**: abbreviations used in film scripts standing for 'Very Long Shot' and 'Close Up' respectively.

33   **Thou hearest me truer... O Christ, O God**: originally 'Thou heardst me truer than tongue confess / Thy terror, O Christ, O God', quoted from stanza 2 of 'The Wreck of the Deutschland'.

33   **lovely-asunder starlight**: quoted from stanza 5 of 'The Wreck of the Deutschland'.

34   **firefolk sitting in the air... kisses his hand**: 'fire-folk' in the original. This is quoted from Hopkins's sonnet 'The Starlight Night'.

34   **kisses his hand**: 'I kiss my hand' in the original. This is quoted from stanza 5 of 'The Wreck of the Deutschland'.

34   **dappled-with-damson west**: quoted from stanza 5 of 'The Wreck of the Deutschland'.

34   **Illgirt:** this word (not listed in *OED*) appears in the 'Lestrygonians' section of Joyce's *Ulysses* (8.687, Gabler, p. 139). It probably means 'shabbily or scantily dressed'.

34   **OS:** a cinematographic term meaning 'off screen'.

34   **Glory be ... a brinded cow:** quoted from Hopkins's poem 'Pied Beauty'.

34   **TWO SHOT:** a cinematographic term referring to a shot encompassing two persons in a frame.

35   **Since, though he is under ... instressed, stressed:** quoted from stanza 5 of 'The Wreck of the Deutschland'.

35   **instressed, stressed:** *OED* quotes the critic W.H. Gardner as follows: 'In the vagaries of shape and colour presented by hills, clouds, glaciers and trees [Hopkins] discerns a recondite pattern – "species or individually-distinctive beauty" – for which he coins the word "inscape"; and the sensation of inscape (or, indeed, of any vivid mental image) is called "stress" or 'instress".'

35   *sotto voce*: spoken or sung in an intentionally lowered voice (Italian).

35   **Gertrude:** St Gertrude, also known as Gertrude the Great, is repeatedly referred to in 'The Wreck of the Deutschland' in conjunction with her attribute the lily (stanza 20), even though she is not directly related to the Franciscan nuns killed in the shipwreck, as she had been a member of the Benedictine order and lived in the thirteenth century.

35   **bring our King ... English souls:** quoted from stanza 35 of 'The Wreck of the Deutschland'.

35   **lush-kept plush-capped sloe:** quoted from stanza 8 of 'The Wreck of the Deutschland'.

35   **flesh-burst:** quoted from stanza 8 of 'The Wreck of the Deutschland'.

36   **Be adored among men ... wrecking and storm:** quoted from stanza 9 of 'The Wreck of the Deutschland'.

36   **American-outward-bound:** quoted from stanza 12 of 'The Wreck of the Deutschland'.

36   **Death on drum ... bugle his fame**: quoted from stanza 11 of 'The Wreck of the Deutschland'.

36   **Wiry and white-fiery ... unfathering deeps**: quoted from stanza 11 of 'The Wreck of the Deutschland'.

37   **name ... among the credits**: Enderby's satisfaction at seeing his name among the credits is understandable in light of the fact that his (unwitting) contribution to another film, *L'Animal Binato*, went unacknowledged according to the narrative of *Inside Mr Enderby*.

37   **storms bugling ... Death's fame**: allusions to stanza 11 of 'The Wreck of the Deutschland'.

37   **Christ, Christ, come quickly**: quoted from stanza 24 of 'The Wreck of the Deutschland'. In the first British edition of the novel Hopkins's Latinate vocative 'O' is erroneously changed to the English interjection 'Oh' (*The Clockwork Testament*, London: Hart-Davis, MacGibbon, p. 17). This edition restores the correct version, in accordance with Burgess's typescript in the archive of the International Anthony Burgess Foundation (IABF), Manchester.

37   **restricted showing rating**: Kubrick's *A Clockwork Orange* was also given an X certificate in the UK and X rating in the USA, the former classifying the film as 'suitable for those aged 18' and the latter meaning that the motion picture in question contained unsuitable content for minors.

37   *The Month*: The editor of the Jesuit monthly *The Month*, Henry Coleridge, found 'The Wreck' incomprehensible and, after some hesitation, returned it to Hopkins. According to the recollections of a contemporary, Fr Coleridge 'read the poem and could not understand it, and he did not relish publishing any poem that he himself could not master'. Quoted in Martin Dubois, 'The *Month* as Hopkins Knew It', *Victorian Periodicals Review*, 43:3 (Fall 2010), pp. 296–308, p. 296.

39   **Tartarean**: 'of or belonging to the Tartarus of the ancients; hence, pertaining to hell or to purgatory; infernal' (*OED*).

39   **Aunt Jemima:** This was an American brand of break-
      fast foods, including pancake mixes. Its logo portraying an
      African-American woman deemed to reinforce racial stereo-
      types, the brand was renamed and its logo redesigned in 2020.

40   **sweet and savoury:** Burgess has the narrator-protagonist
      Toomey comment on this culinary combination in the novel
      Earthly Powers: 'These new French structuralists deny syn-
      chronic sweet and savoury to the cuisine, no part of Western
      culture they say. How about the British, somebody asked.
      Roast pork and apple sauce and so on' (London: Hutchinson,
      1980, p. 647). In a 1961 essay, possibly familiar to Burgess,
      the (as yet) structuralist semiologist Roland Barthes notes
      the unwelcome influence on American cuisine of 'Dutch
      and German immigrants who were used to "sweet-salty"
      cooking'. See 'Toward a Psychosociology of Contemporary
      Food Consumption', in *Food and Culture: A Reader*, ed.
      Carole Counihan and Penny van Esterik (New York and
      London: Routledge, 2013), pp. 23–30, p. 23.

40   **ithyphallus:** 'an erect phallus' (*OED*).

40   **caecum:** 'the first part of the large intestine' (*OED*).

41   **man-hater:** These are the same words with which Burgess
      characterises, in *You've Had Your Time* (p. 269), Adrienne
      Rich, whose Manhattan flat he and his small family rented in
      the absence of the poet-colleague on research leave from her
      teaching job at the City College of New York.

41   **Bayswater:** a district in West London.

41   **MCP:** male chauvinist pig.

41   **Jewish-mother tenant:** an allusion to Philip Roth's *Portnoy's
      Complaint*, a novel Burgess admired for its doing 'for mas-
      turbation what Melville did for the whale'. The trouble, he
      adds in *Ninety-Nine Novels*, with the novel's young protag-
      onist Alexander, 'is the debilitating power of his mother'. He
      finds Roth's novel 'very funny' (p. 106).

42   **androphobic:** man-hating. Not in *OED*.

42   **St Augustine and Pelagius:** St Augustine, an influential
      western Christian theologian, was Bishop of Hippo Regius

(today Annaba, Algeria) from 395 until his death in 430. He features large in *The Clockwork Testament* and elsewhere in Burgess's works (most prominently in *The Wanting Seed*) as the major proponent of the dogma of original sin. He was instrumental in having successive church synods condemn, as heretical, the teachings of Pelagius (c. 354/360–418), who argued against the power of original sin and the essential role of divine grace in salvation. Pelagius was a popular teacher when he moved to Rome around 400. Scandalised by what he saw as the decline of morality in the Roman clergy, he began to preach that Christians should lead a morally upright life, and that they could do so relying on reason and freedom of choice alone (Frank K. Flin, *Encyclopedia of Catholicism*, New York: Facts On File, p. 511).

42   **White Owl**: an American tobacco brand name related to the logo on the container of such cigars featuring a white owl perched on a cigar. Burgess was a heavy smoker, his favourite brand being the Schimmelpenninck Duet cigar. Owls must also have been on Burgess's mind shortly after publishing in 1971 his 'structuralist' novel *MF*, where oneiric and mythical owls play an important part.

42   **Morgan**: the original Welsh name of Pelagius meaning 'seaborn'. The Graecised form Pelagius signifies 'of the sea'.

42   **Sanctitas**: sacredness, sanctity (Latin).

42   **cloacae**: plural of 'cloaca', meaning an underground conduit for drainage, a common sewer (Latin).

42   **effluvium**: 'a noxious or disgusting exhalation or odour' (*OED*).

42   **weeviled**: infected with the beetles called wheat weevil considered as pests. The past participle form is not listed in *OED*.

42   **Eisel**: 'eisel' or 'eysel' is a medieval term for wine or cider vinegar. Not in *OED*.

42   **bonemeal**: 'a coarse powder consisting of crushed or ground animal bones, used as a fertilizer and in animal feed' (*OED*).

43   **Ultima Thule**: 'farthermost Thule' (Latin), with 'Thule' used in reference to a geographical location far up north since classical antiquity. Thule has been identified with such northern islands and countries as the Orkneys, the Shetlands, the whole of Greenland, or Norway. In April 1973, Vladimir Nabokov published a short story titled 'Ultima Thule' in the *New Yorker*. Burgess followed Nabokov's work with keen interest and may well have read the story while in New York.

43   **Favonius**: Roman divinity in charge of favourable winds; also Favonius Eulogius, a Carthaginian rhetorician and a contemporary of St Augustine's.

43   **Boreas**: the god of the north wind in Greek mythology.

43   *sancta urbs*: 'sacred city' in Latin, meaning Rome, the sole centre of western Christianity at the time.

44   **Sperr Lansing**: the anchor of the TV show that Enderby is invited to. The name is apparently derived from Hopkins's last sonnet ('The fine delight that fathers thought; the strong / Spur, live and lancing like the blowpipe flame'). See Geoffrey Aggeler, *Anthony Burgess: The Artist as Novelist* (Tuscaloosa, AL: University of Alabama Press, 1979), p. 95.

44   **Cannon Dickson**: an allusion to Hopkins's teacher Richard Watson Dixon, honorary canon of Carlisle and a fellow-poet with whom Hopkins remained in touch long after his graduation from Highgate School, where Dixon had been an assistant master during Hopkins's boyhood. Doubling the letter 'n' turns the ecclesiastic rank into the name of a large artillery piece (Ca*n*on into Ca*nn*on) which suggests the loud and sometimes militantly aggressive style characterising some of the media personnel Burgess had come into contact with. See, e.g., *You've Had Your Time*, pp. 256–7.

44   **The strong spur ... blowpipe flame**: quoted from Hopkins's last poem.

45   **eschatological**: Eschatology is 'the department of theological science concerned with the four last things: death, judgement, heaven, and hell' (*OED*).

45   **'1844 to 89,' he twinkled:** These are Hopkins's dates (corrected from the typescript-based Hart-Davis, MacGibbon edition where the birth date is given, erroneously, as 1884; p. 25), suggesting that having lived in the previous century he could not possibly be contacted by Ms Tauchnitz in the flesh. The curious detail that Enderby 'twinkled' with innocent joy over being able to produce the relevant dates is explained by a small but significant episode recalled from his student days by Burgess in his autobiography. When the noted Shakespearean H.B. Charlton dismissed, in class, Hopkins as one of those 'modernist upstarts', the young Burgess – or Wilson as he was at the time – pointed out, to the disbelief of his professor, that the dates of Hopkins were, actually, 1844–89. See *Little Wilson and Big God*, pp. 176–7.

45   **Manhattanville:** Also known as West Central Harlem, Manhattanville is a neighbourhood in the borough of Manhattan within walking distance of Enderby's (and Burgess's) New York address.

45   **original sin:** the inherited tendency of all human beings to live a godless, sinful life in consequence of humanity falling out of God's grace due to the first man and woman, Adam and Eve, having disobeyed the divine command and eaten of the forbidden fruit in the Garden of Eden. The doctrine is of utmost importance in Burgess's lifelong engagement with the dichotomy of freedom versus predetermination, an opposition at the heart of the conflict between Augustine and Pelagius in Enderby's dramatic poem in the making.

46   **Grammar of sin:** The treatment of cultural phenomena in general as interrelated elements of a linguistic system comes from such exponents of structuralism as Claude Lévi-Strauss and Roland Barthes, whose influence on Burgess's thinking cannot be exaggerated.

46   **pocula:** cups or drinking vessels (Latin).

46   **podorasty:** a term of Burgess's coinage and as such a *hapax legomenon*, or word of one single recorded appearance.

As the Latin prefix *pod-* refers to feet, as in *podagra, podia-try, chiropody,* the word means 'foot-fetish'. Not in *OED*.

47   **the marvellous milk was Walsingham Way**: quoted from stanza 26 of 'The Loss of the Eurydice', a long poem by Hopkins also addressing the topic of a shipwreck.

47   **our-king-back ... souls**: 'Our King back, Oh, upon English souls!' in the original; quoted from the last stanza (no. 35) of 'The Wreck of the Deutschland'. The line in question can be read as a plea for the conversion of England through the intercession of the martyred Franciscan nuns with Christ for the redemptive gift of a Catholic monarch. See Gerald Roberts, *Gerard Manley Hopkins: A Literary Life*. London: Macmillan, 1994, p. 61.

47   **nates**: buttocks (Latin).

47   **teg**: 'a sheep in its second year, or from the time it is weaned till its first shearing' (*OED*).

47   **cities of the plain**: five Biblical cities on the southern shore of the Dead Sea, including Sodom and Gomorrah, notorious for the supposed homosexuality and/or violent inhospitality of their inhabitants, referenced in the Old and the New Testament (for example, Gen. 18:20; 19:23– 25, Jud. 1:7, Ezek. 16: 50, Mt. 10:14–15). Marcel Proust, recognised by Burgess as an important modernist precursor (see *English Literature*, second edition, Harlow: Longman, 1974, p. 228; *Ninety-Nine Novels*, p. 51), published the fourth volume of his *roman fleuve* 'In Search of Lost Time' under the title *Sodome et Gomorrhe* (1921–22), translated into English by C.K. Scott Moncrieff as *Cities of the Plain* (1927).

48   **Phinehas ... Zimri ... Cozbi**: Phinehas was an Old Testament priest who, intent on preserving the purity of his people's faith, thrust a spear through the Israelite Zimri, who fornicated with Cozbi, a woman of heathen Moab (Num. 25:1–15). Burgess wanted 'the sad love story of Zimri and Cozbi to be given the full romantic treatment' in the television series *Moses the Lawgiver* but apparently in vain (*You've Had Your Time*, p. 289).

48   **Reich, Fanon**: Wilhelm Reich (1897–1957), Austrian-American psychologist noted for inventing the 'orgone accumulator', a sex-box supposedly restoring patients to health with the help of their own organic-orgasmic energy. He coined the term 'sexual revolution', a phenomenon responsible for much of the social-cultural turmoil of the 1960s and 1970s. Ibrahim Frantz Fanon (1925–61) was a French West Indian psychiatrist, political philosopher and armed rebel fighting against the French occupation of Algeria. Fanon's publications exerted a determining influence on post-colonial and Marxist theories. Burgess read the 'Modern Masters' volumes on Reich and Fanon on publication in 1970. Both books survive in the IABF collection.

49   **Tietjens**: Christopher Tietjens, 'the last Tory' is the central character of the novel-series *Parade's End* by Ford Madox Ford. Burgess referred to Ford's tetralogy as a single novel and 'the finest ... about the First World War' (*The Best of Everything*, ed. by William Davis, London: Weidenfeld and Nicolson, 1980, p. 97). Another significant connection lies in the fact that Adrienne Rich, poet, educator and feminist activist, the model of Enderby's landlady absent on research leave, had received, in 1968, the Eunice Tietjens Memorial Prize, a literary award named after a real-life person bearing the name Tietjens, an American poet, novelist, journalist, children's author, lecturer, and editor of the Chicago-based avant-garde magazine *Poetry*, where some major works of Ezra Pound, T.S. Eliot, and William Carlos Williams were first published.

49   **Ford Madox Ford**: the pen-name of Joseph Leopold Ford Hermann Madox Hueffer (1873–1939), a major British novelist of the Edwardian and postwar periods regarded by Burgess as 'the greatest novelist of the twentieth century' (*You've Had Your Time*, p. 130).

49   **halitosis**: Ford Madox Ford's foul-smelling breath, or halitosis, is returned to in Burgess's major novel *Earthly Powers*, where the writer of *Parade's End* plays a walk-on part:

'Captain Ford had breathed in lung-rotting gas, a volunteer infantryman contemned by some of the London literary for his patriotism, a good soldier among despicable scrimshankers' (p. 171). The olfactory symptom of Ford's lung condition receives an unfriendly mention in Ernest Hemingway's memoir *A Moveable Feast*, to which Burgess seems to be responding here and in *Earthly Powers*. It is a noteworthy fact that the Index to Burgess's biography of Hemingway lists five references to Ford, including yet another unflattering remark of Hemingway's quoted from *A Moveable Feast*. See *Ernest Hemingway and His World* (London: Thames and Hudson, 1978), p. 115.

49   **sides-woman**: Burgess's coinage based on 'sidesman', one of the persons elected to the churchwardens of a parish' (*OED*).

50   **xeroxed**: the name of an American company manufacturing and selling digital products and office equipment such as photocopiers, Xerox is a trademark often used generically as a common noun and as a verb in the sense of duplicating a paper document.

50   **respirator haversack**: a gas-mask bag normally made of canvas. Army-issue objects came to be used as fashion accessories in the 1970s, possibly as a statement about the potential of putting military equipment to peaceful use. Ms Tietjens carrying such an accessory can also be seen as a muted suggestion of her relatedness to the writer of *Parade's End*, whose having inhaled poison gas in the First World War is mentioned by Burgess in *Earthly Powers* and elsewhere.

50   **elevenses**: an eleven-o'clock meal or early lunch, mentioned in Burgess's *Honey for the Bears* and elsewhere.

51   **hizzed**: corrected to 'hissed' by the editors of the Hart, McGibbon edition but restored to the form in which the word appears in the typescript as it is likely meant to convey the sound of the pronoun 'his', in which the final letter 's' is voiced in pronunciation.

51 **Sarah Lee**: properly Sara Lee, an American consumer-goods company. Although the corporation went out of business in 2012, the brand name is still used with a number of frozen and packaged foods.

51 *Shehit ... Herisits*: Burgess himself was impatient with what he saw as 'the Anglo-Saxon feminist rage with the English language' (*A Mouthful of Air*, London: Hutchinson, 1992, p. 253). He found particularly objectionable the perception that language in general was a patriarchal creation, its sexist bias manifesting itself, among other things, in the overuse of the masculine pronoun. He pointed out that in several Asian languages gendered pronouns simply do not exist, and that the presumed preference for masculinity in words like *his*tory was more often than not unrelated to the etymology of the vocabulary item in question (pp. 253–4).

52 **infinite Ninth Symphony**: Beethoven's Symphony No. 9 in D minor is regarded by many as the German composer's finest achievement, and Burgess, too, kept returning to 'the glorious *Ninth*' in his non-fiction (most notably in *This Man and Music*) and his novels alike. In *A Clockwork Orange*, the narrator-protagonist Alex rapturously listens to the 'Ode to Joy', the celebrated choral finale of the symphony, during the reclamation treatment he receives at the end of the novel. Stanley Kubrick's film adaptation of *A Clockwork Orange* also exploits Beethoven's famous composition for largely the same purposes as Burgess himself does in the novel. As the critic Galia Hanoch-Roe notes, 'the *Ninth* is heard five times during the film, at pivotal moments, always listened to actively by the protagonist, and always causing violence' ('Beethoven's Ninth: An "Ode to Choice" as Presented in Stanley Kubrick's *A Clockwork Orange*', *International Review of the Aesthetics and Sociology of Music*, 33:2 (2002), 171–9). This is meant to underscore the point, made by Enderby here, that beauty is not to be confused with goodness or truth.

53   **Not to be confused with mere wrong**: The distinction between evil and wrong here owes much to the formulation of the same dichotomy in Graham Greene's work, especially the metaphysical thriller *Brighton Rock* (1938), where Greene 'set up a curious opposition between a secular system of conduct, with right feebly sparring with wrong, and an eschatological code, in which good wars with evil' (*One Man's Chorus*, p. 253). Although Burgess shared some of Greene's fascination with sin, he expressed serious reservations about his fellow-Catholic's theology, which he described as 'heterodox'. While appreciating certain aspects of Greene's art, he stopped short of 'attributing greatness to him' in an anonymously published obituary of Greene (quoted in Biswell, *The Real Life of Anthony Burgess*, p. 383).

53   **killing the Vietnamese**: Burgess made repeated references to the Vietnam War in his public utterances and nonfiction writings such as his open letter of 1972 to 'My Dear Students', *New York Times* (19 November 1972, Section SM, p. 20); in an interview, given the following spring to Charles T. Bunting for the journal *Studies in the Novel* ('An Interview in New York with Anthony Burgess', 5:4 (1973), pp. 504–29, p. 519); and in *You've Had Your Time* (p. 271). Also, Burgess was one of eleven writers who signed a public letter protesting against the US intervention in Vietnam. See 'American Policies in Vietnam' (*The Times*, 2 February 1967, p. 13). See Appendix 2.

53   **ping pong**: a reference to America's foreign-policy initiative known as ping-pong diplomacy, which led to the thawing of relations between the USA and Communist China, following the exchange of table-tennis players between the two countries in the early 1970s.

54   *Wir sind ein wenig frei*: This is a misquoted and rather broadly interpreted quotation from Act 3, Scene 2 of Wagner's opera *Die Meistersinger von Nürnberg*, where Hans Sachs instructs his disciple Walther how to sing properly to avoid giving offence to the elderly in the audience.

These are Sach's exact words: 'Nur mit der Melodei / seid Ihr ein wenig frei' (Only with the melody / are you a little free). The misquotation replacing 'seid Ihr' with 'Wir sind' turns up again in Burgess's later novel *Earthly Powers*, where it is given to a Sister Gertrude (p. 450), whose name happens to be identical with that of the saint mentioned by Hopkins in 'The Wreck of the Deutschland' and with the tall and attractive nun in the film of the same title in *The Clockwork Testament*.

56   **Lancashire**: the county in England which contained Burgess's native city Manchester until the county borders were redrawn in 1974.

57   **From life's dawn ... the same**: quoted from stanza 20 of 'The Wreck of the Deutschland'.

57   **the gnarls of the nails ... lovescape crucified**: quoted from stanza 23 of 'The Wreck of the Deutschland'.

57   **The Bible's a lot of blood-thirsty balderdash**: This chimes in with Burgess's repeatedly made observations about the violent scenes in the Bible on account of which the 'Good Book' might as well be banned – an obvious absurdity meant to illustrate, in his article 'What Is Pornography' and his lecture *Obscenity and the Arts*, how untenable the arguments supporting censorship are. In a talk-show programme he praised Kubrick's adaptation of *A Clockwork Orange* for demonstrating how 'giving the old tolchock to the body of Christ – hammer and the nails' is all that the Bible means to Alex. (See 'Sound on Film: What's it going to be then, eh? A look at Stanley Kubrick's *A Clockwork Orange*', transcript, Brooklyn, USA: Ervin Frankel Productions, 1972, p. 3). With such views, Burgess was certainly not alone among English Catholic writers either. 'The old Book's full of a lot of grand fierce old notions they don't grow nowadays; sort of wisdom of the Stone Age and buried under the Pyramid', says Father Brown, Chesterton's mouthpiece in 'The Arrow of Heaven' (G.K. Chesterton, *The Father Brown Stories*, London: Cassell, 1974, p. 344). 'In some of the Psalms the

spirit of hatred which strikes us in the face is like the heat
from a furnace mouth' begins the chapter on 'The Curses' in
C.S. Lewis's *Reflections on the Psalms* (New York: Harcourt
Brace, 1986, p. 20).

58   **cheeseparing nose**: a miserly, worthless nose. The phrase is
quoted from the 'Lotus Eaters' episode of Joyce's *Ulysses*
(5.183, Gabler, p. 62). A bemused Leopold Bloom makes a
mental comparison of an acquaintance's wife, Fanny M'Coy,
and his own spouse, Molly Bloom, of whom Mrs M'Coy is
no more to him than a poor copy: 'her reedy soprano' may
be 'nice enough in its way: for a little ballad' but has 'no guts
in it'. Fanny emerges from Poldy and Molly Bloom's interior monologues as an example of how ambitious women
of Molly's age and class could fail, in the Dublin of the
1900s, to 'find an alternative to managing domestic affairs'
(A. Nicholas Frangoli and Michael P. Gillespie, *James Joyce
A to Z*, Oxford and New York: Oxford University Press,
1995, p. 147).

59   **Blake sylph**: William Blake's poetry and graphic art are
populated by every kind of supernatural creature – mainly
fairies – but not sylphs. Blake's painting *Urizen in Fetters,
Tears Streaming from His Eyes* comes closest to Enderby's
visualisation of the human condition here.

59   **stolen apples**: a reference to Augustine stealing fruit as a
young man. The story of how he had stolen pears (rather than
apples) is recounted by Augustine himself (*The Confessions
of Saint Augustine*, II iii (8)).

60   **sour apple**: The reference here is made to the forbidden
fruit, eating of which condemned Adam and Eve, and with
them all their descendants, meaning humanity at large, to
the Fall from divine grace. Identifying the forbidden fruit,
left unspecified in the Bible (see Genesis 3:3), is a popular
misconception traceable to Milton's *Paradise Lost* (IX.585,
X.487), but even further back to St Jerome's Latin translation of the Bible known as the Vulgate where the word
malum could mean both 'apple' and 'evil'.

60   **Augustine blushed**: The saintly bishop's embarrassment is caused by his fellow-cleric unwittingly reminding him of his youthful sin of stealing, for the fun of it, fruit from a neighbouring orchard.

60   **benison**: 'that blessing which God gives' (*OED*).

61   **chuck-steak**: otherwise known as a seven-inch bone steak.

61   **Lea and Perrin's**: properly Lea and Perrins, a brand name referring to a British company best known for its Worcestershire sauce, a popular condiment in Britain and elsewhere.

61   **Mensch or Munch**: The German word 'Mensch', sounding almost like the English verb 'munch', means man or human being. Burgess's lasting preoccupation with the idea of 'civilized' cannibalism is documented by his returning to the issue on several occasions. In the 'Epilogue' to his 1978 novel *1985*, he 'prophesises' that in a badly overpopulated and underfed England of the future 'the processed human flesh [will be] sold in supermarkets and [will be] called Munch or Mensch or something' (London: Arrow Books, 1980, p. 230). Commercialised anthropophagia is returned to in a 1982 'Foreword' added to his 1962 dystopia *The Wanting Seed*, where he speculates that 'one day we will find cans of meat in our markets called Mench [*sic*] or Munch, human flesh seasoned with sodium nitrate' (Feltham: Hamlyn, 1983, n.p.). Burgess's avowed inspiration was the 1972 air crash in the Andes, whose survivors kept themselves alive by feeding on dried strips of meat obtained from the bodies of their dead fellow-passengers. However, his intimate familiarity with Joyce's *Ulysses* and the recurrent motif of cannibalism in it may also be behind his near-obsession with the theme. (See, e.g., the chapter 'Hell, Wind, Cannibals' in his *Here Comes Everybody: An Introduction to James Joyce for the Ordinary Reader*).

61   **clavicle**: collarbone.

61   **dysfunctioning of the olfactory system**: Evidence-based medical research has in fact linked olfactory dysfunction,

meaning the faulty detection of smells, to cardiovascular disease in middle-aged and older adults. Burgess associates olfactory hallucinations with neurological disorders in *Little Wilson and Big God*, too (London: Heinemann, 1987), p. 445.

62 **his only own poem**: Rawcliffe, the rival poet, published one single poem not plagiarised from others, but this one appeared 'in all the anthologies'. The poem, rather traditional in form and content, recounts how the poet, jilted by his coy mistress, turns his disappointment into anger, which he decides to vent on his country's enemies hoping that 'Slaughter will wreak a red relief'. Joseph Kell [i.e., Anthony Burgess], *Inside Mr Enderby* (London: Heinemann, 1963, p. 78).

62 **salts drained into alien soil**: quotation from Rawcliffe's poem 'in all the anthologies'.

62 *Aere perennius*: The Latin quotation comes from the opening line of the final poem in Horace's third book of *Odes*. The line 'Exegi monumentum aere perennius' is rendered into English as 'I have crafted a monument more lasting than bronze.' Enderby's meaning is that a poem can outlast any human-made structure, but only if it achieves the formal perfection of classical standards.

62 **swordstick**: As testified by 'The Sword', Burgess's narrative poem of autobiographical content, the writer carried a swordstick while in New York for a conference on literary translation in the spring of 1966. The steel-blade-reinforced cane is described in the poem as 'A third leg, a British sword sheathed in cherrywood / For passive support, no tool or weapon' (*Transatlantic Review*, no. 23 (Winter 1966–67), pp. 41–3; p. 41). The walking aid meant to support Burgess dragging his sclerosis-afflicted leg was only once brandished in self-defence. This happened on Twelfth Street in Brooklyn, where his 'would-be assassins were white and feeble with drugs'. There was no need, he stated, for self-protection in Harlem (*You've Had Your Time*, p. 276).

63   **lilies that fester**: quoted from Shakespeare's sonnet 94. The closing line of the poem reads: 'Lilies that fester smell far worse than weeds.' While the biographical background of the sonnet relates to the poet's special relationship with his patron and – possibly – love, the Fair Youth, a more general interpretation can read into it an admonition to persons in a position of power or authority to lead an ethical life, as corruption of the best can harm the most. For Enderby, the 'best' should be the professors and students of a university.

63   **petromusicology**: a word of Burgess's coinage meaning 'the study of rock music'. The sesquipedalian Latinism pokes fun at the pseudo-scholarly jargon used to lend academic respectability to what Burgess saw as fashionable nonsense.

63   **sociology**: Seen by many as the chief scholarly guarantor of social progress, this branch of the social sciences was a *bête noire* for a number of writers and intellectuals with a stake in preserving the traditional values of the arts and sciences, such as Kingsley Amis or Malcolm Bradbury – and Burgess himself. In an interview he gave to G. Riemer in 1971, he said that the British educational policy of the period was motivated by a 'mechanistic and materialistic' spirit. Aiming to 'get rid of a lot of Latin, Roman, and Greek literature and get down to political economy and *sociology*', this policy 'kills the richness of life' (*Conversations with Anthony Burgess*, ed. by Earl G. Ingersoll and Mary C. Ingersoll, Jackson: University Press of Mississippi, 2008, p. 38; emphasis added).

63   **The elevator depressed Enderby**: What is called an 'elevator' in America is known as a 'lift' by speakers of British English, for whom an elevator may sound as something meant to raise a person's spirits – to elevate them. Hence, an elevator that depresses is an oxymoron.

63   **British shepherd**: These could be the lines half-remembered by Enderby: 'An intermingling of heavn'n's pomp is

spread / On ground which British Shepherds tread' (William Wordsworth, 'Ode, composed upon an evening of extraordinary splendour and beauty').

64   **ruffs**: a 'frill worn around the neck ... characteristic of Elizabethan and Jacobean costume' (*OED*).

64   **Dekker, Greene, Peele, Nashe**: Elizabethan dramatists: Thomas Dekker (c. 1572–1632), Robert Greene (1558–92), George Peele (1556–96), Thomas Nashe (1567–c. 1601).

64   *The Shoemaker's Holiday, Old Fortunatus, The Honest Whore*: plays by Thomas Dekker.

64   **matrical**: 'of or relating to the womb' (*OED*).

64   **seniorsororal**: of an older sister (not in *OED*).

64   **the rash-smart sloggering brine**: quoted from stanza 19 of 'The Wreck of the Deutschland'. A similar phrase appears in Burgess's *A Vision of Battlements*: 'Over the decks salty knouts of broken sea lunged and sloggered' (Manchester: Manchester University Press, 2017, p. 23).

65   **IRT**: short for Interborough Rapid Transit, a company that formerly operated the underground ('subway') system of New York City.

65   **Tellus**: Earth (Latin).

65   **Troubles the will ... rather**: distorted quotation from Hamlet's grand soliloquy in Act 3 Scene 1. Burgess or Enderby has misremembered 'puzzles' as 'troubles' in 'The undiscover'd country from whose bourn / No traveller returns puzzles the will, / And makes us rather bear those ills we have / Than fly to others that we know not of'.

65   **dogmerds**: facetiously Frenchified way of saying dogturds (*merde* being French for excrement).

65   *The Old Wives' Tale*: George Peele's play of 1595, regarded as a burlesque satirising the excesses of contemporary fairy plays and romances.

65   **fumetto**: cartoon (Italian).

65   **chopcherry chopcherry ripe within**: a half-line from a song in *The Old Wives' Tale*, sung by a maid impatient for her hand to be asked in marriage.

65 **Friars Bacon and Bungay**: from the title of a stage comedy written by Robert Greene between 1588 and 1592.

65 **Brightness-falls-from-the-air**: a fragment quoted from 'A Litany in Time of Plague', a poem from Thomas Nashe's significantly titled play *Summer's Last Will and Testament* (1600). The poem is an elaborate update of the medieval motto *memento mori*. The line quoted here is a recurrent point of reference in Burgess's fiction and non-fiction alike, including his critical studies *Shakespeare* (1970) and *Joysprick* (1973), and the novel fictionalising the life of Christopher Marlowe *A Dead Man in Deptford* (1993). Burgess made his own setting of Nashe's poem for soprano, alto, tenor and bass voices in 1969. From an identification of 'brightness' with Icarus *and* Lucifer in the line quoted, and the interpretation of 'air' both as the life-supporting gaseous substance *and* the demotic mispronunciation of 'hair', often infested at the time by plague-carrying lice, Burgess constructs a kind of spiritual physicality characterising the human condition.

65 **Dekker eating a pancake**: In Thomas Dekker's play *The Shoemaker's Holiday* (1599), a group of apprentices eagerly await the ringing of the pancake bells on Shrove Tuesday when they can gorge themselves on these rich delicacies for the last time before Ash Wednesday, the day marking the beginning of the long period of fasting known as Lent. Enderby is no stranger to the culinary self-indulgence represented with forgiving humour by Dekker in the play.

65 **Anthony Munday**: Elizabethan playwright (1560?–1633), older contemporary and occasional collaborator of Shakespeare.

65 **Plowman ... Deverish**: These and their 'plays' are figments of Enderby's imagination running wild. *Gloriana* is an epithet of Elizabeth I, best known from Edmund Spenser's long allegorical poem *The Faerie Queene* (1596).

65 **desiccated**: misspelt in the first Hart-Davis, MacGibbon edition as 'dessicated'

66   **Kickapoo nation**: Algonquian-speaking Native American and Indigenous Mexican tribes.

66   **Pease Pottage**: the name of a village in West Sussex, England.

67   **Moabite persuasion of crypto-reformed Christianity**: No such religious community is known of. Moabites were the subjects of King Moab, ruler of a country often at war with Israel in Old Testament times.

67   **Wyclif**: John Wycliffe (1320–84) was an English scholastic philosopher whose severe criticism of abuses attributed to the Catholic clergy, of which he was a member, made him a forerunner of Protestantism.

67   **Essex rebellion**: In 1600, Robert Devereux, 2nd Earl of Essex, attempted to raise the populace of London in revolt against the rule of Elizabeth I after he fell out of favour with the Queen mainly in consequence of his failed military campaign in Ireland. The rebellion was suppressed, with Essex captured, tried and beheaded. The event features large in Burgess's historical novel *Nothing Like the Sun* (1964) in which Shakespeare himself is marginally involved in the uprising.

67   **Bette Davis**: American actress (1908–89) who played the part of Queen Elizabeth I in the historical romance *The Private Lives of Elizabeth and Essex*, a popular Hollywood film made in 1939.

68   **King Robert the First:** No monarch of that name ever reigned over England; the student probably recounts his garbled recollections of historical rumours concerning the romantic affair between Queen Elizabeth I and her confidant and secret suitor Robert Dudley, the 1st Earl of Leicester (1532–88).

68   **Are you trying to take the –:** Enderby probably stops short of saying, 'Are you trying to take the piss', meaning that the student is trying 'to make something up, to say something ludicrous, to make grand claims, to joke' (Green, *Chambers Slang Dictionary*).

68   **chop**: the stamp of a library, signifying ownership of a book or manuscript.

69   **be for the chop**: be about to be killed or executed (figuratively); derived from the (slang) expression 'get the chop' of the same sense (*OED*).

68   **howlet**: a dialect word for an owl. 'Owl' is a truncated form of 'howl'.

68   **conies**: plural of 'cony', which is an orthographic variant of 'coney', meaning rabbit (*OED*).

69   **Leicester's Men**: a theatrical company, one of the earliest of its kind, under the legal protection of Robert Dudley, 1st Earl of Leicester, but operating as a commercially independent troupe of actors in the 1570s and 1580s.

69   **Earl of Sussex's Men**: a theatrical company in the Jacobean period noted for their association with Shakespeare.

69   ***Lambert Simnel***: a historical figure (c. 1477 – after 1534) achieving some notoriety as pretender to the throne of England. His attempt, as the figurehead of the Yorkist rebellion of 1487, at seizing the crown was thwarted but he was granted royal pardon due to his young age. The play about his 'history' attributed by Enderby to 'Whitelady' is fictional.

69   **Shrovetide Revels**: an event invented by Enderby, possibly inspired by the early seventeenth-century painting *Shrovetide Revellers* by the Dutch master Frans Hals the Elder, possibly seen by Burgess at the Metropolitan Museum of Art, where the picture is on exhibition.

69   **melanonipponese**: The portmanteau word is Burgess's coinage, combining 'melanoid', meaning dark-skinned, and 'Nipponese', signifying Japanese: a person of African-Japanese descent.

70   **Good den**: good even(ing) (*OED*, obsolete).

70   **quatertrey**: In Thomas Nashe's picaresque novel *The Unfortunate Traveller* (1594) it refers to a gambler's four dice or cards with three spots on each (not in *OED*).

70   **coneycatcher**: coney-catcher, 'a swindler, a cheat, a trickster; a perpetrator of confidence tricks; a deceiver' (*OED*). Now archaic or historical.

70   **prigger**: mid-sixteenth to mid-nineeenth century, dated slang for a thief (Green, *Chambers Slang Dictionary*).

70   **troth**: 'a firm promise, an engagement' (*OED*).

71   **Southern colonel**: Colonel Harland David Sanders (1890–1980) founder and former brand-ambassador of the American fast-food company Kentucky Fried Chicken (KFC). The stylised portrait of his goateed face appears on the company's logo. The title 'Colonel' in his name is not a military rank but an honorary title awarded by the Commonwealth of Kentucky.

71   **Schmalz**: 'Schmaltz' is a slang term of Yiddish origin, meaning animal fat, hence 'anything mawkish, over-emotional, esp. in show business use' (Green, *Chambers Slang Dictionary*).

71   **Chutzpah**: a slang term of Hebrew origin, meaning 'gall, cheek, outrageousness, audacity, bravado, nerve, courage' (Green, *Chambers Slang Dictionary*).

71   **Book of Deuteronomy**: literally 'second law' from Greek *deuteros* + *nomos*: the fifth book of the Jewish Torah and of the Christian Old Testament. Neither Schmaltz nor Chutzpah is a Biblical name – 'schmaltz' is a Yiddish word, not Hebrew.

72   **Zeitgeist**: 'spirit of the age' (German). It is a nineteenth-century concept referring to the body of popular beliefs, ideas and fashions characterising an entire historical epoch. Assistant Professor Zeitgeist is likely an academic subscribing to the trends of the day and as such is reminiscent of Howard Kirk in Malcolm Bradbury's campus novel *The History Man* (1972). This ambitious lecturer in sociology is in the habit of answering the phone in his office with the word 'History', ostensibly identifying his university department but also suggesting that he is the very embodiment of the times - the Zeitgeist. Burgess's assessment of Bradbury's achievement with this novel could be a summary of *The Clockwork Testament* itself: 'It is a disturbing and accurate picture of campus life in the late sixties and early seventies' (*Ninety-Nine Novels*, p. 111).

72 **puss**: slang term for face (Green, *Chambers Slang Dictionary*).

73 **Pip pip old boy**: 'Pip-pip' (or 'toodle pip') is archaic British slang for 'goodbye' (*OED*).

73 **mock-British intonation**: In an interview, the novelist and fellow-visiting professor at CCNY, Joseph Heller, recounted how Burgess's students had 'made fun of his [Burgess's] British accent' as well as 'his enthusiasm for literature' (quoted in Biswell, *The Real Life of Anthony Burgess*, pp. 348–9).

73 **And all that sort of rot, man**: 'rot' is British slang for rubbish, nonsense (Green, *Chambers Slang Dictionary*); 'man', used in the vocative is an Americanism.

73 **You ain't nuttin but shiiiiit**: for an account of how Burgess himself 'received coarse threats ... as well as scatological abuse' on rebuking a group of 'nominal students' who had prevented him from giving a lecture on Shakespeare, see *You've Had Your Time* (p. 175).

73 **sweet sweet sweet O Pan piercing sweet**: A line from Elizabeth Barrett Browning's poem 'A Musical Instrument'. Pan is the half-goat, half-man god of shepherds, rustic music and erotic love in ancient Greek mythology.

74 **equivocally**: this is a malapropism – the reviewer means the opposite of what he manages to say: the word fitting into the context is *un*equivocally, or doubtlessly.

74 **Dylan Thomas and Brendan Behan**: Both of these writer-poets acquired notoriety as excessive drinkers; both came from a Celtic background – Dylan Thomas from Wales, Brendan Behan from Ireland – which must have reinforced the prejudice behind the reviewer's hostile remarks. In his 1980 essay 'The Celtic Sacrifice' Burgess refers to poets of an Irish, Welsh or Scottish background as scapegoats castigated in middle-class Britain and America for their 'disease of poetry ... drunkenness and improvidence', and claiming to have seen himself romantically as 'one of the potential Celtic literary victims' on account of his 'Irish and Scots and Lancashire Catholic genes' (*One Man's Chorus*, p. 174).

74   **the aesthetic perversions of Oscar Wilde**: a reference to Wilde's criminal conviction, in 1895, for 'gross indecency', that is, 'the love that dare not speak its name'; with the disparaging remark the reviewer adds homophobia to bigotry. For Burgess on Wilde, see 'Wilde with All Regret', reprinted in *The Ink Trade* (Manchester: Carcanet, 2018), pp. 185–8.

74   **Jolly Old**: short for Jolly Old England, a phrase mostly used by an English person in playfully affectionate reference to his or her homeland. 'Jolly' in this sense: 'Qualifying an adjective or adverb; originally appreciatively, then ironically, with intensive force: Extremely, very. Now colloquial' (*OED*). The American speaker intends this as a sarcastic insult.

74   **escalier**: stairs, staircase (French). This could be a reference to the diagram of vowels, resembling an open-design staircase or ladder, which appears in textbooks of phonetics. See Burgess, *Language Made Plain*, second edition (London: Fontana, 1975), p. 53.

75   **Warhall**: a playfully distorted version of Andy Warhol (1928–87). One of Warhol's best-known works is his 32-piece set of paintings titled *Campbell's Soup Cans* (1962), each a visually faithful representation of another variety of canned soup sold by the company at the time. In 1965 Warhol and his associates shot *Vinyl*, a pirate film loosely based on Burgess's *A Clockwork Orange*. Burgess's obituary of Warhol, part of the uncatalogued journalism collection at IABF, does not mention his adaptation of *A Clockwork Orange*. It is likely that Burgess was unaware of it.

76   **thinking of Ford**: Enderby keeps getting Ms Tietjens's first name wrong because he has in mind Ford Madox Ford's unpleasant character who is called, in the novel *Parade's End*, Sylvia Tietjens.

76   **The poetry is in the pity**: This is quoted from an unfinished preface to a book of poems by Wilfred Owen (1893–1918). Although the preface emphasises content over form, which conflicts with the strictly formalist aesthetic promoted by

Enderby, the quotation fits the context on account of its enunciation of a peaceful and empathic attitude to the victims of war. A biographical detail relating Owen to Burgess is the fact that Owen served in the Manchester Regiment, a military unit formerly stationed in Burgess's native city.

76   **Wilfred**: Misspelt as Wilfrid in Burgess's typescript, Owen's first name appears in its correct form in this volume.

76   **Poetry is made out of words**: This is a variation on the frequently cited words of Stéphane Mallarmé, supposedly spoken to Edgar Degas in response to his painter friend's complaint that he, Degas, couldn't manage to say what he wanted, even though he was full of ideas. 'One does not make poetry with ideas,' went the friendly warning, 'but with words' (quoted in Paul Valéry and Denise Folliot, *The Art of Poetry: The Collected Works of Paul Valéry*, volume 7, edited by Jackson Mathews. Princeton, NJ: Princeton University Press, 1985, p. 63).

77   **whitey**: These provocative ethnic slurs are enumerated by Enderby to suggest how offensive the uninhibited expression of violently anti-white sentiments voiced in Utterage's poem can be felt by the addressee of the student poet's verses.

77   **Catullan**: of or pertaining to the Roman poet Gaius Valerius Catullus (84–54 BCE), noted for focusing in his poems on domestic, not least sexual matters rather than the exploits of epic or mythical heroes and heroines. For Burgess's translations of Catullus, see *Collected Poems*, ed. by Jonathan Mann (Manchester: Carcanet, 2020), pp. 353–4.

77   **old top**: 'a general form of address to a man or woman one knows' (Green, *Chambers Slang Dictionary*).

78   **Prosodic analysis**: a method of prosodic phonology, an approach to the study of the meaningful sound patterns of language in which 'elements are not confined to the narrow segments of the phoneme but might extend beyond these segments to parts of the syllable, the syllable, the word or even a "longer piece"' (Frank R. Palmer, 'Introduction', pp. 1–16, *Selected Papers of J.R. Firth, 1952–59*, London: Longmans,

1968, p. 31). The object of such an analysis is the relationship that obtains between one phonemic unit and another
in a sequence such as the objectionable phrase quoted by
Enderby. Worked out by John Rupert Firth, graduate of the
University of Leeds, education officer in India and finally
the chair of Britain's first department of general linguistics
at the University of London, the system did 'not develop
further after Firth's death in 1960' (*The Concise Oxford
Dictionary of Linguistics*, Oxford: Oxford University Press,
1997, 2007, p. 325), which may be one reason why Enderby's
students have not heard of it.

78   **melanoids**: This nominal form is not listed in *OED*, but is
apparently based on the noun *melanin*, which is defined as a
substance that 'protects the skin from ultraviolet radiation,
and an increase in melanin is responsible for the tanning of
human skin exposed to sunlight' (*OED*). Enderby's use of
such a quasi-medical term to mean 'black' can be seen as a
case of pedantic scholarship masking his indignation or even
malicious intent. It is important that the thinly disguised
racism of the remark should not be attributed to Burgess
himself, who repeatedly and emphatically denounced any
form of racial prejudice; his wholly sympathetic attitude to
'persons of colour' is expressed, among other things, through
the use of a most articulate and intelligent black student as
the narrator of his experimental novel *MF* and the central
role played by the African-American actress April Elgar in
Enderby's Dark Lady, the novel's eponym and most likeable
character.

79   **Sigmund Freud**: The apocryphal story of a young
Freud snubbed by the conservative members of the
Viennese Society of Physicians for 'introducing' the concept
of male hysteria finds its way into Burgess's later novel *The
End of the World News* (London: Hutchinson, 1982). In
this fictional biography a Dr Gauss reminds Freud, amidst
a chorus of vulgar shouts from the audience, that 'hysteria
is a female condition', 'hystera' being 'the Greek word for

the womb' (p. 34). Such an account of the event is based on hearsay evidence dismissed as 'legendary' by the leading historian of psychotherapy Henri Ellenberger, who painstakingly demonstrates in *The Discovery of the Unconscious* (1970) how Freud was treated with professional courtesy at the 5 October 1886 meeting of the Society (London: Fontana, 1990, pp. 436–42). The learned members of this medical association had long recognised the existence of 'male hysteria', only venturing to question the originality of Freud's assertions (based on the findings of the French neurologist Jean-Martin Charcot rather than his own clinical research) and the applicability of the term to what Freud's colleagues preferred to classify as 'traumatic neurosis'. Freud later dropped the idea of male hysteria altogether, and reverted to the conventional dogma of the exclusively female incidence of the condition in *Studies on Hysteria* (1895) co-authored with Josef Breuer, a physician playing a walk-on part in *The End of the World News* as the youngish Freud's mentor.

79   **viking**: in Burgess's typescript the word is spelt with a lower-case initial 'v', possibly meant to suggest Enderby's prejudiced opinion of the student and his background.

80   **binocularly**: with two eyes.

80   **monostomatic**: one-mouthed.

81   **The people who write poems**: Burgess expressed the same ideas in an open letter addressed to 'My Dear Students', published in the *New York Times* on 19 November 1972, during his tenure at the City College of New York, used as the model of the fictional University of Manhattan in *The Clockwork Testament*. He had this to say of the matter: 'the banner-waving students who hold protest meetings are merely indulged. They will, regrettably perhaps, never rule America; America will be controlled by the hard-eyed technicians who have no time for protest.'

82   **Queen and huntress ... bright**: quoted from Ben Jonson's satirical play *Cynthia's Revels* (1600).

83   **vowel-lengthening**: Anatole Broyard, a literary critic of African-American descent, associated with the Beat generation of writers, reviewed *The Clockwork Testament* in the *New York Times*. He accorded some grudging recognition to Burgess's acute ear for black dialect – 'with much African vowel-lengthening'. However, the reviewer sorely resented the author of *The Clockwork Testament* apparently being 'very cavalier in allowing Enderby to make sport of certain "sensitive" aspects of contemporary American life'. See Broyard, 'Poetry Can Kill a Man', *New York Times*, 1 February 1975, p. 25.

83   **silting up of the arteries**: Arteriosclerosis was a condition Burgess himself suffered from, which was one reason why he carried a stick, a fact he noted in his autobiography: 'I travelled with a swordstick, not for defence but as an aid to walking' (*You've Had Your Time*, p. 118). The stick was also remarked on by Graham Greene, whom Burgess interviewed at Greene's home in Antibes in 1980. 'That stick makes you look venerable, Anthony', said the older writer to his visitor ('God, Literature, And So Forth: Interview with Anthony Burgess', *Graham Greene: The Last Interview*, pp. 3–16, p. 15).

83   **monkey-pole**: medical slang: 'a horizontal bar suspended above a bed, which a patient may grasp to aid mobility' (*OED*).

84   **ice**: This word is misprinted as *nice* in the first British edition but occurs as *ice* in the typescript; this edition restores the correct original form.

84   **the legalistic ... vice president**: probably Spiro Agnew (1918–96), who served under President Richard Nixon from 1969 to 1973. Agnew had given up his legal practice when entering politics; his defensive moves meant to reject allegations of corruption in his previous office as state governor could possibly be described as 'legalistic'.

84   **thinking not of the morrow**: Jesus instructs his disciples not to take heed of their earthly needs, as they will be taken

care of by their heavenly father: 'take therefore no thought for the morrow' (Matthew 6:34).

84   **Sufficient unto the day**: quoted from the Bible (Matthew 6:34). In Joyce's *Ulysses* this occurs as 'Sufficient for the day is the newspaper thereof' in the 'Aelous' episode (7.726, Gabler p. 114).

84   **dope**: slang term for 'any preparation, mixture or drug that is not specifically named' (Green, *Chambers Slang Dictionary*).

86   **Seedy Edwardian**: The reign of King Edward VII from 1901 to 1910 is remembered despite certain underlying social tensions, as the last era of undisturbed peace and opulence in the 'Land of Hope and Glory' – the title of a British patriotic song composed by Edward Elgar in 1901, the first year of Edward's reign. Describing Enderby's belated Edwardian elegance as 'seedy' is an ironic comment on the anachronism of his Edwardian nostalgias.

86   **Elgar's First Symphony**: Symphony in A flat major was composed by Edward Elgar (1857–1934), and was first performed by the Hallé Orchestra in Burgess's native Manchester to resounding success in 1908. According to Burgess, who said he had learned symphonic structure from Elgar (see *Little Wilson and Big God*, p. 158), this symphony 'summed up the era', its 'massive soaring melodies' providing 'images of imperial grandeur'. He added that while presenting 'civic order' and 'imperial élan', Elgar had a sense of humour and was aware of all 'the qualifying doubts' (*One Man's Chorus*, pp. 214, 216).

86   **Massive Hope for the Future**: In a comment on his Symphony No. 1 in A Flat, Elgar wrote: 'There is no programme above a wide experience of human life with a great love and a massive hope in the future' (quoted in *Music and Theology in Nineteenth-Century Britain*, ed. by Martin V. Clarke, London and New York: Routledge, 2012, p. 202).

86   **Ichabod**: the son of Phinehas (1 Samuel 4:19–21; 14:3). His name means 'no glory' in Hebrew, and fittingly so as he was given birth prematurely when his mother learned that the ark

of the covenant had been captured by the Philistines and that both her husband and father-in-law were dead. Here its use refers to the waning of British imperial glory.

86   **rutilant**: 'glowing, shining, gleaming, glittering, with either a reddish or golden light' (*OED*).

86   *pax alucinatoria*: a phrase patterned on *Pax Romana* or *Pax Americana*, meaning 'the peace of hallucination' (Latin).

86   **the Algonquin Hotel**: a luxury hotel near Times Square in Manhattan. Warner Brothers reserved a room there for Burgess during his American tour in January 1972, while he was promoting the film *A Clockwork Orange*. In his autobiography, he described the Algonquin as an establishment that 'remains a literary hotel' (*You've Had Your Time*, p. 252).

87   **Gucci**: a fashion house based in Florence, Italy, founded by Guccio Gucci in 1921. The brand name suggests trendiness and opulence.

87   **Maynooth**: a university town in County Kildare, Ireland. It is here that St Patrick's College, Ireland's only Catholic Seminary, is located. Priests trained there once had a reputation of a down-to-earth simplicity, and willingness to mix socially and engage in athletic activities, which endeared them to their rural and small-town parishioners.

88   **Every inch a tar ... sailors are**: quoted from 'The Loss of the Eurydice', Hopkins's second narrative poem on the loss of a shipwrecked vessel. 'Tar' is an old-fashioned slang term meaning 'sailor' (Green, *Chambers Slang Dictionary*).

88   **Hard as ... goldish flue**: quoted from the first line of Hopkins's sonnet 'Harry Ploughman'. That the line was particularly memorable for Burgess is borne out by a reference in the second volume of his autobiography where he recalls how his professor at the Victoria University of Manchester attempted to disconcert him 'with questions like "What is the meaning of 'a broth of goldfish flue' in this poem?"' As usual, Burgess 'could give the right answer' (*Little Wilson and Big God*, pp. 176–7).

88   **Cowley**: a residential and industrial area in Oxford. Along with his other pastoral duties in Oxford, Hopkins had to serve the barracks there in 1878–79.

88   **Can Dix**: a familiar shortening of the fictional Cannon Dickson show.

89   **Born, he tells me... how things will**: lines quoted from Hopkins's poem 'The Bugler's First Communion'.

89   **now well work … quickenings lift**: quoted from Hopkins's poem 'The Bugler's First Communion'.

90   **trouble-and-strife**: Cockney rhyming slang for 'wife' (Green, *Chambers Slang Dictionary*). Its use is a playful allusion to Enderby's Britishness.

90   **A cap of Rosy Lee**: a cup of tea – 'Rosy Lee' or 'Rosie Lea' being Cockney (originally military) slang for 'tea' (Green, *Chambers Slang Dictionary*).

90   **dahn wiv yer rahnd the ahzes**: Cockney rhyming slang for 'down with your trousers' – 'round the houses' or 'round me houses' being slang for 'trousers' (see Green, *Chambers Slang Dictionary*).

90   **ovine**: 'resembling or reminiscent of (a) sheep in appearance, behaviour, etc.' (*OED*).

90   **gill**: a measure of capacity for liquids: 'in Britain, 5 imperial fluid ounces, approx. 0.142 litre; in the United States, 4 US fluid ounces, approx. 0.118 litre' (*OED*).

90   **Though this child's drift … Disaster there**: lines quoted from Hopkins's 'The Bugler's first Communion'.

90   **Low-latched in leaf-light housel … godhead**: a line quoted from Hopkins's 'The Bugler's First Communion'; 'housel' are the consecrated elements of the Eucharist (here = the wafer). See notes to *Poems of Gerard Manley Hopkins*, fourth edition, ed. by W.H. Gardner and N.H. Mackenzie, New York and Toronto: Oxford University Press, 1967, p. 276).

90   **I am gall … have me taste**: a line quoted from the poem 'I wake and feel the fell of dark, not day', one of Hopkins's late 'terrible sonnets', testifying to his darkening mood.

90   **Violence itself is not bad**: In 1973, Burgess wrote a short essay on 'The Nature of Violence' in pursuance of a contract between himself and the Research Foundation of the City University of New York (reprinted as Appendix 5). He expressed views concerning violence similar to those voiced by Enderby here.

92   *TRANSCRIPT*: This is a burlesque of the error-ridden specimens of the genre recorded in a hurry by some of the assistants working for the various television and radio stations where Burgess was invited to discuss issues of popular interest in America and Britain – at the time, mainly the controversial reception of Stanley Kubrick's film adaptation of *A Clockwork Orange*. This compendium of hilariously misunderstood, misspelt or otherwise incomprehensible vocables, reminiscent of D.J. Enright's satirical poem 'The Typewriter Revolution' of 1971 (specimen lines: 'The typeriter is crating / A revlootion in peotry / Pishing back the frontears'), was dismissed by a number of critics as an unlikely exaggeration but was greeted with gleeful joy as something 'marvellously funny' by others. While some of the mistakes may in fact be unlikely to have been made by a professional transcriber of whatever educational background, the presence of some perfectly plausible howlers occurring in similar typescripts is documented by the existence of at least one extant transcription of Burgess's participation in an American talk show' (*'What's it Going to be then, eh' – Sound on Film, Radio Program 17: Transcript*. Brooklyn: Erwin Frankel Productions, 1972).

93   **tail of two cities**: a *double entendre* exploiting the dual meaning of the homophony of *tale* v. *tail*, where the apparent but here irrelevant referent of the phrase is Charles Dickens's historical novel *A Tale of Two Cities*, while the intended significance is 'the whores of two cities', *tail* being a long-established slang term for 'vagina' (Green, *Chambers Slang Dictionary*).

93   **A wise child knows his own**: The proverb 'It is a wise child that knows his own father' is one that occurs in such *loci classici* as Samuel Butler's translation of Homer's *Odyssey*

or James Joyce's *Ulysses* – both works very well known to Burgess but obviously unfamiliar to the transcriber. Burgess's friend Angela Carter later redeployed the cliché in the title of her Shakespearean novel, *Wise Children*, published in 1991.

93   **Cluding**: including.

94   **wheres it got (?) you**: 'where's (where has) it got you' – the source of the misunderstanding here is the different past participle form of the verb 'get' in British and American English: *got* vs *gotten*.

94   **baggers**: 'buggers' – the abusive British term 'bugger' for 'man' must be unfamiliar to the American transcriber, who tries to give, in the manner of folk etymologies, some sense – however inappropriate it may be – to the incomprehensible word. This could also be a reference to *The Carpetbaggers* (1961), a popular novel by Harold Robbins.

94   **term in**: determined.

94   **irreverences**: irrelevances.

94   **priesty nation**: predestination – a concept central, in Burgess's understanding, to Protestantism, to which he opposes the emphasis on freedom of choice in his understanding of Catholic theology.

94   **American plagiarism**: 'American Pelagianism' – the unconditional and excessive belief, supposedly characteristic of the American outlook on life, in the power and sacredness of the individual's freedom of choice related, according to Enderby, to the Pelagian heresy.

95   **monkey**: monk.

95   **Plage us**: Pelagius.

95   **national pensity**: rational (?) propensity.

95   **Errorsy**: heresy. Heretical thinking being an error in the theological sense of the word, this misunderstanding does not go very wide of the mark – it could be a Hopkinsian or Joycean nonce-word.

95   **violets**: violence. This could be regarded as a significant, 'poetic', misunderstanding as Enderby and Burgess himself relate 'violent' to 'violets'.

95   *POMP CIRCUS DANCE*: *Pomp and Circumstance* –
a series of military marches composed by Sir Edward
Elgar (op. 39) associated with British imperial glory and
arrogance – mistakenly, as Burgess argues in his essay 'Elgar
non è volgare', pointing out that 'the title is ironic', as it
comes from *Othello*, where the play's desperate eponym
speaks these bitter words: 'Farewell, the *pomp and circumstance* of glorious war' (*One Man's Chorus*, p. 215; editor's
emphasis).

95   **The Human Engine Waits**: The title of this fictional book
is quoted from the 'Fire Sermon' of *The Waste Land* by T.S.
Eliot, where it appears in a rather different context and not
as a title. Compared to a 'taxi throbbing waiting', the human
mind and body at the end of a working day have been turned
into something of a lifeless mechanism. See Eliot, *Collected
Poems 1909–1962* (London: Faber, 1974), l. 217.

95   **Man Balaglas**: This exotic-looking name is convincingly
'domesticated' by Geoffrey Aggeler, who reads 'ball of glass'
into it – the crystal ball, that is, into which the psychologist
peers to explore the mechanisms of human behaviour. This
is the method of the 'scientific gazer' who, like the arch-
behaviourist B.F. Skinner, of whom Professor Balaglas is a
caricature, plucks out 'the mystery and mechanism' of the
human individual (Aggeler, *Anthony Burgess*, p. 96).

95   **ecommunionicle**: ecumenical.

95   **laminate**: eliminate.

96   **rain forcemeat**: reinforcement – a key concept of behaviourist psychology

96   **killed (kwelled?)**: probably the latter but correctly spelled as
'quelled', meaning 'subdued'.

96   **simple (sinful?)**: probably the latter.

96   **filament**: element.

96   **ethnical**: ethical.

96   **Stands to region**: stands to reason

96   **inhabited**: uninhibited.

96   **irreverent**: irrelevant.

97   **locomotion**: locution, meaning a word or phrase of a par-
      ticular style.

97   **monsters**: monstrous.

97   **ahss**: arse (UK), ass (US). The British pronunciation of
      the word rhyming with *farce* pronounced with a mute 'r'
      may sound incomprehensible to the uninformed speaker of
      American English. Such transatlantic confusion of tongues
      is cited by Burgess as the reason why '*Each Actor on his Ass*,
      straight from *Hamlet* and suggested by [him] as the title of
      a projected Broadway musical, was rejected with horror'
      (*A Mouthful of Air: Language and Languages, Especially
      English*, London: Hutchinson, 1992, p. 223).

97   **ethnics**: ethics.

98   **Inversnaid**: There is no township of such a name in New
      York State; there is, however, a poem written by Hopkins
      named after the village on the east bank of Loch Lomond in
      Scotland.

98   **Oliviers movie of Hamlet**: Balaglas is referring here to
      the 1948 British film adaptation of Shakespeare's *Hamlet*,
      directed by Laurence Olivier, who also took the leading role.
      In his autobiography, Burgess uses Shakespeare as an obvious
      example to illustrate the absurdity of blaming real-life evil on
      imaginative literature 'A man who kills his uncle cannot jus-
      tifiably blame a performance of *Hamlet*' (*You've Had Your
      Time*, p. 257). For Burgess on Laurence Olivier, see his obit-
      uary essay reprinted in *One Man's Chorus* (pp. 328–32).

98   **violentment**: environment.

98   **teetotal Aryan**: totalitarian.

99   **actionary**: reactionary.

99   **Alice in Windowland**: *Alice in Wonderland*.

99   **Leaden Echo … Manshape**: Each of these fictitious film
      titles is an allusion to one poem by G.M. Hopkins or
      another. These are 'The Leaden Echo and the Golden Echo',
      'To What Serves Mortal Beauty', 'Tom's Garland' (contain-
      ing the word 'rockfire') and 'That Nature Is a Heraclitean
      Fire and of the Comfort of the Resurrection' (containing

the word 'manshape'). There's an ironic contrast between the ageing starlet's commercial charms and the sublime but demanding beauty of Hopkins's poetry.

99   **Ermine**: the emphatically feminine starlet's given name can be a tongue-in-cheek allusion to Leonardo da Vinci's celebrated painting *Lady with an Ermine* (c. 1489–91). Also known as the stoat, the mustelid ermine was regarded, at the time Leonardo painted the portrait of his client's mistress, as a symbol of purity and moderation, qualities not readily associated with the starlet Ermine Elderly.

99   **take the (*unintell* piece? pass?)**: take the piss.

100   **Gerald Mann Leigh**: Gerard Manley [Hopkins].

100   **aureate**: 'golden, gold-coloured' (*OED*).

101   **Rhymes ... in sleep-teaching**: an allusion to Aldous Huxley's dystopian novel *Brave New World* (1932) where simple rhymes of an 'educational' content played over loudspeakers in children's dormitories are used as a means of behavioural conditioning.

101   *frisson*: 'a thrill' (French).

101   *oeillade*: 'a wink' (French).

101   **The Hesperus**: 'The Wreck of the Hesperus' (1842) is a narrative poem of Henry Wadsworth Longfellow, recounting how a captain's hubris cost him his own and his young daughter's lives in an avoidable shipwreck on a rock reef off the coasts of Massachusetts. This poem has inspired two feature films of the same title – unlike 'The Wreck of the Deutschland', which is adapted to the screen only in Burgess's novel.

102   **oleic**: 'fatty' (*OED*).

103   **guy on his yacht**: an allusion to the character Dan Cody in F. Scott Fitzgerald's novel *The Great Gatsby*. It is from Cody, while serving on the millionaire's yacht, that a young Gatsby learns how to get rich quick.

103   **Those boys with guitars**: Starting with the frantic transatlantic reception of the music played by the Tornados and such solo instrumentalists and singers as Acker Bilk and Cliff

Richard, the 'British Invasion' of America peaked with the phenomenal success in the United States of the Beatles and the Rolling Stones, to whom the remark probably alludes. Burgess's unflattering opinion of the 'Fab Four' is documented by the satirical portraiture of the band as 'The Cruzy Fixers' in the novel *Enderby Outside* (1968).

103   **Bankside**: an area of London south of the river Thames where the theatrical life of Shakespeare's time was concentrated. The remark seems to be a playfully complimentary reference to the ideals of virility associated with the Elizabethan era but is taken by the audience, probably correctly, as a double entendre suggesting some homosexual tendencies easily associated with the word 'backside'.

103   **homunculus**: 'little man, little person' formed from the Latin root noun *homo* and the diminutive suffix *-culus*. Originally it denoted the figure of a small humanoid a little above a span in height (c. 12 inches or 30 centimetres), created by means of alchemy associated with Paracelsus (c. 1493–1541). Although featuring large in two of Lawrence Durrell's novels, *Clea* and *Nunquam*, the first introduced in Burgess's *Ninety-Nine Novels*, the second reviewed in a magazine article of 1970 by Burgess, it is not so much the homunculus of alchemy that is meant by Man Balaglas here. His meaning has more to do with the 'Cartesian theatre' where an imaginary midget – or homunculus – is seated in the auditorium of the brain to do our visual perception for us. It is remnants of this theory that the influential proponent of behaviourist psychology B.F. Skinner and Professor Balaglas modelled on the former propose to eliminate.

103   **Man *qua* man ... freedom and dignity**: The passage is a verbatim quotation from Skinner's book *Beyond Freedom and Dignity* (New York: Knopf, 1971, p. 200). First published in 1971, the same year as the film adaptation of *A Clockwork Orange* was released, Skinner's programmatic work promoted the idea of abandoning the concept of the 'inner man' and dispensing with such supposedly debilitating ideas as

freedom and dignity. In this argument, purely empirical psychology – 'behaviour technology' – should be allowed to rid society of the ills attendant on modern existence, such as violent crime, antisocial behaviour, overpopulation, environmental pollution, or war itself. Burgess violently opposed what he believed to be Skinner's devoutly wished-for 'death of [the] autonomous man', concluding that 'in terms of the Judaeo-Christian ethic ... he is perpetrating a gross heresy', in fact 'the sin against the Holy Ghost' (quoted in Biswell, *The Real Life of Anthony Burgess*, pp. 360–1).

103   **Man as Thou not It**': Balaglas-Skinner here challenges Martin Buber's opposition of the *Ich-Du* ('I-Thou') type of intersubjective encounter to the *Ich-Es* ('I-It') nexus, where the former enables, through religion, 'a reciprocal relationship of dialogue between one subject and another', while the latter constitutes 'objective relations between subject and thing' (Simon Blackburn, *Oxford Dictionary of Philosophy*, Oxford University Press, 1966, p. 50), thus dehumanising the Other – turning the latter into a clockwork orange, in Burgess's terms.

104   **His abolition ... the human species**: This is another verbatim quotation from Skinner's *Beyond Freedom and Dignity* (p. 200).

104   **No time for comedy**: the title of a 1940 American comedy-drama film adaptation based on the play of the same name by S.N. Behrman.

105   **For how to the heart's cheering ... Of pied and peeled May!**: These are the first four lines of stanza 26 in 'The Wreck of the Deutschland'.

105   **Blue-beating and hoary-glow height ... hearing?** lines quoted from stanza 26 of *The Wreck of the Deutschland*.

105   **home uncle us**: homunculus.

105   **No, but it was not these ... burden in winds**: an unfinished and somewhat garbled version of stanza 27 in 'The Wreck of the Deutschland'.

106   **half American**: Sir Winston Churchill's mother Jennie Spencer-Churchill (née Jerome) was born and raised in

Brooklyn, New York City, before she became a celebrated British socialite and married Winston's father Lord Randolph Churchill. Winston Churchill was a young man when the American writer and war correspondent Richard Harding wrote with vicarious pride in his book *Real Soldiers of War* that Churchill being 'half an American gives all of us an excuse to pretend we share in his successes' (quoted in Martin Gilbert, *Churchill and America*, New York: Free Press, 2005, p. 52).

106   **fag**: The comedic situation of the barfly and Enderby talking at cross-purposes arises from the two, very different, meanings of the word *fag* in British and American slang. Whereas a British speaker would use the word in reference to a cigarette (originally an inferior one), for an American it means a 'male homosexual' (see Eric Partridge and Paul Beale, *A Dictionary of Slang and Unconventional English*, 8th edition, Abingdon: Routledge, 1984).

106   **lucifer**: old-fashioned London slang for a 'match' (Partridge and Beale, *A Dictionary of Slang*).

106   **While you've a lucifer**: a line from 'Pack Up Your Troubles in Your Old Kit-Bag', a marching song of the First World War, written in 1915 by Felix Powell and George Henry Powell.

107   **pretends**: portends

107   **That's why they call it Queens**: This is dismissed as a common misconception by Burgess, who clarifies the issue in his illustrated non-fiction book *New York*, explaining that the borough Queens was 'established as a county in the 17th century and named in honour of Charles II's wife, Catherine of Braganza' (*New York*, Amsterdam: Time-Life, 1976, pp. 66–7).

107   **flageolet**: 'a small wind instrument, having a mouthpiece at one end, six principal holes, and sometimes keys' (*OED*).

108   *integer vitae*: 'upright life' (Latin). These are the first words used as a title-substitute for Horace's *Odes*, Book 1:22, one of the Roman poet's most often quoted poems, positing

that the man of honourable life free of sin has no need for 'Moorish javelins' or any other protective weaponry.

108   **lisle … tippet … pectoral … wimple**: a hard twisted cotton thread, originally produced at Lisle, France; a garment, usually of fur or wool, covering the shoulders, or the neck and shoulders; a cape or short cloak, often with hanging ends; worn on the breast; a veil (*OED*).

108   **veal-to-the-heel**: originally 'beef to the heel', 'a derisive description of a girl's thick ankles, which run from calf to heel in one sad, straight line' (Partridge, *Dictionary of Slang*).

108   **fasces**: 'a bundle of rods bound up with an axe in the middle and its blade projecting. These rods were carried by lictors before the superior magistrates at Rome as an emblem of their power' (*OED*). The Italian derivation *fascio* meaning 'group, association', related to 'bundle', is the root of the term *fascist*.

109   *Gott Mit Uns*: 'God [is] with us' (German). A military slogan used from the early eighteenth century to the period of the Third Reich in Prussia and Germany.

109   **frotting**: 'frot' means 'to rub' in a sexual context (Green, *Chambers Slang Dictionary*).

109   *E conta o que ele fez com ela e tern fotografia e tudo*: 'And tell him what he did to her and have photography and everything' (Portugese).

109   *Um velho lélé da cuca*: 'An old crazy' (Portugese).

109   *Boa noite*: 'Good night' (Portugese).

109   **deuterocaroline dowry**: the dowry received by Charles II. When King Charles II of England, Scotland and Ireland married Catherine of Braganza, daughter of King John IV of Portugal, in 1662, he acquired, as part of his new wife's dowry, the Seven Islands of Bombay (today Mumbai), which, first rented to the East India Company, became the foundation of Britain's colonial rule of India.

109   **WASP**: acronym of 'White Anglo-Saxon Protestant' – a member of the Caucasian elites descending from

English-speaking ancestors and at least nominally belonging to an established Protestant church.

109   **between Plymouth and Plymouth Rock**: Plymouth is a port city in south-west England, while Plymouth Rock is located on the eastern coastline of Massachusetts, USA. In between the two lies the Atlantic Ocean, which was traversed by the Pilgrim Fathers, who set to sail, in the Mayflower in 1620, from Plymouth to disembark, later the same year, at what was subsequently named Plymouth Rock. That the eyes of the young men boarding the subway train here are Atlantic-Ocean blue is indicative of their presumable descent from the first white colonisers of what became the USA. The apparent WASP-ish pedigree of these mindlessly violent hoodlums spectacularly gives the lie to some of Enderby's ethnic prejudices that came to the surface earlier on.

109   **crinal**: 'of, relating to, or characteristic of the hair' (*OED*).

109   **Gerontal**: of or pertaining to the old, cognate with 'gerontology' or 'gerontocracy'; probably Burgess's coinage (not in *OED*).

110   **LOPEZ 95 MARLOWE 93 BONNY SWEET ROBIN 1601**: All three inscriptions appear to be allusions to events and personages of the Elizabethan period: protagonist of Burgess's novel *A Dead Man in Deptford*, playwright Christopher Marlowe died in 1593; 'Bonny Sweet Robin' is a popular tune of the era, sung in *Hamlet* and again in *Twelfth Night*, both dateable to 1601; and the queen's Portuguese-born physician Roderigo Lopez was executed *almost* in 1595 – in fact, in 1594 as is correctly noted in Burgess's non-fiction book *Shakespeare* (London: Jonathan Cape, 1970), p. 137.

110   **Spot-of-blood ... orchard apple**: Correctly 'drop-of-blood' is a line quoted from Hopkins's poem 'The May Magnificat' celebrating 'Spring's universal bliss' manifesting itself in the beauties of May, the Virgin Mary's month.

110   **And thicket and thorp ... cherry**: two lines quoted from Hopkins's 'The May Magnificat'.

110   **blood like a pelican:** In Christian iconography and heraldry, the pelican often appears as a bird feeding its young with its own blood drawn from its own self-wounded breast.

110   **gladial:** pertaining to swords, from the Latin 'gladius', meaning a short sword.

110   **oxter:** armpit (*OED*). See also 'earwax in my oxters' in Burgess's narrative poem, 'The Sword'.

110   **The human condition:** The phrase could be an allusion to numerous well-known works of the arts, literature and philosophy. These include René Magritte's two paintings of the same title (*La condition humaine*, 1933 and 1935), André Malraux's novel *La condition humaine* of 1933 (translated into English as *Man's Fate*) and Hannah Arendt's *The Human Condition*, first published in 1958. The author's thoughts on how violence is an indispensable part of creative human activity whereby the worker interferes with nature to obtain the result of their work make Arendt's philosophical study the likeliest inspiration behind Burgess's choice of words here and his general ideas about the ethics of violent action in relation to the human condition at large.

110   **No art without aggression:** This is a brief summary of Burgess's own position, formulated at about the time *The Clockwork Testament* was being composed. In his essay 'The Nature of Violence' he says that 'violence has always been taken for granted as a means of establishing new ideas and new art-forms. Even the individual act of artistic creation seems to depend on doing violence to a natural form.'

112   **the whorl ... she endured:** quoted from stanza 14 of 'The Wreck of the Deutschland'.

112   **Some blacks chortled inexplicably:** Enderby's experience replicates Burgess's impressions of the audience response he witnessed when attending, *incognito*, a screening of Kubrick's *A Clockwork Orange* at a New York cinema: 'The violence of the action moved them deeply, especially the blacks, who stood up to shout "Right on, man," but the theology passed over their coiffures' (*You've Had Your Time*, p. 253).

112   **with a rope's end ... brave**: quoted from stanza 16 of 'The Wreck of the Deutschland'.

112   **pitched to his death ... braids of thew**: quoted from stanza 16 of 'The Wreck of the Deutschland'.

112   **night roaring ... rabble**: 'Night roared with the heart-break hearing a heart-broke rabble' in the original, quoted from stanza 17 of 'The Wreck of the Deutschland'.

112   **the woman's wailing ... without check**: quoted from stanza 17 of 'The Wreck of the Deutschland'.

112   **a lioness ... babble**: quoted from stanza 17 of 'The Wreck of the Deutschland'.

112   **double a desperate name**: quoted from stanza 20 of 'The Wreck of the Deutschland'. The term refers, in Hopkins's poem, to Deutschland, the name of the doomed vessel as well as the nation that launched the Reformation and expelled the five Franciscan nuns. This is explained by Bernard Bergonzi, who also draws attention to the significance seen by Hopkins of the fact that both St Gertrude and Martin Luther came from the town of Eisleben in Thuringia (Bergonzi, *Gerard Manley Hopkins*, Basingstoke: Macmillan, 1977, p. 160). In the adaptation based on Enderby's 'idea', the doleful suggestion is threefold, as Nazi Germany looms in the background of the shipwreck scene of the film.

112   **beast of the waste wood**: The full significance of the allusion lies in the completed quote from stanza 20 of 'The Wreck of the Deutschland': 'But Gertrude, lily, and Luther, are two of a town, / Christ's lily and beast of the waste wood'. Luther, as explained by Bergonzi, was regarded by Catholics in the 'preecumenical days' of Hopkins, as 'a wholly malign figure' (Bergonzi, p. 160) – hence the implied comparison with Hitler.

112   **Away in the loveable west ... Wales**: quoted from stanza 24 of 'The Wreck of the Deutschland'.

112   **ESPishly**: in the manner of one possessing the gift of extrasensory perception or ESP.

112   **_Vogelgesang_ in Schwarzwald ... Hitlerjugend**: Ordensburg Vogelsang was a military complex where future leaders

of Nazi Germany, members of the youth organisa-
tion Hitlerjugend, were trained. However, the complex
was located in the federal German state of North Rhine-
Westphalia, not in the Black Forest (Schwartzwald) moun-
tain region, which is in Baden-Württemberg.

113   **At this point**: Possibly regarding the repetition as an authorial oversight in Burgess's typescript, the editors of the Hart-
Davis, McGibbon text deleted the second occurrence of the
phrase 'at this point'. Assuming that the repetition is functional in that it verbally imitates a characteristic symptom of
cardiac arrest Enderby experiences here, this edition restores
the second occurrence of the same adverbial phrase.

113   **the critical acumen of Ben Jonson**: Although a playwright
above all else, Ben Jonson was also a keen critic of his fellow
dramatists' work.

114   **Forsyte or Forsyth**: a deliberate confusion of names sug-
gestive of Enderby's disdain for John Galsworthy's multi-
volume series published under the collective title *The Forsyte
Saga* in 1922, and Frederick Forsyth, writer of best-selling
thrillers. Burgess himself was not averse to the 'lighter'
genres; he had this to say of their practitioners: 'a good deal
of my spare time in the last decade has been beguiled by
the reading of authors like Puzo, Forsyth, Higgins, Kyle,
Ludlum, Hailey and Irving Wallace ... A lot of bestsellers are
"fun books", and God knows we all need a bit of fun in our
lives' (*Homage to Qwert Yuiop*, London: Hutchinson, 1986,
p. 483).

114   **In full fig**: dressed up (Green, *Chambers Slang Dictionary*).

114   **By George**: as a variant of 'by Jove' is an obsolete interjection. Its repetition is probably meant to enhance the comic
effect of the missing-denture routine.

114   **Heinemann Award for Poetry**: The W.H. Heinemann
Award (1945–2003), established in memory of William
Henry Heinemann (1863–1920), the founder of the London-
based publishing house named after him, was given to writers
of prose fiction and non-fiction as well as poets. Although

several books by Burgess were published by Heinemann between 1956 and 1990, the award eluded him, as it did Enderby, who even rejected, under hilarious circumstances, the rather obscure Poetry Prize meant for him by 'a famous firm of chain booksellers' (*Inside Mr Enderby*, p. 36).

114   **Major Grey's chutney**: the brand-name of an Indian-style condiment named after the nineteenth-century British Army officer who supposedly created it.

115   **rich tea**: a type of sweet biscuit popular in Britain, where it is usually consumed between meals.

115   **nutria**: 'the skin or fur of the coypu' (*OED*).

115   **coypu**: 'a South American aquatic rodent (*Myopotamus coypus*), nearly equal to the beaver in size' (*OED*).

116   **chastaigne**: chestnut (French).

116   **Goldengrove College**: a fictional seat of American higher learning, whose name, like his visitor's name, is probably derived from the opening lines of Hopkins's poem 'Spring and Fall': 'Margaret, are you grieving / Over Goldengrove unleaving?' The poem was composed while its writer served the parish of St Francis Xavier Church in Liverpool, of which Golden Grove is a district. 'Spring and Fall' is 'about a child's intimations of mortality' (Robert Bernard Martin, *Gerard Manley Hopkins: A Very Private Life*, New York: Putnam, 1991, pp. 326–7), and, while by no means a child, Enderby himself receives renewed premonitions of dying from his caller, the woman of Goldengrove.

117   **Cinna the poet**: Caius Helvius Cinna (died in 44 BC) was supposedly lynched at the funeral of Julius Caesar by a crowd of mourners mistaking him for his namesake Cornelius Cinna, the politician who had supported the assassins of the murdered Caesar. In *Julius Caesar*, Shakespeare has Cinna point out their mistake to his attackers, announcing that he is 'Cinna the poet'; to this, one of the aggressors responds with the cry: 'Tear him for his bad verses!' (III, iii, 28).

118   **Aye, by Saint Anne ... and ginger shall be hot in the [mouth]**: These are lines spoken by the Clown in

Shakespeare's *Twelfth Night* seconding Sir Toby Belch's retort to the hypocritical house steward Malvolio trying to put an end to Sir Toby and his companions' noisy revels. Sir Toby's words are more obvious and more immediately relevant to the situation at hand than the Clown's: 'Dost thou think, because thou art virtuous, there shall be no more cakes and ale?' (II, iii, 108). The Catholic cult of St Anne, mother of the Virgin Mary, by whom Shakespeare's Clown swears, was anathema to the Puritans represented in the play by Malvolio, and in *The Clockwork Testament* by those who demanded ethical responsibility from art and literature – including Enderby's priggish-looking visitor.

119   **Dust hath closed Helen's eye**: a line from Thomas Nashe's 'Litany in Time of Plague'.

119   *jeu d'esprit*: a French expression literally meaning 'play of the spirit' but commonly used in reference to a light-hearted display of wit in a work of literature. Burgess often referred to his own novel *A Clockwork Orange* as 'a jeu d'esprit'. See, for example, *Flame Into Being* (London: Heinemann, 1985), p. 205.

119   **Robert Bridges**: Robert Seymour Bridges (1844–1930), Poet Laureate of Britain from 1913 to 1930, was a close friend of Hopkins, and arranged the first, posthumous, publication of his late friend's collected poems in 1918. Burgess did not think highly of Bridges as a poet, whose crowning achievement, 'The Testament of Beauty' (1929) he dismissed as a long philosophical poem of 'no great depth' (*English Literature*, p. 213). He also thought that Bridges had 'done wrong in delaying the publication of Hopkins's small poetic oeuvre until the end of the Great War' (*One Man's Chorus*, p. 333).

119   *And thy loved legacy, Gerard, hath lain Coy in my breast*: A line partially misquoted from Bridges' untitled *in memoriam* sonnet prefacing the first edition of his friend Hopkins's collected poems. Its last phrase being 'in my home', rather than 'in my breast', the original is a little

less mawkishly sentimental than the (perhaps deliberately) misquoted version.

119 **Geoffrey Grigson**: Geoffrey Edward Harvey Grigson (1905–85) was a British litterateur of many talents working in many genres, including literary criticism. As a practitioner of the latter, he made several important enemies with his strong opinions expressed in an abrasive style. Burgess, who had a Dantesque (or Joycean) tendency of putting his favourite enemies into his fiction, likely makes Enderby dismiss Grigson on account of his, Burgess's, character having been called by Grigson 'coarse and unattractive' in one review and his 'sub-smart funniness ... not at all funny' in another (quoted in *Little Wilson and Big God*, p, 13; *You've Had Your Time*, p. 29). In a mock-translation of one of Giuseppe Gioachino Belli's obscene Romanesco sonnets listing periphrastic synonyms of the male sexual organ, Burgess commemorated Grigson in the closing tercet: 'I would prefer to jettison such junk / And give them Geoffrey Grigsons as a name / If only Grigson had a speck of spunk' (see *ABBA ABBA*, pp. 127–8; and *You've Had Your Time*, p. 243).

121 **a good act of contrition**: According to *An Introduction to Catholicism* by Lawrence S. Cunningham, 'the old "Act of Contrition" ... contains within it the Catholic understanding of both imperfect contrition (loss of salvation) and perfect contrition (love of God)' (Cambridge: Cambridge University Press, 2009, p. 112).

121 **Russian roulette**: In Nabokov's *Pale Fire* (1962), a kind of roulette is mentioned, but there is no reference to 'Russian roulette' as such. Instead, in the scholar-poet John Shade's long autobiographical poem, the poet-narrator's wife, anxious about their daughter's unaccounted-for absence, plays 'network roulette' on her TV set: she clicks the dial from channel to channel at random to mask her agitation (*Pale Fire*, London: Weidenfeld & Nicolson, 1962, p. 49). Noting its immense, though occasionally brutal, humour and its tragedy mixed with satire, Burgess concludes his assessment

of *Pale Fire* by calling it 'a brilliant confection' (*Ninety-Nine Novels*, p. 87).

121   **Camiknicks**: 'an undergarment which combines camisole and knickers' (*OED*).

123   **axillary**: 'pertaining or adjacent to the armpit or shoulder' (*OED*).

123   **Weave a circle round him**: 'Weave a circle round him thrice' is a line from Samuel Taylor Coleridge's poem 'Kubla Khan'.

124   **what a genius he had**: The exclamation 'What a genius I had when I wrote that book' is attributed to Jonathan Swift looking at *The Tale of a Tub* in old age (W.M. Thackeray: *The Four Georges: The English Humourists of the Eighteenth Century*, London: Smith, Elder, 1869, p. 156).

124   ***Wachet auf!***: 'Wake up!' (German). *Wachet auf, ruft uns die Stimme* is a church cantata by Johann Sebastian Bach, first performed on 25 November 1731. Burgess also mentions Bach's choral prelude in the prison section of *A Clockwork Orange* (London: Penguin, 2013), p. 93.

124   **Here stand I ... otherwise**: These are the words, slightly modified to conform to the original German word-order (*Hier stehe ich ...*), reportedly spoken by Martin Luther concluding his resounding refusal to recant his teachings as he stood trial in Worms before Charles V, Holy Roman Emperor, and the papal legatees.

125   **vogelwise**: in the manner of a bird (*Vogel* being German for bird.)

125   **Luther ... had married a nun**: Luther's wife Katharina von Bora (1499–1552) was raised in Catholic convents – Benedictine and Cistercian – but she gradually grew apart from her inherited faith and embraced the teachings of the Reformation. This prompted her to escape from her convent and seek Luther's protection in 1523, eventually marrying him in 1525.

125   **Silenus**: elderly companion of the wine-god Dionysos in ancient Greek mythology; **Falstaff**: Sir John Falstaff, elderly and overweight drinking companion of 'Prince Hal',

profligate heir to the English throne in Shakespeare's *Henry IV*, Parts 1 and 2, also known as the titular character of Verdi's opera of the same name.

125   **Not with a whimper**: This is an inverted and truncated quotation of T.S. Eliot's famous line in his poem 'The Hollow Men' (Eliot, *Collected Poems*, Section V. l. 31). The way the world ends, the poem prophesies, is 'Not with a bang but a whimper'. The tongue-in-cheek *double entendre* here depends for its effect on the double meaning of the word 'bang' referring to a sudden, loud noise and the sexual act.

125   **Cry, clutching heaven by the**: Corrected and completed, the line quoted from Francis Thompson's poem 'In No Strange Land' reads like this: 'Cry, – clinging to Heaven by the hems'.

125   **Rhine refused them ... ruin them**: quoted from stanza 21 of 'The Wreck of the Deutschland'.

125   **Francis Thompson**: English poet and Catholic mystic (1859–1907). Thompson merits a brief mention by Burgess in *English Literature* as one of the poets of the late Victorian period who 'sought a new meaning for life in the Catholic faith' (p. 208).

125   **So fagged, so fashed**: This is a line-fragment quoted from Hopkins's poem 'The Leaden Echo and the Golden Echo'. Although it is hard to hear any erotic undertones reverberating in the poem, here and in *A Clockwork Orange* the quotation sounds at least somewhat risqué. See the note in *A Clockwork Orange: The Restored* Edition, London: Penguin, 2013, p. 210.

126   *Enderbius triumphans, exultans*: While this may sound like a parody of Church Latin, it has no one-to-one equivalent in Catholic liturgy. The phrase can be interpreted as a piece of dog Latin referring to heraldry, the English cognates meaning the same as do their Latin originals: Enderby triumphant, exultant.

127   **Spenglerian parabola**: an allusion to German philosopher Oswald Spengler's magnum opus *The Decline of the West*

(1918–22) in which the downward trajectory of every culture is compared to a parabola. Enderby has a poem on this
theme, 'Garrison Town, Evening'. See Burgess's commentary
on Spengler, quoted by Jonathan Mann in his introduction
to Burgess, *Collected Poems* (pp. 12–13).

127   **Poughkeepsie:** As the invited guest of a BBC talk show
in London, Burgess was informed, in the spring of 1972,
of a rape that had occurred in the New York town of
Poughkeepsie, allegedly inspired by the film adaptation of *A
Clockwork Orange*.

127   **Gadarene filth:** filth associated with Gadara, a Biblical city
in today's Transjordan, where Jesus cast out demons from
two 'demoniacs', and sent the demons into a herd of swine
(Matthew 8:28). It is the swinish quality of the filth that the
Bible-educated cleaning lady has in mind.

129   **Obtrincius ...:** fictitious character, as also Fabricius, Flaccus,
Tarminius, Atricia later in the passage.

129   **fetor:** 'an offensive smell; a stench' (*OED*).

128   **Engels:** Friedrich Engels (1820–1895) German Socialist
thinker, author of *The Condition of the Working Class
in England* (1844) and co-author, with Karl Marx, of the
Communist Manifesto (1848). Lived and worked in Burgess's
Manchester. Although unsparingly critical of the capitalist
system, Engels remained dedicated to the successful operation of the factory he had inherited from his father. The tag
'pie-in-the-sky-when-you-die' is cited from 'The Preacher
and the Slave', a song written by Joe Hill in 1911 to pour
scorn on 'long-haired preachers' making empty promises of
bliss in the hereafter to pacify the hungry and angry work-
ers here and now. The juxtaposition of the line from the
anti-clerical song with the name Engels (which in fact means
'angels') is that the ideology of Communism, not unlike some
traditional religions, is meant to keep the exploited masses at
bay with dreams of a distant and unknowable future.

131   **kirtles:** 'a man's tunic or coat, originally a garment reaching to the knees or lower, sometimes forming the only

body-garment, but more usually worn with a shirt beneath and a cloak or mantle above' (*OED*).

132   **POV**: point of view

133   **one apple**: This is a reference to the forbidden fruit the eating of which resulted in the expulsion of Adam and Eve from the Garden of Eden and the consequences of their Fall for the whole of humanity original sin.

133   **Moonwashed apples**: a reference to John Drinkwater's poem 'Moonlit Apples': 'And stiller than ever on orchard boughs they keep / Tryst with the moon, and deep is the silence, deep / On moon-washed apples of wonder'. Quoted in *The Century's Poetry 1937–1937: An Anthology*, vol. 2, ed. by Danys Kilham Roberts (Harmondsworth: Penguin, 1940), p. 332.

133   **Burning burning burning burning**: a line from 'The Fire Sermon' in T.S. Eliot's *The Waste Land*. See Eliot, *Collected Poems*, l. 308.

132   **atoned**: This word occurs as 'atone' in the Hart-Davis, MacGibbon edition but as 'atoned' in the typescript; this edition restores the correct original form.

134   **They go down with the sun**: allusion to Spengler's *The Decline of the West*, whose German title, *Der Untergang des Abendlandes*, could be literally translated as the downfall ('going down') of the lands of the West ('lands of the evening').

138   **creepystool**: also, creepie, creepie-stool, or creepy stool. 'A low stool' (*OED*).

139   **The Goths have arrived**: The sack of Rome by the Visigoths led by Alaric occurred in AD 410. Pelagius escaped to Carthage from their onslaught on Rome. Augustine's *The City of God Against the Pagans* was written to console his fellow Christians after the devastations of the event.

140   **Unforeordained**: This word is misprinted as 'unforedained' in the Hart-Davis, MacGibbon edition but occurs as 'unfore-rordained' in the typescript; this edition restores the correct original form.

142   **The Duke of York**: This snippet of etymological information is returned to in Burgess's coffee-table book of 1976,
New York (p. 12), but there is a Duke of New York in *A
Clockwork Orange*, too. It is the name of a pub frequented
by some old 'baboochkas', or elderly women, bribed with
free drinks by Alex into providing him with an alibi.

142   *Protestant* **king**: George III, indeed a Protestant monarch,
was the king, referred to by Burgess as 'the man who lost
America' in the title of a discarded proposal for a novel.

143   **postcoital tristity**: commonly known as post-coital tristesse
or, in modern sexology, postcoital dysphoria: the sadness
or anxiety experienced after sexual intercourse. 'Tristity' is
Burgess's coinage.

143   **fashed fag-end of his days**: This is likely a dual allusion to
the phrase 'so fashed, so fagged' in Hopkins's 'The Leaden
Echo and the Golden Echo' and the line 'To spit out all the
butt-ends of my days and ways' in T.S. Eliot's 'The Love
Song of J. Alfred Prufrock' (*Collected Poems*, p. 15).

143   **nunc dimittis**: Latin words quoted from 'Simeon's Canticle'
(Luke 2:29–32). In the Vulgate, the whole sentence reads:
'*Nunc dimittis servum tuum, Domine*', meaning 'Now thou
dost dismiss thy servant, O Lord'.

143   **heaven-haven**: the title of a poem by Hopkins, significantly
subtitled 'A nun takes the veil'.

144   **Andrea**: This is the name of Burgess and his wife Liana's
son Paolo Andrea (Andrew) Burgess-Wilson (1964–2002),
repeatedly mentioned in Burgess's account of his stay in
New York during his visiting professorship at City College
New York in 1972–73 (see, for example, *You've Had Your
Time*, p. 270). Burgess adopted Liana's son, whose birth
name was Paolo Andrea Halliday, shortly after the family
moved to Malta in 1968. His novel *The Kingdom of the
Wicked* (London: Hutchinson, 1985) is dedicated to Paolo
Andrea.